ROMANTIC SUSPENSE AT ITS BEST!

MORE . . .

MORE

"A relentless page-turner with plenty of enticing plot twists and turns." —*Seattle Post-Intelligencer*

"[A] fast-paced and intricately plotted tale of danger, deception, and desire that is perfect for readers who like their romantic suspense adrenaline-rich and sizzlingly sexy." —*Booklist*

"Adair has done it again! The chemistry between Hunt and Taylor is red-hot, and the suspense is top-notch." —*Rendezvous*

"A very sexy adventure that offers nonstop, continent-hopping action from start to finish." —*Library Journal*

"Get ready to drool, sigh, and simply melt. . . . Fascinating characters, danger, passion, intense emotions, and a rush like a roller-coaster ride." —*Romance Reviews Today*

Also by
CHERRY ADAIR

Undertow

Riptide

Vortex

CHERRY ADAIR

St. Martin's Paperbacks

VORTEX

Copyright © 2012 by Cherry Adair.

All rights reserved.

For information address St. Martin's Press, 175 Fifth Avenue, New York, NY 10010.

ISBN: 978-1-61793-974-7

Printed in the United States of America

St. Martin's Paperbacks are published by St. Martin's Press, 175 Fifth Avenue, New York, NY 10010.

This one is for my BFF Deborah McGuire. Words cannot express how much I love you for all you are, and for all you do. If friends were flowers, I'd always pick you.

Acknowledgments

Thank you from the bottom of my heart to copy editor extraordinaire Martha Trachtenberg for years of meticulous editing. Thank you for not (*too* vocally) mocking my awesome ability to get every number I use completely wrong. Every time. Your patience, nitpickiness, and wonderful sense of humor make what I love to do even more enjoyable.

And thanks to my Awesome Street Team for all the fun and names on Facebook.

One

She fought him off like a feral wildcat, their bodies rising and falling in the swells. Grappling to get a secure grip on the woman's slippery, flailing limbs, Logan Cutter struggled to restrain her, keep her face out of the water, and not drown himself in the process.

Over the surge of the roiling, moonlit-speckled black water, the warning bells sounded. Three long rings, followed by the ship's whistle, alerted everyone there was a man overboard.

Woman overboard in this case.

Except there *were* no women on board *Sea Wolf* this voyage.

If not for his dog barking, and that fleeting glimpse of the white strobe on the woman's life vest seen briefly in the vast darkness, he would've gone to bed, none the wiser.

Salt water stung the scratches she'd already scored across his throat and face. "Lady, stop fighting me!"

Sirens bleating. The slap of the waves. She could do little more than gurgle now and again as the sea filled her mouth. But she fought him with such intent, he was afraid he would have to knock her out to save her. The other alternative was to swim away until she went under. A little water in her lungs wouldn't kill her. But it might shock her into awareness. Or not.

The floatation device she wore wasn't foolproof, as was evidenced by her repeatedly sinking below the surface.

Logan grabbed whatever he could—her hand, this time—hauling up so her head breached the surface chop. She coughed, gagged, fought harder for purchase. She tried to climb his body.

"I'm trying to help—Shit!" Her thrashing leg found his groin. He managed to close his fingers around her upper arm. *Now* she shrieked bloody murder, grabbing at his hair, his face, his reaching hands. She was as slippery as an eel as she battled to scale to the highest point. His head.

He went under. Came up spluttering, peeling her octopus arms off him, so he could control where they went and how. "I get it." He managed to grasp both slender wrists in one hand. "You're terrified. I won't let you drown, hear me? I got you. Just let me—"

Mindless with fear, she was out of control. Dangerous to them both as, despite—or because of—his hold on her, she planted one foot on his extended leg and started climbing his body again. "—ver hit—wom—my life," He bit out. "—ut, lady, if—don't—rescue you,—gonna—ave—slug y—. Your choice." None of his threat came out in a neat stream, as he, too, was gagging and spitting out water. His words washed out of his mouth the minute he uttered them.

Moonlight shone on the woman's pale, wet face, glinting in her terrified eyes as she batted at his hands. Logan doubted she even saw him. She was in full-on panic mode. Her instinct for survival primal, she was too afraid to hear his assurances. He grabbed a handful of long hair as she went under again, pulling her head to the surface. He jerked his face out of reach—too late—and was rewarded with her elbow smacking him in the mouth.

Their bodies rose with the next swell—he saw the lights of his ship—then sank into the next dark trough.

It wasn't uncommon for drowning victims to use their rescuer as a floatation device. "Damn it, we'll both drown at this rate!" He was already hoarse from the salt water and so much yelling. He could've saved his voice. She was too panicked to hear him. "Settle dow—" His nose got in the way of the top of her hard head. "Ow!"

He grabbed and twisted the cord of her life vest in one unyielding fist, holding her at arm's length and kicking out, dragging her with him. Her head went under again. He tried to hold it up, but getting her to the ship took precedence over worrying about her swallowing a little water. "My ship is two hundred yards away. Stay still and I'll get you there. Keep fighting me, and I'll haul your unconscious ass the rest of the way." At least that was the way he heard it in his head; to her, it was probably disjointed babble.

She sank, and this time when he hauled her head up she wasn't fighting, but hung limp in his grip. Exposed to the cold water for who knew how long, she was now unconscious, the vest keeping her on her back, head mostly out of the water.

Logan spat out water as a wave slapped him in the face. Where the hell were his men with the dinghy? He struck out for the lights of the *Sea Wolf* in long, sure strokes. She was damned lucky he was a strong swimmer. Exactly what she needed right now. She could sue him later for manhandling her.

He wasn't a particularly inquisitive guy, but the

woman's presence begged the question: What the hell was she doing in the middle of the Pacific Ocean at midnight a hundred miles from land?

The fishing trawler he'd noticed earlier had disappeared before dark, and that was hours ago. If she'd been out here that long, it was a miracle anyone had found her. If it hadn't been for Dog, Logan would have finished his nightly exercises and gone to bed, none the wiser.

Finally able to do his job without her fighting him tooth and nail every step of the way, he wrapped an arm across her chest, tightening his grip as they rose and fell with the waves. He fought to keep her head out of water as best he could by grabbing ahold of her long hair, which stuck to her skin like seaweed. Logan tucked her against his hip, waited until a swell lifted them, and scanned the area between himself and the lights of the ship for a sign of the dinghy.

He heard muffled shouts, and the throb of an engine, more lights flashed on from his ship, the searchlight strafing the water a few feet ahead. He and the woman went down into a dark trench. He kicked, swimming one-armed, holding her tightly to his side.

"Who is it?" Galt, one of his divers, yelled, bringing the inflatable dinghy alongside Logan and the woman.

"Not one of us." Logan treaded water as he maneuvered the dead weight into position for his friend to pull her over the side. "Good?" he asked, as Galt grunted, hauling the body over the lip by her vest and easing it into the bottom of the raft.

"Yeah."

"Haul ass. I'll swim back."

"Didn't doubt it." Galt's teeth and bald head glinted

in the moonlight. He used the motor to power back to the *Sea Wolf*, leaving Logan to follow.

"Wow. A mermaid. Is this our lucky day or what?" Daniela Rosado stayed limply silent as she listened to guys' happy tones. Her chest hurt. Someone had thumped her lungs, and she vaguely remembered spitting up a lot of water. It was a miracle she hadn't inhaled half the ocean. Her throat and lungs burned. Her body ached, and she was freezing.

Furious and freezing.

"A mermaid with hypothermia," a deep authoritative voice pointed out, not sounding pleased. "Harris—where are those warm blankets? Dell, bring the first-aid kit, then go find her something dry to wear. The rest of you clear out. Wes, you stay. We have to get her out of these clothes."

Oh, no you don't. No one's stripping me. It took every ounce of reserve she had to remain limp, not stiffening in resistance at their comments. She just needed a few more moments to gather her thoughts.

She was no longer in the water. A plus. Cold and wet, she lay on an equally cold and wet flat surface. Not the hard deck this time, but a bed. Streamers of wet hair covered half her face, water dripping down her throat, to pool in her ears. Her teeth chattered as she shivered.

"Where the hell's Harris? Good man." A heated blanket was wrapped around her by large, sure hands. It was then tucked tightly around her body, sealing the icy wet fabric of her clothing against her wet, chilled skin.

Was she on board the *Sea Wolf* after all? The last

few hours were foggy, and her brain felt sluggish and uncooperative. If she *was* on board, it was more fluke than meticulous planning. The idiots could've drowned her.

A pulse throbbed on her forehead. Point of contact where they'd hit her. She'd do a little hitting herself when she caught up with them. But before that, Daniela had to gather her wits and come up with a story to explain how she'd ended up in the water.

As several men in the room made suggestions as to what to do with her, she drifted as if she was still in the current. It was really hard to put together two consecutive thoughts, let alone plan a course of action, and she let herself float.

Why hadn't they just *listened* to her? Taken a few extra days to formulate a plan?

Because they were idiots, that's why.

"Hand me that other blanket." A deep, take-charge, make-it-happen kind of voice.

"Her clothes are wet, maybe I—"

Whatever the softer toned man had been about to say was cut off as Mr. Take Charge started chafing her body with hard, rough hands. He didn't seem to care much where he rubbed, but at least she was warming up. Maidenly hysterics weren't appropriate right now. Getting warm was somewhat of a priority; she'd been in that water a long time. Brain sluggish, responses too slow, didn't matter. Daniela knew she had to think, and she had to think *fast*.

She was so angry she was surprised her fury wasn't turning the water on her skin to steam. The morons. The idiots. The scumbags. They'd thrown her overboard. *Hit* her, and thrown her overboard.

No warning, no discussion. She was going to kill them.

Now she had to decide—while she still could—what the best course of action was. Open her eyes and say hi? Stay limp and mute as she figured out what to do next? The longer they thought she was out of it, the longer she had to make up a plausible story. And the more time they had to strip her naked.

Limp it was. Unless stripping was imminent.

The man with the rich, deep voice got up from the side of the bed at her hip, leaving a cold spot. "Wes, she's all yours. Get the lead out, she's still shivering. Call me when she's tucked in."

"Why does Wes get to tuck her in?" another man demanded, amusement lacing his words. He sounded a bit farther away than the others.

"Because our mermaid's modesty is safest with him. Give a holler when she's dry."

Several pairs of footsteps retreated, a door closed.

A firm hand placed on her shoulder gave a little squeeze. "You can open your eyes now."

Daniela's sea-salt encrusted lashes fluttered, and she let out the shuddering breath she'd been holding.

The man crouching down beside the bed was in his late thirties, muscular, with a sandy brown buzz cut. Even with a smile, "Wes" didn't look safe at all. His broad shoulders blocked her view of the room she was in. They were alone.

"Hi, how're you feeling?" he asked gently, moving a hank of wet hair off her cheek. Cold water ran down her neck.

"Cold." She shivered. Her teeth clicking together like castanets made it obvious.

"Like some hot tea?" He picked up a steaming mug from the table beside the bunk, in a hand the size of a turkey.

"Please." She was annoyed at how weak her voice sounded. Weakness was the last damn thing she wanted to show. *Ever.*

Cupping the back of her head, he tipped the mug to her lips. The tea was sweet and warm, not too hot. Daniela drank greedily, her throat parched from the salt water. Even the act of swallowing was exhausting. "Enough."

He took the mug from her lips. "Want help getting out of those wet clothes, or would you rather take a hot shower?"

No. But she wanted the heat enough to say, "Shower." She was as breathless as if she'd been running, instead of just lying there in a damp puddle on the clammy blankets. God, she hated feeble. She didn't do weak and feeble or wimpy. People took advantage if there was one second when your guard was down. Took advantage of—She cut off the thought mid-whine. Enough!

"I'll help you." The giant got to his feet, then leaned over to scoop her up in his arms. Strong. She stiffened. "Don't worry," he said cheerfully. "I won't drop you. Two steps and we're in the head—That's bathroom to you." He let her slide to her feet, but kept an impersonal arm around her shoulders to steady her as he turned on the shower. "Need help?"

This coming on board the *Sea Wolf* had been an *insane* idea when they'd proposed it. She'd argued vehemently that it wouldn't work. Daniela knew if she was given a couple of days to think it through she could come up with a better plan. Of course the better plan

was not to be near her cousins at all. *That* would've
been the intelligent plan. But she'd been desperate and
out of options.

Now look where she was.

"I can close my eyes and help you with those buttons
if you like. Promise not to peek."

She shook her head.

His eyes crinkled, his smile pretty cute, as he said
cheerfully, "If it makes you feel better, I'm gay."

Daniela held onto the sink to keep her balance. She
didn't trust his smile or care about his sexual orienta-
tion. He was a head taller, and at least eighty pounds
heavier than she was. She backed up.

"Tell you what," he said gently. "I'll leave the door
open a crack, and wait right outside in case you need
me. Take your time. Get warm." He gave her a worried
look. "Are you sure . . . ?"

"Yes." Sure that she didn't want to be naked and
vulnerable in such tight quarters. He was between her
and the door.

"Okay." He backed out and pulled the door so just a
sliver of the cabin beyond showed.

The tiny bathroom was already filled with steam. It
would be ridiculous to stay in here shivering when she
didn't have to. But she'd be quick and keep her eyes
trained on the door the whole time. She snapped the
door closed, then locked it. Then, still shivering and
shuddering, she stripped off her soaking wet shorts, sleep
shirt, and panties, dropping everything into the sink.

"Oh, don't you look attractive?" Her lips twitched.
She looked like a drowned rat. A pale-faced, big-eyed,
drippy-wet drowned rat.

Rubbing her palm over the foggy mirror, she lifted

her bangs to inspect the swollen lump on her forehead. It throbbed in time with her erratic heartbeat. There was a giant bruise as well as an oozing three-inch cut over her left eye. That explained the pain and the headache, but those were the least of her problems.

They'd snuck into the *locked* cabin and hit her while she was sleeping, the miserable scum-dog cowards. She stepped into the pounding water, careful not to let the hot water beat on her forehead. All she needed was to pass out, necessitating that someone come in and rescue her. Again. She carefully lathered her hair. What the hell had the idiots hit her with? She was fortunate they hadn't killed her before they'd tossed her into the water.

They were fortunate they hadn't killed her, Daniela thought grimly as she used grapefruit-scented gel to wash the salt water from her skin and hair.

She had a fairly recent aversion to water, but she'd been on the swim team in high school, and once in the water, even slightly dazed by the blow to the head, she'd let the life vest do its job. Until the realization had struck her that she couldn't see any lights, and might very well drown out there in the middle of the Pacific with no one being any the wiser.

There was a good reason *her* side of the family had nothing to do with *their* side of the family her whole life. Her cousins were not only criminals, they were *stupid* criminals.

"How're you doing in there?" Wes yelled over the sound of pounding water.

"Great. Be right out." Getting out, and feeling considerably more herself, Daniela turned off the water.

"I'm going to hand you some clothes, ready?" Her guard/babysitter said through the door.

"Thanks." Wrapping the towel tightly around her body, she unlocked the door, wedging her bare toes against the base so that it couldn't be pushed open more than a few inches. It was false security, as she well knew, because if he wanted to, he could shove the door open any time he wanted. The idea of that big guy in this minute bathroom, with her *naked*, made Daniela sick to her stomach. Her armpits prickled with nerves, and a sheen of sweat made her skin clammy in the steamy bathroom. Her own reaction pissed her off.

Still, she almost slammed the door those scary few inches. And then what? Stand here naked forever?

The clothing was stuffed through the crack in the door. Bunching the fabric in one hand, she murmured, "Thanks," then firmly shut and locked the door again, immediately letting out the breath she'd been holding. If she had a prayer of pulling this off, Daniela knew she had to get a grip. Center herself. Remember what was at stake.

She dropped the towel and quickly dressed, men's boxers still in the store's plastic bag, socks, jeans, a plain gray T-shirt, and a fleece hoodie sweatshirt. She didn't care how anything fit, it was clean and dry, and baggy enough to hide her braless state. She unlocked the door, combing her fingers through the wet strands of her dark, shoulder-length hair as she stepped into the dimly-lit cabin. "Thanks, I feel much—" Her heart stumbled, then started beating double time.

Instead of the muscle-bound "I'm gay" Wes, there stood a dark-haired man with the face of a pirate, the shockingly blue eyes of a fallen angel, and the mouth of a sinner.

Where Wes was all bulging muscle, and a dopey grin,

this guy was tall, lean, and muscled like a well-honed athlete. This was power and strength on an understated level, all the more frightening because his strength was subtle.

Daniela's heart started doing calisthenics as every cell in her body went on red alert. She took an instinctive step back, stumbling as her back hit the bathroom doorjamb.

"Whoa," he said, reaching out to grab her arm. His deep, vaguely familiar voice sent a frisson of alarm up and down Daniela's spine, and the familiar cold clench in the pit of her stomach made her entire body feel cased in ice. *Oh, no no no.*

Where was the exit? Behind him. Trapped. The polished wood door was hard against her back. She dug her stockinged toes into the short nap of the carpet.

Her rational mind knew she was overreacting. She wanted to calm down, but her body knew the consequences of letting down her guard. Better safe than sorry.

He held up both hands and backed away. There wasn't much room in the small cabin for retreat. "Are you hungry? Wes went to find you something to eat."

"I'm not."

"Here. Sit down before you fall down." He moved out of the way, and indicated one of two bunks. "Wes replaced the wet sheets and added plenty of blankets in case that shower doesn't do the trick." His voice was low and calm, but he was still positioned between herself and the only way out.

There was a small window—a square of ink black—in the paneled wall over one of the bunks. She shifted a few feet to lean against the polished teak wall beneath it because her knees felt soft. She was angry at herself for her reaction to this man. He'd given no indication that he'd harm her.

He meant nothing to her, or she to him. No axes to grind, no points to be made. She tried to breathe through her fear. "I'll stand for a bit." Shaky and ridiculously weak, she felt her heart thud in a hard, slow, uneven rhythm. All of which annoyed her. She'd grown beyond this knee-jerk reaction to being trapped. She wasn't trapped. He wasn't a threat. Breathe. Just breathe through it.

Daniela pushed her wet hair off her face with jittery fingers. *Go away. Just get the hell out of here so I can breathe.*

There was absolutely no rational reason to believe he'd do her any harm. Daniela wished her body would get the memo. She took a deep, albeit, shuddering breath, hanging on to reason with both hands.

"Sure." He sat down on the other bunk, arms braced on his thighs, hands clasped loosely between his knees. He wore jeans and a black T-shirt that fit snugly across his broad shoulders and muscled chest. His skin was deeply tanned, his strong forearms covered with crisp dark hair. Even sitting still and seemingly relaxed, he looked virile, predatory, and dangerous as hell.

Daniela could barely inhale as she tried to make herself as inconspicuous as possible in her borrowed clothes. Acutely conscious that she wasn't wearing a bra, she folded her arms over her chest, then thought better of it and dropped her arms to her sides.

"You're perfectly safe here, I promise. I'm Logan

Cutter, and you're on board my ship *Sea Wolf.* Who are you, and how did you end up in the water hundreds of miles from anywhere?"

"My name is—" Oh, no. If she gave him her name, one inquisitive click of the mouse on his computer would dredge up everything. She touched the lump on her forehead. "Annie?" Close enough to her pet name Dani not to trip her up.

His forehead creased in a frown. "Don't you know?"

She shrugged, keeping her expression bland. She eyed the mug of tea on the table between the bunks six feet away, throat so dry she could barely swallow. "It sounds right."

He reached out, snagged the mug, and rose off the bunk to hand it to her, handle out, then sat down again before she could flinch at his nearness. "How did you come to be in the water, Annie?"

Wrapping both hands around the tepid mug, she gave him a blank look. His frown deepened. "What *do* you remember?"

"Waking up right there." She indicated the bunk beside her with her crooked elbow, then sipped the sweet tea.

"Before that?"

She mimicked his frown, trying to read what he was thinking from his inscrutable expression, as she whispered, "Nothing." Churning black water. The sure knowledge that she was going to drown.

He got slowly to his feet. "Take a seat. I want to check that gash on your head."

If she knew nothing else, she knew she did not want this man to put those well-shaped hands on her. Anywhere. "It's okay."

"You might have a concussion, and probably need stitches. Let me take a look." After a few seconds' pause, and a nearly imperceptible tightening around the eyes, he said quietly, "Please."

Boxed in and out of options—for the moment—Daniela walked around the foot of the bed, and sat down on the edge of the mattress. She stiffened, body braced as he sat too close right beside her. The heat of his body was a furnace blast all the way down her left side. The smell of spicy soap on his skin indicated he'd also showered recently.

How in God's name was she going to explain this situation to him? The answer was, she couldn't. Eyes downcast, all she saw were his muscled jean-clad legs, and his hair-roughed forearm. All she could think was, *danger*. In bright red, flashing neon.

"Turn into the light." His deep voice stroked along her ragged nerve endings like a fur glove.

Eyes closed, Daniela suppressed a shudder, turning her face up toward him. Willing herself not to flinch, she started as he placed the edge of his hand under her chin to turn her head so he could see her injury. Little sparks of electricity zinged between his fingers and her skin. His touch made her skin heat, and was far too intimate.

"Honey, you need to breathe or you'll pass out. Just relax. I won't hurt you." A false assurance she'd heard one too many times.

She breathed in the smell of his clean skin, and a shiver pebbled her skin. "It's just a bump."

"The salt water did a good job of disinfecting it, but there's a cut that may need stitches. I'll put some antiseptic on it just in case, and a couple of butterfly bandages until we get you to the hospital in Lima and have you checked out."

Her eyes sprang open in alarm. "No!" God, he was so close, just inches away. Dani had never seen such intensely blue eyes in her life. They did not fill her with confidence. Just the opposite.

"It'll just sting for a second, I promise—"

"No hospital in Lima. No hospital." She grabbed at his hand, poised over her face. Wrapping her fingers around his wrist, she held on tightly. She didn't want to touch him, she really, really didn't want to touch him. His skin was hot, her fingers unable to circle his wrist. "Please. Don't make me go to Lima."

"Why not?"

Shit. Why not? "I don't know." She let go of him, and instantly felt cold again. "It scares me. Something bad . . ." Daniela let her voice trail off. The tears flooding her eyes were from exhaustion and frustration, and were real. Possibly the only honest thing she could share with him. He could read into them whatever he liked.

He fingered aside a strand of wet hair where it had fallen over her eye. "Something bad happened to you there?"

"Yes." She touched the headache pulsing in time with her erratic heartbeat. "No. Maybe. I don't remember." The sick feeling in her stomach intensified. This not remembering would only work if Logan Cutter bought into it. But the intelligence in his eyes made mincemeat out of *that* idea. Not to mention Daniela was pretty sure amnesia didn't last forever. Still, it would certainly work for tonight. Tomorrow was another day.

He applied antiseptic sharp enough to sting her nose. "How did you manage to fall overboard, Annie?"

A hot, annoying tear rolled down her cheek as she forced herself to meet his incredible, piercing azure eyes. He was far too damn close. The heat of his coffee-scented breath tickled her cheek. "I don't remember."

Gentle fingers adhered a couple of butterfly bandages across the cut. It almost didn't hurt like hell. She gritted her teeth.

"All right. Let's not worry about it tonight. It's late, and clearly you're traumatized as well as exhausted. The cut and bump are taken care of for now. Have a good night's sleep. Nothing bad is going to happen to you on board the *Sea Wolf*, I promise."

Daniela prayed he was right.

Two

"How's she doing?" Wes whispered, as Logan partially closed the cabin door and stepped into the companionway. His two best divers, Wes and Jed, and his captain, Piet Vandyke, were waiting for him. Dog wagged his tail violently as Logan emerged from the cabin. The animal, a salt-and-pepper wolf/Alsatian mix, was reasonably civilized, but he was leery of strangers. Logan figured the woman had had enough trauma for one night. She could meet Dog tomorrow.

"Annie doesn't remember much more than her name right now," he said quietly as Jed let go of the dog's ruff and the beast padded over to butt his head against Logan's hip. "Either from the trauma, or from that knock on the head. I patched her up, but she refuses to go to the hospital. Thank Dog for seeing her. I sure as hell didn't."

He'd been doing tai chi on the aft deck before turning in when the dog had barked manically and refused to stop until Logan went to the rail to see what the hell he was going on about.

"You wanna fly her in, or you want me to do it?" Jed asked. Logan noticed the two unopened beer bottles in his hand. "Chopper's ready to go."

Dog's tail beat a fast rhythm as he looked at the partially open door. Logan absently slid his fingers into the animal's thick pelt, massaging Dog's muscled neck.

Dog groaned his appreciation, leaning against his legs. "Leave it out, but I don't think we'll need it tonight." The helicopter was folded neatly, and had to be brought up to the helipad by elevator to the deck.

"She polished off the tea, then conked out, exhausted." And she'd fought sleep as if the hounds of hell were after her. It was only after he insisted she lie down, and at least close her eyes and rest, that she'd reluctantly done so. Her breathing had changed almost instantly, indicating her exhaustion. He'd covered her with a light blanket and left the cabin to come out and talk with the guys.

Logan braced his feet against Dog's considerable weight. "We'll let her sleep. See how she's doing in the morning. Even with the memory loss, whatever she experienced was powerful enough to scare the crap out of her. She begged me not to return her to port."

"Drop anchor again?" Vandyke, a slight, sandy-haired Dutchman in his mid-forties, had been with Logan for twenty years.

Logan felt the deep-throated throb of the engines beneath his feet, rumbling in preparation for a move to a new dive location. Hopefully *the* new dive location. "Yeah. For now."

They'd be going in the morning, because this location had yielded zip—a big, fat, fucking zero—and the crew and divers were bored. The *Nuestra Señora de Graza* was exactly where Logan had calculated she'd gone down, but they'd found none of the treasure that had been listed on the manifest. Not a single doubloon, gold bar, or emerald. It was as if the galleon had made her return trip from Lima to Spain—empty.

They'd done as much as they wanted to do with the

wreck and debris field; time to move on. Logan had reached that conclusion just before he'd pulled Annie from the water.

"Will do." Piet left to return to the bridge.

"Well," Jed said considering. "Fishing a beautiful woman out of the drink will relieve the boredom some."

Boredom wasn't good on a ship, even one the size of *Sea Wolf*. Frustration had frayed tempers, even though they were used to the challenge of painstakingly searching for treasure ships. Yet Logan had been so sure his quarry was right where no one else had thought to look. Damn, he hated being wrong. But wrong he was.

"Regrouping and finding our treasure will do that," he told his friend shortly. "When Annie remembers what happened, one of us can fly her into Lima."

"Sure."

Wes wore a worried frown. "Think she fell from one of the cruise ships? Or possibly one of the sports fishing boats?"

"Catch and release as if she were a black marlin?" Logan didn't think anyone in their right mind would see this woman and throw her away. "No idea. She might be a tourist, but I suspect she might be local."

"She doesn't *sound* local, but, yeah. Maybe. I checked the labels in her clothes. Nothing distinctive," Wes told him, then added, "Wherever she came from, she should be watched. Concussion or whatever." He shot a worried frown at the partially open door. His white T-shirt stretched over his wide chest and bulging biceps. "I don't mind staying with her tonight. She should be woken up every half hour or so."

Logan shook his head. "Go ahead and turn in. I'll let you know how she's doing in the morning."

"You su—Yeah. Okay. Night."

"That was pretty decisive," Jed murmured, amused when Wes's cabin door shut further down the corridor. The two men were close in height, but where Logan's hair was dark, and a bit too long, Jed's was a streaky surfer blond and fell to his shoulders. "Your mermaid has a powerful allure, everyone including Dog wants to protect her."

"There's nothing here she needs protecting from," Logan pointed out testily.

"She doesn't know that."

Logan slid his fingers in the front pockets of his jeans. "She's skittish all right." *More than.* "I'm not sure I believed her about the memory loss. But that knob on her head says she *might* be telling the truth. And honestly, even though most people do, I couldn't think why she'd lie. If I hadn't seen her out there in the dark, the questions and answers would be moot. She'd be dead right now."

"Not prepared to take her at face value?"

Jed knew Logan's stance on liars well. The two men had been friends for more years than Logan cared to count. The rest of the guys on board were all friends as well as employees. Most had been with him since he bought his first dive boat after he made his first major find and became a multimillionaire at seventeen.

He trusted all of them, but Jed more so than the others. Logan kept offering his friend his own ship, and Jed kept refusing. He liked to dive, but didn't want the responsibility and all the rest of the shit that was involved in running his own dive team, ship, and crew. The arrangement suited them both.

"Let's just say I reserve judgment."

Jed handed a beer over, since neither would be flying tonight. "Fair enough. Pirates?" he asked, his voice low as he leaned against the polished teak wall opposite Logan.

Logan popped the cap. "Christ, anything's possible out here." He took a pull of the cold brew. Like an apple, he had one a day, if that. His father had been many things; a drunk was just one of them.

"There wasn't any indication of another ship nearby, though," he pointed out. "Just that fishing trawler while we ate dinner, and that was four to five hours ago. The mysterious Annie doesn't look like the kind of woman who'd enjoy an excursion on a working fishing boat to me."

"Vandyke's looking into that, right?" Jed drank his beer, then indicated the open door with the bottle. "Shouldn't be too hard to track down a fishing boat."

"Unless it was up to no good," Logan said grimly. "Could be a kidnapping attempt gone wrong—God only knows there's plenty of bad shit for people to do way the hell and gone out here if they have a mind for it. Drugs. Pirates. Piet will track down the registry of the trawler, ask some discreet questions of the cruise line. Could be she fell from a pleasure craft day-tripping. Drifted on the tides . . ."

"Someone is sure to have reported her missing," Jed speculated, drinking. "We have no idea how long she was in the water."

"She had the life vest, but as you saw, it wasn't fastened properly, and could easily have slipped off her in the swells. It's a fucking miracle she survived."

Realizing they weren't going to move to Logan's

comfortable cabin next door, Dog sighed and lay down at his feet. "Hell of a long shot finding anything, but Piet's checking the chatter on the radio and the news to see if that's the case. I don't want to send up any red flags and alert the wrong people to her location if her fear is founded."

Jed's expression was thoughtful. "Any chance this is something cooked up by Case?"

"That's what I'm thinking." Rydell Case was Logan's nemesis, and while setting some sort of trap was a very un-Case-like thing to do, it wasn't out of the realm of possibility that he'd use an attractive woman as the bait. The man was devious and dangerous, but usually chillingly direct. Still, Logan didn't trust him farther than he could throw him. "I don't put anything past that son of a bitch. But he's never given the impression that he's stupid, just the opposite. If he put her in the water for me to find—and God only knows for what purpose—it was damned risky. If Dog hadn't seen her, she would've died out there."

The fear in her eyes hadn't been fake, Logan was sure of it. Her amber-brown eyes had looked at him with very real emotion. Whatever had happened to her was probably even more frightening for her because she couldn't remember. *If* she couldn't remember.

"Hell, for all we know she's a damned good actress, and she has an agenda worth almost dying for."

Jed smiled. "If you truly believed that, I'd be flying her to Lima right now."

Every protective instinct Logan had had leapt to the fore when her cold fingers curled around his wrist to hold him at bay.

Jed pushed away from the wall. "Maybe she'll remember more in the morning."

"Yeah, maybe. We'll stay put for tonight. But after I talk to her again tomorrow, we'll have to head to port to make some discreet inquiries. Someone must be looking for her."

"Could be the someone who tossed her overboard," Jed pointed out.

Logan agreed. "Based on the way she freaked out when I mentioned heading into Lima, it's something to take into consideration." A crime, not an accident? Had she been pushed, not fallen?

"I'm beat." Jed stretched and yawned. "Let me know if there's anything you need me to do."

"Let's all get some sleep, and see where we are in the morning."

"We're going to have to go to Plan B," Jed pointed out with a rueful shake of his head.

"That, too." Logan slipped inside the small cabin, Dog as his shadow, and closed the door. He'd left the light in the head on, and that door almost shut, so that just a sliver of light fell in a golden pinstripe on the carpet between the two bunks.

He leaned over to check on her. She shot straight up, letting out a bloodcurdling scream, and punched him in the eye. At the same time, Dog scrambled onto the bunk beside her, barking madly, ruff raised, yellow eyes narrowed at his owner as he protected the woman.

"Hey hey hey. It's just me. Logan," he told her quietly, backing away to give her room. As he did so, he made a "down" hand gesture to the protective dog. Dog stopped barking, but still stood defensively beside her, watching Logan with the same suspicious eyes as the woman. Well, hell.

Her eyes glinted wildly in the semidarkness as she splayed her hand to her throat, breathing as if she'd just been running. Half damp dark hair curled around her shoulders, and her large, expressive dark eyes were stark with fear. A sheen of perspiration made her pale olive skin glow in the dim light.

Christ. No woman had ever been scared of him in his life. He didn't like the feeling one damned bit. Especially since it wasn't warranted.

"What are you doing here?" she demanded, eyes flickering nervously from Logan to Dog standing on the bunk beside her.

He didn't point out the obvious. His ship, he could be anywhere he damn well pleased. "You have a concussion. Have to check you to see how severe."

"Back up, please. You're too close." She sat up, cautiously and slowly, holding the cotton blanket to her throat with both hands. Her lifted chin and defiant eyes were undermined by the way she wobbled even though she was sitting. "I'm neither dizzy, nor nauseous, and I can see you quite clearly."

Feisty must mean she was doing better. "Can you tell me your last name?"

"No. Does your wolf bite?"

"He's protecting you. Your bodyguard, if you will. He feels responsible for saving your life." Logan touched a finger to his abused eye. Not buffered by water, this punch was solid. He was probably going to have a shiner for his trouble. "Do you know where you are, Annie?"

She gave him an are-you-kidding-me look. "A boat."

"How'd you get here?"

She shrugged and lay down again, pulling the blanket up to her chin like a Victorian maiden. "I'm tired." Dog lay down beside her, flopping his head across her belly with a put-upon sigh. The crafty animal was positioned between Annie and his master. The man who'd saved his scrawny, malnourished hide when he'd been left, tied up, outside a wharf-side eatery in Tokyo three years ago. The man who'd stood between the dog and three dockyard thugs and had the crap beat out of him for his trouble. The man whose bed he shared every night. So much for gratitude.

To get to her, Logan would have to go through his dog.

"Please don't chew on me," she whispered, not touching the animal, but not moving away. Not that there was anywhere to move in the narrow bunk. "I've already had a shitty day." She turned her head as Logan stretched out on the other bunk. "What do you think you're doing?" she demanded in a normal, if irritable tone.

He stacked his hands beneath his head. "That knot on your head could mean serious business. You probably have a concussion. Someone has to watch you in case you fall into a coma."

"I appreciate your concern, but I'm sure I *don't,* and if I do . . . I'm willing to risk it. Please go."

"Close your eyes. I'll wake you in half an hour."

"I—"

"I'm not leaving," Logan told her mildly. Staring into the semidarkness, he listened to her indignant breathing as she fought to stay awake. It didn't take long for it to slow as she was dragged unwillingly into sleep.

Interestingly, he didn't feel in the least bored now.

* * *

Directed by a crewman, and with the dog padding down the corridor beside her, Daniela found Logan Cutter's office. She'd showered and pulled on a fresh T-shirt and the jeans she'd been given. Then she decided that since she had no bra, two T-shirts would be better. It wasn't that she was large-breasted, she was quite compact. But she didn't want to wander around the ship with her boobs bouncing. The less of a sexual being she was while she was here, the better. She didn't want to draw attention to herself, or any part of herself.

Would her amnesia story hold up in the light of day? Especially under the scrutiny of Logan Cutter's blue eyes? Of course, they couldn't be as blue, nor as penetrating as her memory painted them. She tried to picture the rest of him, but all she came up with was a murky image of a big, annoying, dark-haired hulk.

The light had been dim, and God only knew, she was traumatized about being thrown into the ocean. She rubbed her arms. It didn't bear thinking about—how deep the water was, or what would've happened if someone hadn't come in after her and hauled her to safety. She had absolutely no memory of the rescue, but remembered everything leading up to it in living color.

Given the choice of nearly drowning and spending the night three feet away from Logan Cutter, Daniela was almost sure which she would've chosen. Too freaking bad she hadn't been given a vote in either decision.

The dog nudged his nose against her leg to get her attention. He must be half wolf, half some giant dog breed, with a thick pelt of gray-and-black fur and a white muzzle. Just because his pink tongue was lolling as if he was smiling at her, didn't mean he couldn't go for her throat at any second. Daniela liked that she could see right off that he was dangerous. No hiding behind the benign appearance of a King Charles spaniel and then ripping out your throat for this guy. He looked more than half wild, and extremely dangerous.

Daniela had to respect that, though she'd still keep a careful distance. She wished humans didn't have the capacity to hide their true selves behind civilized masks. It would make spotting a predator much easier.

He turned narrow gold eyes on her as they stopped outside the door, and sat, politely waiting for her to knock. "Are you really as tame as you're acting, or just toying with me until you pounce and have me for breakfast?"

His tail wagged, and he showed sharp white teeth and a long pink tongue.

Daniela took a calming breath, her fist inches from the polished teak door as she hesitated, girding herself before knocking. Cutter's dedication to her health meant he'd woken her every freaking thirty minutes to make sure she wasn't dying. They'd both been relieved when he'd finally decided she was going to make it.

Despite being the bedmate of a woolly mammoth, Daniela had slept the last three hours, after Cutter left, like the proverbial log. She rapped smartly on the door.

Her off-the-cuff strategy to lie about not remembering anything was all well and good, but she figured "regaining" her memory—that was, lie a different lie through her teeth—would net faster results. "Come," a deep voice ordered.

"Good morning." Daniela entered his inner sanctum with a smile. It wilted a little when she saw him. Her first real view of him came as a rude surprise. Logan

Cutter first thing in the light of day was a jolt to her senses. The fact that she felt an instant, albeit unwelcome, curl of awareness came as a shock.

He was everything, and more than, she'd remembered. His slightly shaggy dark hair was several months past a cut, and he needed a shave. The dark shadow on his strong jaw just enhanced the piratical look of him, making him appear untamed and dangerous.

Fortunately, Daniela had been handling *dangerous* for quite some time now—not always *successfully,* but she was getting the hang of it. Still, his bland once-over made her insides contract, and left her feeling decidedly unsettled.

Never let them see you sweat. She wasn't sure what to expect. Last night there'd been so many unfamiliar faces that they'd all blended together. Defenses down, she'd reacted without thinking. This morning she had her armor firmly in place. Ready for whatever the day threw at her.

Just a woman thrown from a moving boat by bad guys. One who'd better come up with a logical explanation *fast*.

The dog circled the desk, tail wagging, and Cutter took his hands off the laptop keyboard. "Morning," he said pleasantly, rubbing the animal's ears while studying her. "Take a seat. How're you feeling?" His voice was rich and deep, and unintentionally, she was sure, seductive. Tightly leashed power hummed around him like an electrified fence.

"I'm—" Her mouth went dry as she suddenly noticed that the skin on his face and strong brown throat were scored with long red scratches. It wasn't a giant leap. "Are you the one who found me?"

"Dog pointed you out. He saw the beacon on your vest."

"He didn't manage to get me on board, I know. No opposable thumbs. So, did you . . . ?"

Cutter shrugged his broad shoulders. "I was in the right place at the right time."

She might have known that Logan Cutter himself would swim out to get her. "Thank you. I'm sorry I scratched you. And, I think, gave you a black eye?"

He touched the slight bruise. "Understandable under the circumstances, don't worry about it."

His eyes were bluer, and far more penetrating, than she remembered. He was more striking than handsome, his expression impassive. She got the uneasy feeling that she'd been judged and found lacking as his eyes brushed over her like a physical touch on her skin.

The hair on her arms lifted in response to that mild stare. Everything about him was dark except those X-ray eyes. If there was any emotion in them, it was challenge. A trick of the light, she was pretty sure. They'd barely exchanged a dozen words throughout the night. He couldn't suspect her of lying, she'd hardly told him anything. Yet.

He was all hard, lean muscle in a black T-shirt that announced in acid yellow, EAT. SLEEP. DIVE. As if he needed a T-shirt to tell the world he was at home on the ocean.

She looked away, glancing casually at the items on the shelves. Boy, the guy was neat. Everything in its place and shipshape. Her mother, who'd always despaired of Daniela's housekeeping skills, would approve.

A slab of unpolished, ancient-looking wood served as

his desk. It was positioned beside a large picture window framing a spectacular view so he could look out while he did whatever he did that required an office on a boat.

Daniela wasn't interested in the pretty day or the sparkling, infinite, blue water view. She casually looked around as she headed for one of two mismatched black leather guest chairs near his desk. He had some interesting artifacts on the ceiling-to-floor, wall-to-wall shelves. Various ancient tools in enclosed, dust-free cases. A few small fossils, some bones, some kind of stringed musical instrument. Bits of rock and blobs of a mysterious fused metal. Not what she . . .

Her heart did a hop, skip, and jump as she saw the translucent jade-green bowl on his desk. The sunlight streaming through the vessel pooled a delicate liquid emerald shadow on the roughly scarred wood surface.

My God, could it be that easy? If there was a hard way, and an easy way, somehow she always seemed to go for the hard. It was a huge, and unexpected, piece of good fortune to see the bowl she wanted/needed, prominently displayed in plain sight.

"I'm feeling much better, thanks." The bowl was why her idiot cousins had risked her life. She shifted the chair a little farther away from the desk, pulled her eyes from the artifact, and sat down. The dog padded away from Cutter to come and flop down on her foot. With a massive sigh, he put his large head on his paws and closed his eyes.

Her host indicated the dog with a tilt of his chin. "I see your new bodyguard is taking his job seriously. How's the head?"

"Apparently pretty hard." She smiled ruefully as she

touched the bump on her forehead. A slight headache was the least of her problems. "Thank you for saving my life. If you hadn't seen me . . ."

Cutter didn't quite smile. It was an interesting illusion. Daniela suspected that, like his dog, he was making only a nod to civility.

"As I said, you have Dog to thank. If it was up to me, you'd still be out there. Couldn't see anything in the dark, but he insisted."

Before he asked her about her memory, she grabbed the ball and ran with it. The best offense was a good defense, her dad, a tax attorney, always said. "When I woke up, I remembered."

"Remembered . . . ?"

She gave him her best, most charming, guileless smile. "Hi, my name is Annie Ross." She'd been using that name for the past week and knew she'd answer to it.

"Good that you figured out who you are." The small smile he gave back didn't reach his eyes. He didn't trust her, and he didn't care if she knew it. "If you still had that concussion, we'd be heading into port right now, whether you wanted to go to Lima or not."

Daniela forced herself to stay completely relaxed. Calm. Friendly. Trustworthy. "I have good reason not to want to go there, so regaining my memory was extremely fortunate for me." She shrugged, and regretted it when his attention flickered to her chest, making her annoyingly aware of the shape and weight of her unbound breasts. "And it saves you a trip," she added when his attention returned to her face.

The dog lifted his head and snuffed.

"We'll see. I see you and Dog have bonded."

Apparently, the three of them had slept together, all

night. Logan on the bunk just a few feet away, the wolf-dog spooned around her body on the narrow bunk like a thermal blanket. She wiggled her bare toes under the animal's hairy belly to no effect. "His name really is Dog?"

Logan shrugged broad shoulders. "Couldn't come up with anything more creative at the time, and it stuck. So, do we head to Lima anyway, Annie Ross? I'm sure people must be worried."

She met his stunningly blue eyes, and saw awareness simmering in the ocean-colored depths. That attentiveness made her mouth go dry, and caused the knot in her belly to tighten one more notch. "Nobody will be worried, I assure you," she told him evenly.

Not too many details, she reminded herself. Keep it simple. She kept her hands loosely clasped in her lap, and consciously stopped her foot from bouncing by slipping it beside the one wedged beneath the dog's belly. Nerves hummed through her like live wires. Her palms were damp, her mouth dry.

She felt as though she had a blinking neon sign over her head proclaiming her a big fat liar. *Hell*, she kept her eyes steady and her chin lifted, *what was one or one hundred more in the grand scheme of things?*

"Do you have family in Peru?"

Holy crap. *What?* She opened big, innocent eyes. "No, why do you ask?"

"Just wondered if you're Peruvian."

"My mother's from Mexico City." *Sorry, Mom.*

"Won't she be worried about you?"

Daniela shook her head. Easier to be an orphan, but she wasn't willing to kill off her mother to enhance her story. She settled for, "We haven't spoken for a while."

A month since her parents had left for their Mediterranean cruise.

"Were you part of a tour group on one of the cruise ships?"

"I was working on the—on a ship as a cruise *director* for a wealthy man and his friends. They'll think nothing of my disappearance."

"Does that man happen to be Rydell Case, by any chance?" His voice was steel, as his gaze went from cool to flinty. Clearly he didn't like the man he was asking about. She instinctively froze at his tone. Dog's head lifted from his massive paws, and he looked up at Logan, then swiveled his head to look at her. After a moment he put his head down again, closing his eyes.

Daniela suspected that Cutter, like his dog, could be a dangerous enemy.

After a nanosecond spent trying to decide if the other guy he mentioned was worth throwing under the bus, and deciding he was another complication, Daniela said honestly, "Never heard of him."

Logan leaned back in his chair. "The name of the ship?"

"I'm sorry, but I'd rather not say." She'd considered making up names to fit the story, but the less detail, the less chance he'd find out she was bullshitting. She could tell he wasn't her biggest fan, and they'd barely exchanged a dozen words.

"And the name of this 'wealthy man'?"

There was a fine line between giving too much information and not enough. It would be harder for him to catch her in a lie with too little information, but she had to give him something. Her mind raced. "I'd prefer not to tell you that either. Look, it was a job that went horribly wrong from the start." *God. Perfect. Yes.*

"It was a three-month cruise, on a ship similar to this one. I was hired to cater to the whims and entertainment of the guests. Arrange card games, excursions, make sure the food and wine were as they liked it . . ." What else did someone like that do? She had no freaking idea. Not sleeping with the boss was the point here. That would cover evasion, dislike of being too friendly, what she was doing here—Oh, yes. *This* was the perfect cover.

Or not.

"And?"

"Things were okay for the first few weeks, but he was bored with his current mistress and put her ashore—" Cutter cocked a dark brow for which port, but she repeated firmly, "Put her ashore. Then he decided I was fair game. I wasn't. I was polite, then I was adamant, then I started getting annoyed, then I was frightened."

She shuddered realistically, and, because she couldn't resist, picked up the bowl from his desk to stroke her fingers over the smooth rim as she spun her story. She'd read a book years ago about how to spot a liar. But she was trying so hard not to show any of the tells—or at least any she remembered—that she probably looked guilty as hell of lying through her teeth anyway.

She looked down at the bowl. "This is lovely," she murmured, trying to regroup. The artifact was stunning. The size of a large shallow teacup, it was as if it was made to fit in the palm of her hand. Heavy for its size and delicacy, it weighed over three pounds. Carved, she knew, from the original five-pound lump of emerald straight out of the ground in Muzo.

Its three short legs, pared from the solid piece, were fanciful fish. Emeralds were soft stones, and the bowl, once glass smooth, was now pitted by time. The ring of ships carved in beautiful, and delicate, bas relief circling the outside, were still easy to identify.

Nuestra Señora de Garza. La Daniela, San Isidro, and *Conde del Mar.*

"Yeah, it is." She glanced up to see him watching her intently. His steady, penetrating gaze made her feel transparent. It was as if he could see right into her lying, mouse-in-a-maze brain. "He attacked you, then threw you overboard?"

Daniela forced herself to maintain eye contact. Once, lying had been practically unknown to her. These days, she was becoming quite proficient at it. Practice made perfect.

She smiled slightly. Project calm, cool, honest. "No. I attacked him, and jumped overboard." She swore that when she discovered which idiot had clocked and almost killed her, before tossing her into the water, she was going to kick his ass.

His lips twitched. "Brave woman."

"*Desperate* woman," she corrected as Dog rolled over on his side, legs spread out in front of him, paws crossed. "Look," she told his owner. "Obviously I don't have any money on me, hell, I don't even have shoes. But can I stay on board for a little while?" *Two weeks four days, to be precise.*

The cousins might've forced her into this situation, but being on board Cutter's ship served *her* purpose as well. Might as well use it to her advantage. "Until I'm sure he's long gone at least? I'd be happy to work for my passage in any capacity. Except in your bed, of course," she tacked on calmly, just in case her story gave him any ideas.

"Of course." Cutter's tone was Sahara dry. Daniela would've preferred if he didn't watch her as if she were a bug under a microscope. "It would be no hardship to carry an extra passenger, we've got the room. Sounds like with your experience, you're a Jill of all trades. You're welcome to stay on the *Sea Wolf* until you deem it safe to"—he paused—"go back to your life. I'm sure we can find something for you to do. But go ahead and take a couple of days off first. How does that sound?"

"Fantastic, thanks. That's very nice of you. I haven't had a vacation in years. It will be nice not to be at someone's beck and call morning, noon, and night." And wasn't that the truth?!

"Are you and your friends on vacation?" she asked casually. "What are you doing out here? Game fishing?"

"We eat what we catch." His smile was electrifying. Had he decided to believe her? Or was that the same smile a shark gave when circling closer and closer to dinner?

"The *Sea Wolf* is a salvage ship. We're searching for a four-hundred-year-old Spanish galleon. *Nuestra Señora de Garza*." He leaned back in his chair. The sunlight beaming through the open window highlighted the blade of his nose and made his eyes look eerie and otherworldly. "She was returning home to Spain, loaded with gold and emeralds, but sank after a storm incapacitated her, leaving her to be finished off by a fierce battle with local pirates. A double whammy."

"She was obviously in the wrong place at the wrong

time." *Wrong ship, buddy, but the right load. Now, just turn around and head south down the coast.*

Daniela stroked her thumb over the smooth surface of the carved ships on the emerald bowl. The *Nuestra Señora de Garza* in front, followed by the three smaller gunboats like a mother hen by her chicks.

A little buzz of warning rang in her brain. Wait a minute—There was absolutely no way a man like Cutter, and she didn't even know him well, would give a total stranger that information. Tell someone he didn't know, who happened to be stuck on his ship, that there was the potential of scoring what amounted to millions of dollars in booty?

Either he was stupid. Which she was sure he was not.

Or very trusting. His eyes said not.

Or he was telling her so he could see what she would do next.

Playing cat and mouse could be exhausting. She'd thought she was done with it.

Daniela leaned forward, the green bowl, worth more than a king's ransom, held loosely in her hand as she lobbed the ball back into his court. "You're a treasure hunter? Wow. How cool is that?"

"Usually I'm a treasure *finder*," he said dryly. "But my prize this time around is proving to be elusive. We found our wreck, and some debris field—three miles of it—but not the treasure. We were going to move to another location this morning, but fishing you out of the water delayed us while we decided just what to do with you."

Lovely; she was like a lost and found package. "There's no reason to stick around here if you want to go somewhere else. I'm pretty good at unraveling puzzles.

Maybe I can help you find your big fish." She smiled and held up the bowl. "Are you following this map?" Her question sounded innocent, she hoped, but it felt loaded and weighty to her. There was no subtle way to work *that* into the conversation.

Of course he wasn't following the damned map. If he was, he wouldn't be hundreds of miles off course, parked in the wrong place, and she wouldn't be sitting here with a painful egg on her forehead, and a dog the size and weight of a moose cutting off the circulation in her feet.

"I have a copy of the ship's log, and from all our research the *Nuestra Señora de*—" He frowned slightly at the non sequitur. "What map?"

Daniela tilted the bowl so he could see the lines and markings scored inside. "This appears to be a map to . . . something." To my namesake, *La Daniela*.

His frown deepened, and so did the suspicion that she'd been too caught up in her own fabrications to heed the warning in his eyes. "What makes you think it's a map?"

She pretended to inspect the swirls and notations carved on the inside. "Maybe it isn't? That's disappointing. Well, it looks like a map—Longitude and latitude right here, landmarks, et cetera."

She'd never *seen* the bowl, but she'd heard her fill about it all her life. Her side of the family had never had possession of it. Generations of the bowl's owners had, for various reasons, never managed to retrieve the treasure for themselves. Instead, they'd passed along the story until it had reached mythical proportions.

Even when her cousins had told her they'd gotten the bowl into Cutter's hands, she hadn't been sure if they'd handed him a Tupperware container or the real deal.

The real deal, apparently.

She looked up and pulled a disappointed moue. "Probably not. I was reading something just last month in *National Geographic* about how hundreds of years ago, people used whatever they had to make maps so their descendants could find hidden treasures."

His smile disappeared. A shiver raced across Daniela's nerve endings. He wasn't going to go for any of this. Maybe if she'd had some damned heads-up that she'd be sitting here chatting with the man this morning, she would've come up with a smoother transition. Right now she was winging it.

It had all made sense when she'd lain there last night, just a few feet from a sleeping stranger, and concocted a story that now had more holes in it than Swiss cheese. But if she didn't keep dropping hints, Logan Cutter would head off in an even more wrong direction, or worse, give up the search and move on to something else, and she'd be quite literally sunk.

"Wouldn't it be incredible if this was the key to finding the wreck you're looking for?" She let her voice trail off doubtfully.

It *was* an emerald off the treasure of *Nuestra Señora de Garza,* given for safekeeping to the captain of the gunship *La Daniela* to take home to Spain with a fortune of gold and emeralds, right under the noses of unsuspecting pirates.

The smaller ship had slipped away from the pirates pursuing the larger ship, exactly as planned, with no one, including Logan Cutter, the wiser. Only to encounter El Niño hundreds of miles south, which had dashed it against the rocks. There'd been only one survivor. Her great, great, great whatever. A thief, a scoundrel, and oh, yeah. Probably a liar.

"That would be a one in a million chance and a hell of a coincidence." He held out an elegant hand. "May I?"

It was no coincidence, and it had apparently taken weeks of planning and attention to detail to get the damned bowl into his hands. Although, having interacted with the men responsible, Daniela wouldn't have thought to put "careful" or "planning" of any kind into their vocabulary.

They'd sold Cutter the bowl. Then waited. And waited. For him to change course. For him to head to where the bowl indicated *La Daniela* had gone down. For him to get a freaking clue. So far, nothing had gone according to plan. She hadn't wanted to be involved in this harebrained scheme in the first place. So they'd taken the choice out of her hands.

Daniela rose without disturbing Dog, and leaned over the desk to hand Cutter the bowl. Their fingers brushed. An electrical shock zinged up her arm, and she sat down on the chair with a thump. Holy Mother of God, what was that?

He turned the bowl between his hands. Stroked a finger inside, along the ridges and swirls. His face was obscured as his hair fell forward, but she read excitement in his shoulders, and the reverent way he cradled the bowl. "Interesting."

He placed it gently on the desk. "Stranger things have happened on the way to great finds." He tapped several keys on his keyboard.

Daniela held her breath.

* * *

She looked better this morning. Much better, Logan thought. Her eyes were her best feature, long-lashed and amber brown, the color somewhere between chocolate and aged whiskey. Her nose had a little bump on the bridge as if it had been broken, but it didn't detract from how appealing she was.

Her olive complexion shone with vitality and good health, and looked temptingly smooth and strokable. Her shoulder-length hair was the rich color of bitter chocolate, and slightly wavy. The bump on her forehead was covered by a sweep of glossy dark hair that brushed her long eyelashes.

Even in borrowed jeans a few sizes too large and a cotton T-shirt, she looked as if she wore designer clothes. She hadn't arrived wearing a bra, and she wasn't wearing one now. Her breasts were small and firm, her nipples small peaks against the gray fabric. Not that he was looking.

There was something defiant about her bearing, as if she was waiting for someone to challenge her. Was that a normal characteristic for her? Was she used to people doubting her? Was she a pathological liar and therefore expected people to doubt what she said? Or was her attitude a by-product of her fabricated story?

Or—stranger things could happen. He shifted his attention from her breasts to the bowl. The story was just preposterous enough to be true. She was exactly who she claimed to be, and her story was the real deal.

And he believed in happy endings and unicorns.

He pulled up the charts for the coastline of Peru on his computer, taking his time while he mulled over this

latest development. Miss Annie Ross had brought a lot
of questions on board with her.

Nuestra Señora de Garza was said to have first
encountered El Niño, and then, when she'd been left
vulnerable with her sails shredded, she'd been hit by
pirates.

The *Sea Wolf* was experiencing La Niña now, the
meteorological opposite of the El Niño that had sunk
Logan's Spanish galleon hundreds of years ago. She was
characterized as normal, even drier weather than usual,
with stronger offshore winds and a return of colder
water offshore.

Annie's story wouldn't be that hard to validate. If
the ship she'd been on went into port, they'd have to
register. Someone would know which ship and where.
Piet would find out everything necessary about the
shipping traffic in the time frame Annie could've been
thrown, or jumped, overboard.

This whole business with the bowl had come out of
left field. He'd known it was carved from a grapefruit-
sized emerald; the pitting in the soft surface of the gem
was unmistakable. He'd paid a couple of hundred bucks
to a persuasive seller on the wharf in Lima when he'd
arrived last month.

A pretty artifact, he'd thought. A look through his
jeweler's loupe later had surprised the hell out of him.
The stone was a high-quality gem, very old, and without
a doubt, out-of-the-stratosphere valuable. Clearly the
seller had had no idea of the value of what he'd sold.

Logan had immediately put out discreet feelers to
see if the bowl had been stolen. It was beyond price,
and worthy of gracing any reputable museum. But as of

yet he hadn't heard anything about it one way or the other.

Then in walks a woman he doesn't know, with a suggestion that the same artifact was a map. Call him a skeptic, but that stretched the bounds of coincidence to a whole other level bordering on science fiction.

He liked pretty things, and his new guest was certainly that, with her soft mouth and wealth of shiny dark hair. How much of her story was true? If she was lying, she was good. A trait Logan didn't find commendable.

He didn't give a shit if the lie was important, or to cover someone's ass. He demanded straight talk from his business associates, employees, friends, and family.

He was a hard-ass about it and didn't give a fuck if people liked his rule or not. If he caught anyone in a lie, the association was over. Done. Finished. Forever. He cut them out like a cancer and didn't look back.

So, liar or not, Annie Ross?

Not too many facts to trip her up, a little self-deprecating humor, and a studious suppression of her not inconsiderable sex appeal. He couldn't, wouldn't let the fact that he found her sexually appealing cloud his bullshit radar.

He was already predisposed to doubt her veracity because she'd been found floating in the ocean miles from anywhere and was strangely cagey when he'd asked how she'd ended up there.

Yet if this was some sort of nefarious scheme, it was a pretty dangerous one. She hadn't cried out when she was in the water. If not for Dog, Logan wouldn't have known she was out there.

"Well?" she asked eagerly, leaning forward.

"I'm checking the location to see if it's even possible." Peru was the third-largest country on the central west coast of South America, and unless this "map" was specific, it would be like searching for a needle in a 1,500-mile-long haystack. "But if these three marks here are what I think they are . . ." His voice trailed off as his heartbeat accelerated.

"What marks? The little ships behind the big one?"

"No, inside. There are four tiny uninhabited islands several miles off the coast down south that are spaced apart just like this. With a fifth about—" He ran the tip of his finger down inside where the fifth, and smallest, island would be. He couldn't see it on the surface, but he thought he felt a slight rough spot. "Hmm."

"Well?"

Or it could be wishful thinking. "Maybe there's another bump. But it might be a divot in the stone." He wouldn't tell her that the bowl was an emerald, or it might disappear. Or did she already know what it was *and* its worth? Was this what she'd come for? If so, it wasn't smart to bring its importance or value to his attention this early in the game.

"What about the ships on the outside? Do they correspond to what you know of the ship you're looking for?"

Logan's lips twitched as he turned the bowl in his fingers. She was stopping just short of hitting him over the head with whatever she was attempting to convey. Not subtle. But in spite of himself he was intrigued by her game. So much so that he was curious enough to let her keep going just to see where she thought he'd follow.

There was a galleon, followed by three smaller

gunboats. His heartbeat kicked hard against the wall of his chest in excitement. He'd seen the carvings, but it had never occurred to him that the four ships depicted could be *his* ships. Lima was an ancient seaport that had seen ships coming and going for centuries. What were the chances?

Annie was very interested, and apparently suddenly quite knowledgeable about the details on the artifact. Yes, there were markings inside, but how would she know that the rings were longitude and latitude unless she had spent time studying maps?

Or unless she knew about the bowl before she'd been hauled aboard his ship.

Logan smelled a con. A Rydell Case kind of con.

He had two choices. Toss her back overboard, with a "fuck you" note pinned to her chest, for his nemesis to retrieve.

Or keep her close and find out what kind of con was being run on him. Then he'd deliver the note himself.

He held the bowl up to the sunlight streaming through the window. "The *Nuestra Señora de Garza* was protected by three gunboats. *La Daniela, San Isidro*, and *Conde del Mar.* Ninety guns apiece. All said to have been blown off course by the storm, then attacked by pirates." There was no record of the ships splitting up. "All hands dead—"

"Or there was at least one survivor, who grabbed a chunk of emerald and made it home." Annie's eyes glowed with excitement. Seemed she understood the monetary value of the bowl as well. And how could that be when she'd just seen it here in his office? How did she know it was an emerald, for that matter? Had Case told her to keep her eyes peeled for emeralds as evidence that Logan had found the treasure?

"Maybe he carved in what he remembered of the location of the ship carrying the treasure."

"The *Nuestra Señora de Graza*." Logan tried to make the pieces fit—which they didn't. It was a nice fairy tale, but his ship had been sunk too far out to sea for anyone to have survived, let alone make it back to dry land. He shook his head, back to reality. "No one could have survived the attack, and certainly none of the ships were left intact after the storm hit, so even if someone had managed to escape death, there was no way they could've made it to land."

"Maybe the four ships weren't together. Maybe one sneaky little ship carried all the treasure on board for just the eventuality that they'd be attacked? Maybe she made it and went the other way."

He tilted his head to stare at the opinionated stowaway. "No. They would've stuck together, that's why the gunboats were with the galleon. They wouldn't have left her alone. Not in the storm, and not at the mercy of pirates. They were the muscle on the trip to and from Spain."

"Oh." She sounded disappointed. Why wouldn't she? She'd woven a romanticized story about what had happened hundreds of years before. "That's too bad. But what if?"

She was a dog with a bone, which made him even more suspicious. "Tell you what." Logan rose, and Dog rolled onto his back with a yawn that showed a lot of large white teeth. "I'll work with my team and see if the lines inside match any actual latitudes and longitudes, and if these bumps correspond to the outcroppings along the coast. I have some work to do topside first."

Tempted to lock the now intriguing bowl away, he decided against it. Wanting to see what she'd do next, Logan placed it back on his desk next to the photograph of himself arm in arm with his brothers. The photograph, the last taken by their mother, showed three kids in swim trunks grinning from ear to ear.

Annie stood too. Dog lumbered up beside her, pushing his massive head under her hand so she could scratch behind his ears the way he liked. Logan had to grab her arm so the dog didn't push her over as he leaned against her hip in ecstasy.

Her naturally olive skin was as silky smooth as satin, and cool to the touch. "I'll remember to brace myself next time," she said with a smile, shifting out of his hold to stroke a delicate hand between Dog's eyes. Logan smelled soap on her, and a female scent that teased his senses. The muscles in her arms were well defined, as if she used them for more than dumbbells at the gym.

He was glad she'd moved, because he was tempted to stroke her skin and linger in his sun-warmed office. "Dog will pin you to the ground and insist on ear rubs all day long if you indulge him." He indicated the door, and she and his dog preceded him into the companionway.

"As long as he doesn't suddenly decide I look like a meal, we'll get on fine." She looked at Logan under the sweep of her bangs. "He's never, um, tasted anyone, has he?"

"He seems to have a taste for you."

Her smile widened. She had pretty teeth, almost

straight except for a charmingly crooked eyetooth. "That didn't exactly answer the question."

Neither have you, honey. And until she did, Logan had no intentions of letting his guard down. No matter how attractive his mermaid was.

Three

They'd provided her with socks, but no shoes. Daniela chose to go barefoot, and the highly polished floors felt cool and smooth beneath her feet. Cutter, who wore deck shoes and no socks, spared her feet a glance and kept walking. He was wearing black boardshorts with his T-shirt, and he had hairy, strongly muscled, tanned legs. For some odd reason, looking at his legs made her feel fluttery inside.

She shoved her hair back from her face. She felt naked without at least the little bit of makeup she habitually wore. Mascara and blush would help. She'd seen in the mirror how pale she looked, and while the bump on her forehead had gone down considerably, leaving a thin red scab surrounded by purple, it still throbbed in time with her heartbeats. She reminded herself she wasn't here to impress. It was merely her own vanity that wanted a little color on her skin.

The *Sea Wolf* was a magnificent ship, spacious and well appointed, with plenty of sparkling glass windows giving uninterrupted views of the water. The interior looked more like someone's home than a ship. He had some excellent artwork: oils, watercolors, Japanese woodcuts, and several bronzes—he favored headless female nudes. That must say something about him, she wasn't sure what.

If she wasn't here under freaking duress, she might enjoy taking a leisurely tour of his works. *If* she wasn't here under duress.

Being pissed off at her cousins was counterproductive. She was here now and might as well make the best of it. Not that she had much choice. Daniela vowed she'd keep well out of Logan's way and be as inconspicuous as possible. God only knew that was a skill she'd honed in the past few months.

Usually she enjoyed other people's living spaces. What they chose to share their environments with told her who they were, or in some cases, who they wanted the world to think they were. In the last few years, she'd dealt more with the latter. She knew the type well; they came into her upscale Dupont Circle gallery, Blue Opal, every day. The art gallery and small retail store were located on the first two floors of a row house, her apartment on the third. Her building was situated in a well-established, tree-lined neighborhood, surrounded by brownstones, high-rises, galleries, bars, clubs, and trendy boutiques.

She wondered if she'd ever see any of those things again, as she walked through the sleek modern interior of Cutter's ship.

He didn't have a lot of "stuff" cluttering up the beautiful teak paneling or white painted walls. From the look of things, he liked life without complication—simple, easy, clean. Was this who he really was, or a façade created by an expensive designer trying to please her client?

To be honest, right now Daniela didn't give hoot about the décor of Logan Cutter's fancy boat. She could be back on the smelly fishing boat with the Idiots for all she cared. Being here was merely a means to an end. A means to two ends.

One was a minor blip on her radar, or had been a minor blip, until the Idiots had taken matters into their own inept hands. Her cousins were unpredictable, and far more dangerous than Daniela had suspected.

They were a different kind of villain than she was used to. Muscle, no brains. Still, she'd been a fool to let down her guard just because they were family. She sure as hell hadn't seen them as killers, but as soon as she'd refused to participate in their plan, they'd taken the choice out of her hands by hitting her over the head and dumping her overboard to get eaten by sharks or climb on board the *Sea Wolf* and do what they wanted her to do.

Trust no one was her mantra for a damn good reason.

Two weeks and four days.

She'd follow through on their scheme, because doing so suited her purposes, but she'd do it her way.

Stay hidden. Stay alive.

Those were *her* goals.

If she could manage that for the next two weeks and four days, she'd be home free.

Dog padded happily at their heels while Logan kept up the small talk as they walked through various large rooms and down several flights of stairs. A few black-and-white, artistically framed photographs—mostly of divers—graced the walls in one long corridor.

There were bookshelves everywhere, filled with a wide variety of neatly lined-up reading material, and hermetically sealed boxes holding interesting artifacts, she presumed from some of his dives. Daniela had never seen so much highly polished teak and brass in once place.

He told her there was a gym and a movie theater on one of the decks, but didn't show her. She suspected that, unlike Wes, Cutter didn't need the gym to pump up his muscles. He looked like a natural athlete and had the long lean lines of a swimmer. She kept her eyes off his legs.

They passed several men wearing white shorts and T-shirts. Daniela presumed they were crewmen, but they seemed relaxed as they greeted her and Cutter. Must mean that Logan was a decent man to work for. That boded well for the next few weeks.

"You okay?" he asked, slowing his steps as they wound their way through groupings of deep, comfortable-looking, white canvas slipcovered chairs in what looked like a library cum business office cum family room, all done starkly and dramatically in black and white. Wide windows gave an almost three-sixty panoramic view of cobalt blue water and a cloudless azure sky. Several open doors allowed a light breeze to play through the fronds of tall palms in glossy black pots strategically placed about the room.

"Yes, sorry. Just admiring your artwork. That's a Stephanie Kayne, isn't it?" She indicated a large un-framed oil painting hung away from direct sunlight and positioned between two ceiling-to-floor bookcases. Three curls of smoky black on a white background. One had to stand twenty feet away to see that the curls were the curves of a woman's naked back. It was one of the artist's most iconic works.

"It is. You have a good eye. I have several of her pieces. You enjoy art?"

Daniela shrugged. "Some of it." All of it. It was one of the biggest disappointments in her life that she had no artistic talent or even technical ability herself. She'd spent most of her adult life nurturing and promoting the talent of others in her DC gallery, and on a slightly lesser level, in the retail space where she showcased Peruvian artists and artisans.

The room needed color, but perhaps Cutter thought the never-ending blues outside were enough. If this were her space, Daniela would hang an MM Beck over by the long sofa for a splash of crazy color, and place a Fredricks Sher bronze for warmth on that little glass table over there . . . And . . .

It wasn't her space, she reminded herself with a pang that physically hurt her chest. The artwork that fueled her passion, and filled her life with color and purpose, might not be waiting for her when—if—she ever made it home again.

Don't, she told herself as tears stung her eyes. She looked up at the ceiling and blinked them back. One thing at a time. One foot in front of the other.

Two weeks and four interminable days.

She could do it.

"Have you always worked on ships, Annie?" Logan indicated they stop at a lavish buffet set up near the door leading to the deck. Carafes held fresh-brewed coffee and various labeled fruit juices, and trays bore artistically displayed cut fruit. Chafing dishes held fluffy pale yellow scrambled eggs, thick slices of savory ham, crisp brown bacon, and several other dishes, while ice containers held chilled pink shrimp, bright white-and-yellow deviled eggs sprinkled with a rust of paprika, and pale green and pastel orange platters of sliced melons and fat red strawberries. Pretty fancy. A regular upscale restaurant brunch buffet. He fed his crew well. Daniela wasn't hungry, but she knew she should eat something.

Beyond the windows a group of men sat under a black-and-white striped awning, their voices a pleasant bass blur accompanied by the susurrus and slap of waves against the hull. This deck was close to the waterline, and she was surprised at how noisy the calm water was.

A chill danced across her skin when she looked at all that water. It was a miracle she'd been seen. She rubbed the goose bumps on her arm, and turned her attention to the spread.

Grateful for the distraction, she poured fragrant, steaming hot coffee into a large, thick mug and added sweetener and a splash of cream. "For the last five years or so. It's a great way to see the world, or rather, I'd always thought it would be a great way to see the world. I didn't take into account that while my various bosses played, I'd be working. No weekends off."

My God, she almost believed herself. Suppressing a smile, she helped herself to a plate of fresh fruit and a napkin, then added a container of Greek yogurt for some protein.

Logan waited while she made her selections, a mug of black coffee in hand. No sugar. No cream. Plain. Simple. Uncomplicated.

"And what did you do to keep body and soul together before that?" It was a casual question weighted with a challenge.

"Oh, odds and ends." The look he gave her was unsettlingly direct, and nerves danced in her stomach. She reminded herself firmly that the man couldn't read her mind. "Mostly temp jobs," she told him vaguely, falling into step, taking a tentative sip of hot coffee as they walked, to hide her expression.

"But you have a home base?"

"I got bitten by the travel bug early. I'm kind of a nomad. I bunk on friends' sofas between jobs, then take off on my next crazy adventure. I love it." When this was over, maybe she'd become a fiction writer. The reality was that she'd always been pretty much a homebody. Her idea of a good time had been an evening with a good book, or an exciting movie, with her cat Piewacket on her lap—*Oh, damn. Don't go there.* Had been. *Had.*

Her idea of bliss, Daniela thought, feeling the acid of rising fury grind in her stomach, was to wake up early, and take her first cup of coffee down into the gallery before any of her staff arrived. To feel the coolness of the cement floor beneath her bare feet, and hear the hum of the forced air as she walked through the current exhibit, Pie winding around her ankles.

Not that she'd had a lot of nights at home in her apartment above the gallery in the past few months.

Then it had all gone to hell in a handbasket and crashed down around her.

Would she ever feel that sense of pride and accomplishment again? Or had Victor taken that from her, too?

Two weeks four days.

What had been done to her, how she'd been used, pissed her off no matter how often she told herself to stay in the now. She was safe. Now. All she had to endure, for now, was the passing of time. She wondered in what state she'd find her life when the dust cleared.

Logan touched her arm. The same zing she'd felt in his office earlier shot from her elbow into her fingers.

"Maybe you should sit down a minute, you look a little flushed."

Here. Now. Don't project.

Daniela forced her shoulders to relax, and loosened her stranglehold on her mug and small plate. "Just the hot coffee, I promise I'm feeling great." She felt an unexpected lump in her throat, and tried not to let on how his consideration affected her. She hadn't realized how much she'd missed simple human kindness in the last few months.

They walked out onto the deck. It was already in the mid-eighties, the sunlight brilliant as it bounced off the calm water and reflected off the white surfaces of the spit-and-polished ship. The fresh air smelled deliciously clean and salty, and she breathed in deeply, then let it out slowly.

The *Sea Wolf* was a terrific place to hide. She might as well enjoy the moments while she was here.

The animated conversation at the table stopped dead as they approached.

Two men sat on the dive platform below, removing their gear, and the others sprawled on the comfortable chairs surrounding an oval glass-topped table. As soon as they approached, the men all got to their feet. Like Cutter, most wore little more than shorts or swim trunks, and they were all deeply tanned and fit-looking. A glance at *their* legs and chests didn't make her breath catch as it did when she glanced at Cutter.

"Dive team. Annie Ross," he introduced her to the men as he pulled out a chair for her, and everyone rearranged themselves to accommodate them. "You remember Wes?"

Daniela smiled at Wes. "I do. Thanks for taking such good care of me last night."

Wes grinned back. He had the thick neck and bulging muscles of a weightlifter, and a sweet, boyish smile set off by a dimple. "It's not every day we pull a mermaid from the sea. Have the memories come back?" He gave her an inquiring look.

"In living color." She smiled, then nibbled a slice of pineapple. The heat of the day was mitigated by a slightly cooler breeze that lifted her hair off her shoulders. The pineapple was sweet and juicy and tasted like tangy sunshine on her tongue. Just as she took another bite she glanced up. Cutter's gaze was fixed on her mouth.

"Officially, I pulled the mermaid from the sea," a bald giant of a man in his forties told her cheerfully. She had to divert her own glance when the guy held out a hand as big as a Christmas ham. "Steven Galt, ma'am." His touch was gentle as he pumped her hand.

"Oh, God! Don't smile at the man," a tall, good-looking blond guy warned from across the table. He looked as though he should be carrying a surfboard under one arm and a bikini-clad blonde under the other. "He's engaged to marry the exquisitely beautiful, kind, sexy—but not too sexy—Kym Fullen back in Murrysville, Pennsylvania, in a couple of months, and he'll show you pictures of her from birth to the day they met in seventh grade and beyond. Ad nauseam. Fair warning."

He raised a soda can, a cheer, as he teased his friend, then gave her a bright white smile. A charmer, Daniela thought, not affected one way or another. He knew he was ridiculously handsome, and very sexy with all that beachy blond hair and those broad, tanned shoulders.

He did absolutely nothing for her. His type were a dime a dozen where she came from.

"Jedidiah Jones, the glue that holds this miscreant bunch together while Cutter works too hard moving his money around and being the boss of us." Jones shot Logan a friendly sneer.

Logan just sipped his coffee and smiled, his eyes reflecting the color of the water behind him. In the sunlight, the faint scratches on his strong brown throat, and the faint purple skin beneath his left eye were more obvious than they had been when she'd first seen them. Her heartbeat thudded uncomfortably. The event itself was nothing more than a frightening blur, snapshots of watery terror. She didn't really remember anything between being tossed overboard and being brought on board the *Sea Wolf*.

What she *did* remember was the heat of his touch on her cold body, and the unexpected sense of safety she had felt, hearing his steady breathing as he lay in the bunk just a few feet away from her all night.

Daniela drank her coffee, enjoying the camaraderie of the men. Earl Horner appeared to be the oldest. Early fifties perhaps, not quite as jovial as the others, he was pretty quiet as Logan and the others talked over each other. The men introduced themselves, adding bits of information like colorful confetti into the conversation.

Izak Vanek was from Czechoslovakia via Boston, and insisted on showing her a creased picture of his three little girls back home. She was more interested in how recently he'd *been* home.

"I've never been there," Daniela lied through her teeth. The moment he'd said Boston, her heartbeat had sped up and her hands had gotten clammy. God, six degrees of separation? "I hear it's very pretty. Do you manage to get home often?"

The unasked questions tasted bitter on her tongue, but she dared not ask them. They weren't questions one could ask a total stranger. Like, are you following the election primaries? Who'll get your vote?

"Not for the last six months, but for sure after this salvage." He grinned. "But my family sailed with us recently, so I don't get too homesick."

He didn't appear to recognize her, but her appearance had changed quite drastically since leaving DC. From blond back to brunette. Chances were that seeing her here would be out of context, and he wouldn't recognize her.

The air she was holding in her lungs hurt, and she let it out slowly. *Don't buy trouble.* She wrapped one hand around her mug. *Breathe. Smile.*

Aaron Cooper introduced himself as the youngest member of the team. He was in his early twenties, with a surprising six-pack for such a thin guy. He wore his long dirty-blond hair in a long skinny ponytail down his long skinny back.

It was clear to Daniela that the men had all been friends for a long time. They joked with ease and finished each other's sentences and teased like siblings.

A man dressed in white shorts and a white polo shirt with epaulets on the shoulders came outside and waited for a lull in the conversation. In his forties, he had short, sandy hair, and a deeply tanned, craggy face. Cutter introduced him as the captain, Piet Vandyke. He'd come out for his orders.

Daniela held her breath, her mug suspended between the table and her mouth.

Go south!

"We'll stay put until tomorrow. I have something I want to check out before we move our location," Logan told him easily.

Yes!

The captain went back inside, and Cutter gave her a considering look. "I suppose we can cobble together some clothes for you. This is an all-male ship, so it'll be slim pickings, but I'm pretty sure we have some women's odds and ends lying about, and everyone could contribute to your wardrobe. But perhaps we need to send someone into Lima to do a little shopping for you."

The last damn thing she wanted was someone going into Lima and mentioning to the wrong person that they'd fished a woman out of the sea. "Thanks, but there's no need to go to all that trouble. A pair of shorts and a couple of T-shirts will do."

Wes met her eyes and gave a small nod before shoving his chair back. "I've got cabin fever, why don't I make a port run? I can be back by late tonight." He looked over at Logan for approval.

Logan nodded. "Who else needs some shore leave?"

A couple of the men got to their feet. "God, yes," Aaron said fervently.

Izak tossed his empty soda can in a receptacle nearby and got to his feet. "I'm in. I saw a shop selling locally dressed dolls. The girls will love 'em."

The beautiful brown-skinned, dark-eyed, black-haired dolls, dressed in Peruvian alpaca wool textiles, with their intricate designs and vibrant colors, were popular at the Blue Opal Gallery. With a lump in her throat, Daniela sipped her coffee.

Wes walked around the table. "We can leave in an

hour. Annie, wanna come and give me a list of essentials?"

She glanced at Logan as she got to her feet, Dog beside her. "Are you sure . . . ?"

"Use the company credit card," he told Wes. "Might as well check with Hipolito to see if he needs anything for the galley. Hell, make an announcement. Anyone who wants to go, can go. Twenty-four hours." Logan paused. "Wes—Annie doesn't want anyone to know she's on board. Tell the others. Come and see me before departure."

"Well, one thing I can say." Jed cupped his clasped hands behind his head and shot Logan an annoyingly cheerful smile across the table as Annie walked off with Wes. The two of them disappeared inside. "You don't look bored to tears anymore."

"I've never been bored a day in my life. I'm too busy to be bored," Logan told his friend, his tone light.

"Our little mermaid is going to provide—days? Weeks? Of entertainment. I can't wait. What's her story?"

Logan took a sip of the steaming brew in his cup. The woman could say anything she wanted to, but he knew fear when he saw it, and could almost taste her desperation. "A story is probably exactly what it is—pure fiction. My bullshit meter is in the red zone."

Jed gave him a bogus look of shock. "That sweet girl, BSing you? Say it isn't so."

Ignoring his mocking, Logan filled Jed in on what Annie had shared with him, then paused to give Wes instructions when he returned to say he and the others were taking off. "Where's Annie?"

Wes smiled. "Helping Hipolito with lunch."

"We might all be dead by the time you get back to-morrow." Logan told him, only half joking. Rydell Case would love that.

"She did look like she knew her way around a butcher's knife." Wes's smile widened.

Great. Everyone was amused by the situation. "Go before I change my mind. And buy her a bra, for God's sake."

"Yes, sir." Wes went.

Logan found it annoying as hell that they were all so entertained just because a mystery woman was now on board. He frowned at Wes's retreating back. "Maybe they *should* take her to Lima and leave her there."

"When she's clearly afraid of someone?" Jed's brows rose with surprise. "With no money, and not even a pair of shoes?"

"All of which could be resolved with the swipe of a credit card." Why the hell couldn't they just find the treasure of the *Nuestra Señora de Garza* and be working their asses off bringing up a boatload of emeralds and diamonds right now? Then he'd be too involved, too damn busy to be distracted by a pair of guileless, whiskey-brown eyes and pale, slender feet.

"What if she's telling the truth, and some amorous, and clearly dangerous, man is really after her ass? Will your credit card protect her then, even if it is black?"

Logan set his mug down with an irritated chink on the table. "Could be she conked herself on the h—Okay, that doesn't make sense either. Not that she couldn't have done it to herself, but wouldn't she have fastened the vest correctly before doing so? Fuck. I have no idea what game she's playing."

Jed sat back in his chair, irritatingly silent for longer

than Logan liked, assessing him. "If she's playing a game at all. For once in your life, can't you just accept someone at face value and enjoy the ride?"

Logan couldn't just sit there. He got up and walked to the railing, curling his fingers over the smooth wood, staring into the cool, clear water. Too bad not everything in life was so damn transparent. "No. Because I smell a rat. And that rat could very well be Case, so I won't let my guard down. There are too many of us invested in this project. I won't allow that dick to fuck it up."

Jed hefted himself out of the chair and came to stand beside him. "We didn't *find* the treasure, so it's not as though he'll swoop in and steal it from under our noses," he pointed out in an annoyingly reasonable voice. "Last we heard, he was on the other side of the world, near the Cape of Good Hope, on trial for stealing *that* treasure."

Logan glared at him. "Whisper *Nuestra Señora de Garza* a bit louder, and the son of a bitch will be hovering like death on the horizon." He cocked his head as the mechanical whir of the helicopter doors opened overhead on the upper deck.

Jed shook his head. "You are one cynical bastard, you know that? I find it fascinating that your protective instincts are still fully intact even though you hate liars and don't believe a word our mermaid says. Why didn't you just send her to shore with the guys? No skin off your nose, right?"

The loud mechanical noise of the helicopter rising from beneath decks halted their conversation for a few minutes, then the whop-whop-whop of the rotors starting up blocked out conversation for a few more. The sound changed as Cooper lifted off. The chopper skimmed overhead, whipping up the water, and their hair, as it hovered low before ascending.

Logan watched them skim over the water toward Lima until the sound of the rotors faded. He leaned over, hanging his wrists over the rail, and turned his head as Jed continued the conversation as if there hadn't been a break. "If she's lying, why not jettison her before things get even more complicated?"

"I want to see how this unfolds."

"That makes two of us, Wolf, my man." Jed's eyes lit up. "In the meantime, if you're determined to hold her at arm's length, may I say dibs?"

"Don't be an ass," Logan told his best friend coldly. "She's on board my ship, and until I decide otherwise, under my protection."

Jed's eyebrows rose a fraction. "Really?"

"Really."

"For the duration?"

Logan narrowed his eyes. "Are you trying to piss me off?"

Jed had the audacity to grin back. "Is it working?"

"Not at all." Logan pushed away from the rail and went back to the table and sat down, stretching his legs out beneath the table. Where his damned dog should be.

Jed followed. "Can I at least flirt a little? I'm getting out of practice. Remember flirting? You used to be pretty good at it until you went all serious on my ass."

The past year, his brothers had had . . . issues, which, because they were so close, affected them all. But worse, and more immediately, his nemesis Rydell Case had recently ripped off one of his salvage teams near Cape Town, South Africa, to the tune of seven million dollars and change.

Right now Logan had the bastard tied up in court there. Not nearly satisfying enough as far as he was concerned. Case should be thrown in jail, and the key tossed in the sea. If he'd sent Annie, Logan wanted to know why.

Logan acknowledged that juggling ninety-nine things at once was his norm—he liked making order of chaos. He ran pretty much every aspect of Cutter Salvage, dealing with the numerous headaches, large and small, that went into running a multimillion-dollar business with employees and investors.

Usually he thrived on the disorder of life's curveballs. But the last few days he'd been feeling—inexplicably—flat. He tried blaming it on not finding the treasure this trip, but knew that wasn't really at the bottom of his listlessness.

His brothers depended on him to be a rock. Unmovable. Always there. He took his job as the oldest seriously. Maybe sometimes he went a little overboard, but his family and friends always knew that his word was his bond, that he would shoot straight on any issue. That his integrity, unlike his old man's, was one thousand percent there when they needed it. There was no room in his life to play.

"Life *is* serious. People depend on me."

"This is unfortunately, and too frequently, true." Jed sobered. "Okay, what do we do if and when we find the boat she was on?"

Logan bypassed the carafe of coffee in the center of the table, and reached over to snag an iced bottle of water from the cooler. He missed having Dog at his feet, damn it. If anyone needed a bodyguard it was himself. Annie's braless state had about given him brain freeze. He didn't need her here to remind him he hadn't had sex, not with anything other than his fist, in almost a year. Jesus. He needed shore leave himself.

"Work backwards" he told Jed, trying to shove the image of her small, plump, unbound breasts out of his usually bland imagination. "Find out who else was on board, start digging, get some answers, dig for more. The gash on her head is real. Her being in the water for hours is real. The rest is up for conjecture."

"What happened to your zero-tolerance policy?" Jed asked, curiously. "Think maybe it's time to realize that sometimes a little bullshit is necessary to make the world go around more smoothly?"

"Prevarication is never necessary." Logan had been raised by a man who lied just because he woke up in the morning. Everything about his childhood had been built on a mound of fabrications and half-truths. "I have a new half-brother to prove it."

Still, it had taken years of negative reinforcement before he got the memo, and pared his life down to a couple handfuls of people he trusted.

"You like family," Jed pointed out. "Why's this new brother an exception?"

"This character worked for Nick for years before presenting himself. I'm predisposed not to like *this* family. We'll see."

"The problem with people who have no vices is that one can pretty much figure they're going to have some pretty annoying virtues. Just sayin'." Jed tossed his empty soda can into the bin. "The sooner we find our wreck, the happier you'll be. Hell, the happier we'll all be."

"Damn straight, and on that happy note, our mystery guest had something interesting and unexpected to offer. She claims that emerald bowl I bought last month is a map. A map, coincidentally, to the treasure we're looking for."

"Seriously?" Jed laughed. "Now I'm with you on the bullshit meter."

"Come up to my office and let's see what the bowl tells us."

Still grinning, Jed got to his feet. "Maybe we should call in Madam Mermaid to interpret our reading."

Logan's eyes narrowed. "No, we'll figure it out without a slanted editorial. Get the lead out. We have a mystery to unravel, and a treasure to find."

Four

Daniela was on her way back to her cabin from the galley, a steaming mug of tea in one hand, a plate of warm brownies mounded with melting vanilla ice cream in the other, Dog a shadow beside her.

The corridor was quiet, the movement of the ship barely noticeable at all. On this deck were the cabins of the dive team. Half of them had gone with Wes that morning to buy her a bra. Dinner had been several hours ago, and she was so bored she was ready to run laps around the deck.

Her cabin was at the end of the long corridor, apparently right next door to Logan. Lucky her.

It was decent of him to allow her to stay on board, especially since he was making little attempt to hide his suspicion.

She was lapsed, but the whole Catholic guilt thing made a hard knot in her belly when she thought of everything she was doing to stay alive. Justified? She hoped Father Morgan would be proud that after all this time, she still felt pangs when she lied. He'd done a good job.

Her parents must be sick with worry. They knew some of why she'd run, but not all—thank God—and not where. Senator Victor Stamps had a very long reach and a way of persuading people that terrified Daniela, making whatever she did to protect her family worthwhile. Anything.

Her parents were enjoying a Mediterranean cruise. They'd return to New Mexico in three weeks. That was cutting it awfully close, but she'd had no say in the matter.

Thanks to Logan Cutter, Daniela felt safe, too. At least for the moment. Well, as safe as she could feel with two hundred pounds of muscular brooding male watching her every move. Right now all she needed to do was figure out how to outsmart her cousins before she repaid Cutter by bringing danger and mayhem to his pretty ship.

It hardly seemed fair. But then sacrifice was supposed to bring one closer to God. Cutter might very well be up for sainthood when she was through with this nasty business.

Even eating an elephant required one bite at a time.

Locate the bowl. Check.

Give said bowl to Cutter. Check.

Give him the broadest clues she could without hitting him over the head with said bowl or actually drawing him a map. Check.

Now it was up to him to decide what to do with the information. Logically, in her mind at least, he'd believe her, and hotfoot it down the coast in the other direction to see if maybe she was right. But since he didn't appear to be the trusting sort, she suspected they'd stay parked right where they were. "In the middle of the ocean until hell freezes over, right, Thor?" She tried out a new name for Dog. He didn't appear to like it one way or the other.

In their short twenty-four-hour acquaintance, Daniela had come to some conclusions about her reluctant host.

"Would you say intractable, stubborn, and believes he's always right? Yeah. What I figured." Her dad was the nice version of the characteristics, so Daniela had cut her teeth on the breed. Still, experience hadn't prepared her for Victor, who practiced the dark side of those traits.

The next step, if necessary, was a club over Cutter's thick head, then wrest the steering wheel out of the hands of the nice captain, and move the ship herself.

"On the other hand," she whispered to an oblivious Dog. "Why do I care if he believes me or not? I don't give a flying fig if we stay anchored here for the next two and a half weeks. In fact, that would be even better. What do you think?" No treasure would ensure the cousins stayed away.

"It's not as if he can salvage all the treasure in one day, right?" she quietly asked the dog beside her.

The dog didn't share his opinion, just cocked his head and perked up an ear. Judging by the hopeful glances he kept giving the dish in her hand, he was anticipating some of the ice cream melting off her plate as she walked.

Various scenarios galloped through her head. Right now she didn't doubt that her idiot cousins were just over the horizon, waiting for the *Sea Wolf* to move. The second Cutter retrieved all the treasure, they'd swoop in and take it. She'd tried to reason with them, and they'd agreed to split the treasure fifty-fifty with Cutter.

Even she wasn't that gullible. In fact, Daniela had never been that gullible. Which was why she couldn't figure out how she'd ended up in the mess that was her ex-lover, Victor.

Thank God he didn't know where she was.

That was a terrific place to be.

The cousins wouldn't make a move until Cutter had

the treasure. That could take weeks, or months, or . . . years? By which time, please God, she'd be back home in DC. Or wherever.

Victor's people were beating the bushes for her in New York, San Francisco, anywhere an upscale art dealer might normally go. She'd spent the last month zigging and zagging across the country, using buses, trains, and ferries to cover her trail. He'd had two fluky, lucky-for-him breaks, but she'd managed to elude his thugs both times.

Victor's minions wouldn't think to look for her in the middle of the Pacific. Nobody, other than the cousins, knew she was here. And she'd given them a fabricated reason and the same fake name she'd given Cutter. Even if by some twist of fate they tracked her down to Lima and the eight million people there, they'd never think to look for her out here in the middle of the damned ocean. Victor, of all people, knew how she felt about the water.

While it felt as though she juggled a bowling ball, an egg, and a swiftly moving chain saw, all while blind-folded, Daniela figured the respite Cutter was granting her would give her a chance to catch her breath, stop looking over her shoulder, and come up with a plan for her future. It seemed like a fair trade-off to be stuck in such close proximity to a man who clearly didn't trust her. Which was just fine by her; the feeling was mutual.

She'd claimed exhaustion as an excuse not to eat with the men—Okay, not to spend any more time with X-ray-eyes Logan. Nobody had asked her "exhaustion from what?" She hadn't done a damn thing all day but do her best to be invisible, sit around flipping through guy magazines, and try not to anticipate a hundred things going horribly wrong.

She wanted to find a TV and watch the news for any new developments. Better still, she needed a phone. There were several TVs about, so as soon as she thought the coast was clear, she'd go and see if she could find international news. BBC or CNN. There was nothing she could do about the phone. She almost smiled. Logan would be delighted to lend her his, she was sure. And then he'd know more than she wanted him to know.

The less he knew, the better, and the less she interacted with him the better. He had a way of looking at her that made the hair on the back of her neck stand up. Okay, made her nipples stand up as well. The bra would help with that problem.

She'd had dinner in her cabin, accompanied by Dog, who'd watched her chew every bite of chilled pasta salad as she tried out a dozen names on him. He didn't appear excited by any of them. After dinner, he'd taken a nap on her foot as she read a stupefyingly boring book about big game fishing in the South Pacific, the first book she'd grabbed when Logan had come into the library to tell her dinner was being served.

Half the divers had gone to Lima with Wes, and the other half were now playing poker in the library. Logan would win, Daniela decided as she approached her cabin. He had the steely poker face down pat. Perhaps the man didn't actually *have* emotions.

The beautifully paneled teak walls of the corridor were well-lit and spotlessly clean. From the spacing of the doors, each cabin was as roomy as the one they'd given her. Some even bigger. Someone had left his cabin door ajar, as she'd done, with the latch wedged between the door and the frame so she didn't need a hand opening it on her return trip from the galley.

"Are you allowed in there?" she asked Dog as he nosed the door open and pushed inside. He could probably go anywhere he pleased, but she called his name. "I don't blame you for not answering to Dog. That's a silly name. Come on, Sam, we'll keep trying until we find one you do like. Come on." She gave the cabin an inquisitive glance as she encouraged Dog to back out.

She didn't know whose cabin it was. Whoever he was, he'd left his cell phone on the tiny wedge of a desk by the door.

Torn, Daniela hesitated. She needed that phone. But did her need justify stealing it? Reluctantly, she continued down the corridor, passing a few more doors. She nudged her door open with her bare foot, then set her dishes on the same wedge-shaped desk inside her cabin. Dog came in and jumped up on her bunk, and she kicked the door shut. "He's going to want you back sooner or later, you know."

He lay down, his head on his paws, watching her with ice-cream-hungry puppy eyes.

"Wes told me in no uncertain terms when he was asking my freaking bra size, mind you, that I was not to feed you people food. Ice cream is people food, Dogbert. Can't help you. Damn it. I need that phone," she told him. Needed contact with the outside world. Needed to know that Victor's still in DC. Need to know that the authorities are closing in on him. That, damn it, I'm really safe.

Even on board a ship, in the middle of the ocean, Daniela felt the target on her back no matter what kind of soft-shoe shuffle she was doing to avoid going mad waiting.

If she sat down and slowly ate her dessert, and sipped her tea, and if the other door was still open when she was done . . .

Father Morgan wouldn't be satisfied with forty Hail Marys for stealing—no, borrowing—the phone. On the other hand, those forty, added to the hundreds of others she owed, were a drop in the bucket. Perhaps she could take a couple of months to recite them all at the same time when this was over.

She perched on the edge of the bunk across from Dog.

The brownies were tasteless, the ice cream bland.

Guilt was a terrific diet.

She wished she hadn't seen the damn phone.

Daniela sipped her tea, draining the cup.

She wished Whoever hadn't left his cabin door ajar. "He left it open because he doesn't expect to be robbed," she whispered, praying she'd resist temptation.

What if Victor's goons had somehow followed her to South America? She'd run from DC by such an arduous, circuitous route that she didn't see how they could've. "He doesn't even know I have family in Peru, Meatball. Distant certainly, but how hard would it be for him to find out with his connections? Not hard at all."

She showcased Peruvian artists and artisans as much as she could in her gallery, so she also had friends and dozens of business connections in Peru and elsewhere in Latin America. He knew she came to South America, and Peru in particular, at least twice a year. There was a trail to follow. Not that she'd been in contact with anyone she knew even peripherally since she'd arrived.

She'd never mentioned her Peruvian cousins, because

she'd never set eyes on them until she'd looked them up a week ago. They hadn't even known her name. "Still don't, Slaplilly."

She wasn't paranoid; people really were after her. And the consequences of them finding her this time were too terrifying to contemplate. Victor Stamps was a psychopath with a firm handshake, a winning smile, and some very powerful friends. When it came to Daniela Rosado, he liked to mete out his punishment personally.

The brownie/ice cream combo became a lump of cement in her stomach. She got up to put the dishes on the desk, then sat beside the big dog on the other bed. Pressing her fist to her sternum, she doubled over, resting her forehead on her knees, the dog's warm body a small comfort against her hip.

Go get the phone.

She couldn't use it and return it. The numbers she called would be on there for all to see, even if she deleted them from Recent Calls. There were ways to track the numbers, she knew. Victor had gotten numbers from her phone, which was how . . .

It's just a phone.

"That doesn't belong to you," she could just hear Father Morgan's gentle voice now.

It wasn't the item. It was the magnitude of how low she was sinking in a bid to stay alive.

Dog had abandoned him. Half his men were in Lima drinking and carousing, having a great time. His best friend was finding the whole situation amusing, and Logan had a woman on board whom he didn't trust, but couldn't stop thinking about.

"Aren't we centered and relaxed enough?" Jed complained, doing a tai chi Snake Creeps Down.

Logan, performing the same stretching lunge, told him unsympathetically, "Feel free to get lost any time."

"Misery loves company."

"I presume you're referring to yourself? I'm in a stellar mood, and will sleep like a baby after this."

"It's too slow."

"That's the point. One must practice slowly if one wishes to be fast. It's a balance of yin and yang. Black and white. Dark cannot exist without light. Life is defined by death. Everything in balance."

"You're not going to go all Karate Kid on me, are you?"

Hiding his smile, Logan ignored the oft-heard refrain and moved into the next form. They could've turned on any number of outdoor lights, but he enjoyed the moonlight. Thinking time. A delicate southerly wind moved his hair across his face, like ghostly female fingers.

Perfectly balanced, he moved from Brush Knee to Parry and Punch.

They'd ascertained that the emerald bowl *was* the map Annie claimed it to be. Crude, it wasn't a complicated, incomprehensible cypher, just straightforward lines of longitude and latitude scribed into the soft gem on the inside curve. A few landmarks here and there made it fairly easy to pinpoint the location of . . . whatever.

If the crude map was correct, and the ship had sunk where indicated, they were five *hundred* miles too far north. They needed to head south down the coast off Punta de Bombon. Every indication was that *Nuestra Señora de Garza* had been heading north to return to

Spain by taking the land route with her treasure. Had one of the swift gunships slipped away unnoticed and gone south instead, intending to sail around the tip of South America unnoticed?

If this map was to be believed, she'd never made it, and lay waiting beneath the water at least five hundred miles in the opposite direction.

Clearly, whoever had taken the emerald and scribed the coordinates inside it, thought the treasure worth considerably more than selling what had originally been an uncut emerald weighing close to five or six pounds, or about ten thousand karats. A hefty score even four hundred years ago.

"Doesn't appear that she lied about the bowl." Jed's voice was quiet on the warm air as he read his friend's mind. Which at times was damned annoying.

"Keep moving," Logan instructed when Jed planted his feet to chat. He waited until Jed glided into the next form. "No, but how did she know of its existence?" That didn't mean she wasn't lying about everything else. She was a good liar. Not many tells. But then he'd learned to be an excellent lie detector from an early age. He had acute lie-dar, and with Annie it had hovered in the red zone from the beginning.

He and Jed had spent the afternoon researching her claim that the bowl was a map to a new location. "It certainly *appears* to be accurate for the time period. The carving's quite accurate. Crude, and worn in spots, still, it's close enough to make me a believer."

"Which ship sank off the coast, though?" Jed asked. "One of the gunboats? Think the *Nuestra Señora de Garza,* anticipating a pirate raid, loaded her treasure onto one or more of the smaller vessels and sent them at a fast clip in the opposite direction?"

"Or was it some other ship altogether and nothing at all to do with our *de Garza*? If we follow the map, will it lead us to A, nothing? B, gold or silver bars? Or C, the wealth of emeralds and gold we're looking for? That's the million-dollar question."

"Well," Jed said dryly, reaching for a bottle of water, clearly done with exercising for the evening. "We aren't getting any younger or richer just standing here, are we?"

"We could follow the map to—Nothing," Logan pointed out again, taking the bottle Jed handed him. "The Spanish plundered all the treasures from the area. The ship, if there is one, could hold anything."

Jed's teeth glinted in the moonlight "Or everything. But I suspect a four-hundred-year puzzle isn't nearly as intriguing as finding out how our uninvited guest knows about the emerald bowl in the first place. *And* how she knew it was on board the *Sea Wolf*. Come on, admit it. Even you must be curious."

"Clearly Annie Ross's—if that's even her name— presence on board is no accident." He knew the why. To lead him to a treasure so someone else could scoop it up. "The big question is—did Rydell Case send her?" He found the idea of Annie and Case together—in any capacity—repellent.

A lamp suddenly turned on in the library, shedding a pool of amber light on the deck outside the windows. A few moments later the flickering glow of the television and the muted susurrus of voices broke the stillness of the night.

Jed's teeth glinted in the moonlight. "It appears your mermaid has insomnia."

"Probably from a guilty conscience." Logan straightened, his workout now rendered useless. He didn't feel either relaxed or at peace.

"Why don't you go in there and apply the thumbscrews? You'll feel better. I'm gonna go and soak in the hot tub . . . He picked up the towel he'd tossed over a chair back, then straightened to glance Logan's way. "Unless you want to apply said screws in the hot tub, in which case I'll go to the sauna—Unless—?"

"Fuck off, Jedidiah."

Laughing, Jed ambled off.

Logan swiped his face and chest with his towel, tossed it on the table, and went to see who was watching television.

Annie was curled up on the end of the couch, her feet tucked up under her, Dog's large head in her lap. She paused, stroking the dog's pricked ears as Logan strolled in. She gave him an indecipherable look from big brown eyes beneath her bangs. "I didn't realize you were outside." Her voice was talking-in-the-middle-of-the-night quiet.

Her eyes looked dewy in the dim lighting, and her flushed skin appeared as fine as a baby's. Logan wondered what it felt like, and stuffed his fingertips into the front pockets of his shorts to resist the urge to reach out and grab what he wanted. She was a woman made for moonlight or candlelight. He was tempted to turn on more lights to dispel the intimacy of the room.

Dog appeared to be in a blissful sleep, but opened one eye briefly to look at him, then closed it again.

"I like to exercise before hitting the sack. Couldn't

sleep?" he asked, rounding the sofa. She'd showered and he smelled that clean woman smell that made him think of crisp, sex-rumpled cotton sheets, and hot, smooth, tangled limbs. He patted Dog's butt as he sat down.

Her gaze flickered to his bare chest, then darted back to his face. "It's been a long day." She tried to straighten, but the dog's weight pinned her in place, wedged against the arm of the sofa. Her dark hair was still damp, curling slightly against her shoulders. The lamplight limned the curve of her cheek and the plump bow of her lower lip. "Just trying to unwind a little before I go up."

He leaned over and picked up the control from the glass coffee table, pointed it at the giant screen and turned the volume down. "A tsunami in Asia? The political debates? Riots in Atlanta? Not exactly conducive to relaxing before bed. No ill effects from that bump?"

"No." Her gaze flickered to the screen, then back to him. Her lashes were long and dark, spiky shadows on her cheeks, which were sprinkled with intriguing pale gold freckles "I'm fine. Really."

Logan put his bare feet up on the table, ankles crossed, then laced his fingers over his belly, letting his gaze drift over her. She was sitting too still. The kind of still a rabbit sat when a wolf was at the door. But her dark eyes didn't look fearful as she tilted her chin and met his gaze unflinchingly.

The woman had *cojones*, he'd give her that.

He followed her gaze to the flickering TV, where a London bobby was shoving some guy into the back of a paddy wagon. "What magazine did you say had that article that gave you the idea the bowl was a map?" The scene switched to the London anchor, then switched to news from around the world. Her head moved before her eyes followed to look at him as he talked. What was so fascinating about the news? Something she wanted to catch, or was it a way to not have to look at him? "I'd like to read it."

The pulse at the base of her pale, slender throat throbbed, as she said evenly, "It was fascinating. Sorry, I don't remember. Some magazine I picked up in the doctor's office a while back."

Logan leaned his head against the back cushion on the sofa. "If you remember the title or author, I can do a bit of research online."

"Ah—Mary or Molly Edwards or Edmonds, maybe . . . Sorry, I don't really remember. It was months ago . . ." Her voice trailed off, then she rubbed her hands over her mouth and cheeks, and gave him a tortured look. "Oh, damn it," she whispered roughly, shutting her eyes, then opening them again. "I can't do this, it's nerve-wracking!"

"Watching television? I admit the reception isn't g—"

"I made that up."

He rolled his head to look at her straight on. Her posture might look relaxed, but every nerve and tendon in her body was poised and ready for flight. "You made up the magazine article?"

"Well, yes. That too. I lied about reading about the bowl for starters."

Logan's brow shot up. That he hadn't expected. "You lied?"

"I didn't need to read about it. I've heard the story of the treasure of *La Daniela* my whole life. My great, great, however many greats, uncle was a seaman on board *La Daniela*. He was forced to accompany the men back to Spain with the treasure. He was on the gunship when she was hit by the storm.

"He was one of two survivors. The other man died a few years later. According to family history, *Nuestra Señora de Garza* was really a decoy. The treasure was switched to *La Daniela* after they left port, and were far out to sea. The big ship headed north with two of the smaller ships, *La Daniela* went south . . ."

Logan swung his feet to the floor, turning fully to face her. So she had lied. It pissed him off that he was disappointed, even though he'd known. He hadn't wanted to be right.

He cut to the chase. "Are you saying you believe the smallest gunboat carried the treasure, ostensibly back to Spain, and she was the ship that sank down the coast?"

"That's the family story." She toyed with Dog's ear, something he usually hated; he didn't even twitch.

Despite his fascination with her story, and trying to sort out truth, half-truth, and outright bullshit, Logan wanted her hands petting *him*. Crazy shit. He dragged his attention back to her cockamamie story. Or what could be the truth, if he listened to his gut.

His lie-dar wasn't giving him an accurate reading. She was good, Logan thought, watching her, his own expression neutral. Very good, in fact. She displayed just the right amount of hesitation and eagerness. Just the right amount of calm curiosity. Maybe it was part of the truth. Not all of it. If Logan had been less intuitive to the liars of the world, he might even have been fooled by her. Oh, she was still lying all right. He just didn't know about what.

"*La Daniela* was long gone when the storm came

up, and then the pirates attacked *Nuestra Señora de Garza, San Isidro,* and *Conde del Mar.* The story goes that my great-great-uncle was pressed into service, and when the storm hit, driving *La Daniela* against the rocky reef, he and another sailor jumped ship and somehow made it to shore."

She rubbed between Dog's ears, and the animal groaned his pleasure.

Crap. He was jealous of his dog.

"The two men made it back with the biggest piece of the treasure they could carry," she continued. "The emerald. Apparently the other guy was a woodworker, and he carved the map. He died. I suspect my distant great-great-uncle got his hands on it and returned to scoop up the rest of the treasure that nobody knew about. But when he went out in his fishing boat the water was too deep, and he couldn't get to it. The story was passed on. Of course, we never believed it for a second."

"We?"

"My mother's side of the family going back several generations. *La Daniela*'s treasure has always been a bone of contention in my family. Sort of the line in the sand between the good guys and the bad," she added wryly as her attention, strangely, returned to the television. Some Kennedyesque DC politician spouting something with utmost sincerity, tears in his eyes.

Logan returned his attention to her. "Were you behind the guy who sold me the bowl?"

She shook her head, then gave him a worried frown. "No. I was an unwitting participant because my cousins couldn't get you to turn around."

"Turn around?"

She was distracted by the news, which was always

the same crap. Logan clicked it off and the screen went dark, plunging the room into the amber glow of the one lamp by the window. She blinked at him like a sleep-walker.

"Do these cousins have names?"

"Look," she said earnestly. "I don't want you to report them to the authorities. They haven't done anything—yet, and hopefully you can do a better job than I did of dissuading them from swooping in and stealing you blind."

A nerve pulsed in his tightly clenched jaw. "Names?"

She let out a breath. "Piero, Angel, and Hugo—" she hesitated, and he encouraged her with a hard look. "Apaza."

At least it wasn't Rydell Case. Logan committed the names to memory. "They the ones who hit you and tossed you overboard?"

"They told me we were coming out to your ship to tell you about the bowl. Once we left the harbor, we had . . . a difference of opinion."

He felt a sudden fury churn up inside him, and said savagely, "Your life vest was improperly fastened."

She gave him an unhappy look. "I'm fortunate they put one on me at all."

"Yeah. Fortunate. Why has no one bagged the trea-sure already? They've had the map for hundreds of years. Surely someone in all that time must've had the smarts and wherewithal to dive for it?"

"You'd think so, wouldn't you? Apparently, at the time of the wreck no one had the capability of diving so deep. That's why they carved the map out of the emer-ald, so that they'd never forget the location. It was no use knowing *where* if they didn't have the technology to get at it. Then the emerald seems to have disappeared for a century or two. I suppose it's possible that their branch of the family—like mine—thought it was all a big myth."

"Why didn't these cousins dive themselves?"

"They couldn't afford the equipment, not to mention, they had no idea how to go about a salvage of this magnitude," she said dryly. "Plus it's so much easier to let you do the all work and go to the expense. They plan to stroll on board and grab it after you're done."

"So, that's been the plan all along? I go south, find the treasure, then the Three Stooges swoop in and relieve me of it?"

"Apparently. I'm really, really sorry." She looked sincere, But that could be part and parcel of the whole con. "I tried reason and threats. But they've waited all their lives to retrieve the treasure."

"Unfortunately," his voice was cold, "they're shit out of luck, since I claimed the treasure as my own a year ago and did it all legally. They should've thought of that. The papers are signed and sealed, and as official as death."

She gave a small two-shoulder shrug. "They think they have a right to take it."

"It's a popular misconception held by several people in my line of work. Their thinking is erroneous."

Her fingers flexed, digging into Dog's ruff. "What are you going to do?"

Logan leaned forward, elbows on his knees. Casual enough, but it brought him closer to her. "Talk to my lawyers, then go find the treasure. Your cousins and I will iron out the details first, however."

Her eyes widened a fraction. "You're going to make

a deal with them? I hate to sound un-family-like, but these guys are crooks."

Logan couldn't help but grin. Exactly what did she think he'd been doing as a treasure hunter and salvage operator, paperwork? Danger didn't scare him. "Thanks for the heads-up."

"No, seriously. My side of the family hasn't spoken to their side of the family in over thirty years. I'd never even met these guys until a week ago. If there's an easy way for them to do something, believe me, they'll take the low road. These are *not* nice people."

Logan pinned her with an unwavering gaze. "And you think I am?"

Five

He had a smile like a shark. How had he pulled the story out of her when all he'd done was sit there, watching her like a lazy, blue-eyed predator? A smart woman would dive overboard and start swimming back to Lima. But a smart woman was damned if she'd run from a man ever again.

She'd made her line in the sand. Logan Cutter's ship just happened to be straddling it.

His seductive superpower was his unwavering disregard for bullshit. Unlike her ex, Victor, who oozed fake charm and faux emotion, Logan let her know exactly how he felt. If what she read in his eyes was true, then Cutter still thought she was a big fat liar, and he made no pretense otherwise.

Daniela felt bad enough about the situation already. His look just summed up what she'd been feeling since she'd been pulled from the sea. Guilt. The great motivator. Father Morgan would be so proud. No wonder she'd leaked her story like a broken faucet.

Victor had his own methods of persuasion. Humiliation. Cold mockery. Disdain. Cutter's stillness was just another form of coercion. The ding to her conscience came from the fact that she was still lying by omission. But one step at a time.

"How dangerous are these guys?" His even tone

suggested he wasn't particularly concerned. There was a lot of him, and most of it was a lot naked since he was only wearing loose-fitting gray shorts.

His skin gleamed like smooth bronze in the far-too-intimate lamplight. His dark hair was a bit shaggy and looked as if a woman had spent a happy hour or two running her fingers through it. And if she allowed herself to go down the—Holy crap, look at the man's rock-hard six-pack, and the crisp dark hair on his pecs, and . . .

Mouth dry, Daniela dragged her gaze up his flat belly, passed his pecs, and moved up the strong, tanned column of his throat. Her gaze landed on a pair of inquiring cobalt eyes. Really, the man was a whole other kind of lethal. He should be forced to wear sunglasses. And a shirt.

"I don't know," she said slowly, willing her galloping heartbeat to slow down before she passed out. "They're petty criminals. Certainly they're lazy and greedy. They struck me while I slept and threw me overboard, so I suspect that, yeah, they might be more violent than I gave them credit for."

No wonder her mother always crossed herself when she mentioned her older sister Jimena and her husband, who was in prison more than he was out. And her mother had never met her three nephews either. Even Lady Clairol wouldn't be able to prevent her from turning gray then. *Be safe, Mom. Please be safe.*

Daniela's speech was slower than usual, because while she was talking, she was thinking, God. She'd stood up to the world's most devious, terrifying intimidator, and Cutter, without lifting a finger, or making a threat, had managed to get her to spill her guts without even trying.

"I certainly don't trust them. That said, I don't know them." At all. She'd met the Three Stooges a week ago. And what she'd seen of them she didn't like. Liked them even less for hitting her and tossing her into the ocean. It was a mixed blessing that she'd been in flat-out panic mode from the moment she'd hit the water. To say she had an aversion to having her face in water was the understatement of the century. Daniela masked a full-body shudder by stroking both hands down Dog's back.

"You don't consider them violent?" he asked incredulously. "They struck you hard enough to almost kill you, and dumped you overboard like yesterday's garbage." Strangely, he sounded furious. Or as furious as a cold-blooded shark could sound.

"Well, yeah. You have a point there," she said tightly. He'd need more than sexy feet and impossibly blue X-ray eyes to get her real motivation out of her. But talking about her cousins was better than telling him why she'd hooked up with them in the first place.

Three words.

Senator. Victor. Stamps.

She had just about had a coronary seeing his handsome, oh-so-sincere-politician's face on the big screen right before the commercial break, with the crawl that he had an important announcement to make. The press might think he was about to announce his bid for the presidency. But Victor was smarter than that. He knew how powerful anticipation was. He wasn't going to declare for two more weeks.

No, he was going to say something about *her*.

They'd give him a sound bite, and probably flash her photograph up beside him, as he wept crocodile tears for his missing fiancée. Thank God Cutter had turned off the TV in the nick of time.

Daniela felt as though she'd had the most narrow of escapes. Surreptitiously, she wiped her sweaty palm on Dog's thick fur. He lifted his head and licked her wrist. Foolish tears stung her eyes. She looked up just in time to see the muscle jump in Logan's jaw.

Midnight-blue eyes watched her unblinkingly, as he drawled, "We'll see just how petty they are when I contact the cops in Lima."

She found she couldn't look away from those startlingly blue, suddenly predatory eyes. A shiver of apprehension or anticipation skittered through her. Of course he'd contact the authorities. Except Daniela didn't want anyone to know she was involved, however marginally. "Of course you'll do as you like. But since you haven't even headed out to the site, or found anything yet, why not wait a while?" She kept her suggestion casual.

"I'm sure they won't do anything until they see you've salvaged the treasure. That could take weeks or months, right?"

"Sometimes *years.*" Absently, he rubbed a hand across his chest.

Daniela flexed her fingers, almost feeling the damp glide and the crispness of the hair there, as if it were her hand touching him instead of his own. Dog lifted his head, and she realized she'd fisted her fingers in his fur. She stroked an apologetic hand down his back, and he put his head back on her curled legs with a sigh.

"Since I presume their intent wasn't to kill you," Logan said, "aren't they expecting you to contact them?"

"No." Daniela wanted to go back up to her cabin. Her

life was fraught with complications already, and her hyperawareness of Cutter wasn't helping. It was as though he was sucking all the air out of the room, making it hard for her to breathe, or swallow, or think rationally.

A hell of a time for pheromones to kick in.

Another minute or two to finish the conversation she'd started, five minutes tops, and she'd excuse herself. "These guys aren't the brightest. I presume they'll follow you to the location and skulk while you do all the work."

Even in the muted lighting, his eyes were an impossible shade of cobalt, and disconcertingly direct, making Daniela want to fidget. She stroked Dog. One of them might as well feel soothed, because she sure as hell wasn't anything close. She felt wired, and so jumpy, she wanted to have hot, wild s—Wanted to go for a long hard *run*.

"I suspect you're right." Cutter showed not an iota of the tension she was feeling. He was as relaxed as a big cat on sunny tree branch in the savannah. He looked as though he was settled for the duration, but Daniela didn't want to sit there in the far-too-intimate semidarkness with him. His hot gaze felt as tangible as warm honey on her face, her throat, her chest . . .

Her breasts felt heavy, and she was insanely aware of him. His contemplation was as possessive as if he was running his hands all over her, and that look filled her with an aching, nameless longing.

No, not nameless at all.

Inappropriate. Inconvenient. Wrong time, definitely wrong place.

Her body wasn't getting the memo.

He smelled . . . hot. Salty. His skin was still sheened

with the sweat he'd worked up doing whatever he'd been doing out on the dark deck earlier. Dear God. It should be illegal, if not immoral, for a guy to look as mouthwatering as Logan Cutter did. She could barely catch her breath. Everything about him tantalized and aroused her senses.

Easy.

Get up.

Walk out.

Now.

She'd told him about the cousins. Warned him. Told the truth—that bit of it anyway. Time to remove herself from temptation. She yawned, not totally faked, and stretched out her legs slowly, dislodging Dog, who groaned and cast her a reproachful look as he found himself on his feet between the sofa and the coffee table. Daniela slid her feet to the floor, and stood.

Ow! Ow! Ow! Her feet had gone to sleep, and the rush of blood to them felt like thousands of pins and needles stabbing her skin. Logan's gaze drifted up her body to rest on her face. Slightly light-headed from lack of oxygen, she wiggled her toes to get back some feeling. "It's been a long day. I'm going to turn in."

She kept her voice cheerful, determined to escape without giving anything else away. "Thanks for the hospitality. I'm sure you want Poseidon to stay with you. Night."

"Poseidon?"

She looked at the dog. The dog looked back. Daniela sighed as she kept wiggling her toes. She didn't trust in her ability to walk away in any sort of dignified manner while her feet were still numb. "Yeah. I see he's not crazy about that name either."

"He has a name." Logan's lips twitched ever so slightly. Possibly a trick of the light. But his amusement, or her demandable imagination of it, brushed like a cat's tongue across her nerve endings. Amused or not, tension pulsed in the air between them.

"Dog is not a name." Her voice sounded soft and breathless She cleared her throat. "If his name was Cat *that* would be a—"

With all the dignity of a clown getting out of a clown car, she toppled over Dog as she shuffled on numb feet, trying to make a graceful exit.

She was at least three feet away from Cutter, who lounged at the other end of the sofa, but when she fell, somehow she landed hard against his chest, her hands splayed on his flat belly, her legs sprawled between his.

Hot skin. Engulfed by sizzling sensations.

A predatory gleam sparked in his eyes. Tilting her chin up with his fingertip, he watched her from beneath lowered lids and murmured, "Well, hello, Annie Ross."

Daniela blinked as his lips descended. "Who?"

Her lips were slightly puckered, and petal soft as Logan brushed her mouth with his. He moved his lips over hers in a slow, lingering exploration. When he swept his tongue into the warm cavern of her mouth he tasted chocolate, and something elusively sexy that aroused him as if they'd been having foreplay for hours.

He felt the galloping of a heartbeat against his chest, and wasn't sure if the heavy, rapid beat was hers or his own. He threaded his fingers through the silky strands of her dark hair, tilting his head for better access. She canted her head the other way as she swept her slick warm tongue over his, giving no quarter and expecting none in return.

Her cool fingers flexed against his belly, ratcheting up his heat. Logan wanted to twist their bodies so she lay beneath him along the length of the sofa, but a tiny part of his reptilian brain that could still function, remembered, despite her response now, the way she'd retreated from him in the cabin the night before.

That small show of nerves could be anything. He didn't know her well enough to know what might be a hot button, but he didn't want to spook her. Not now when her body molded against his, soft where he was hard, smooth where he was rough. Her touch sparked fire on his skin and sent arcs of heat racing through his veins.

Careful not to scare her, he kept his body relaxed, no matter how hard, literally, it was not to take control of the situation.

He savored the soft shape of her mouth with a sweep of his tongue, enjoying the silky glide of hers as she explored. He drank her in, caressed her mouth when he wanted to caress her body. Logan disciplined himself to keep his hands in the luxuriant fall of her hair. It was a lesson in restraint, but he shook with it.

It took several rapid heartbeats before he realized she was no longer engaged, and that she was trying to break free, her body stiffening in resistance. Logan immediately untangled his fingers from her hair, lifted his hands as she sputtered, "Mfft!" and jerked her head away.

She rolled off him so quickly that he had to shoot out a steadying hand to prevent her from crashing into Dog, or the coffee table behind her. She held up her hand, and he dropped his as she scrambled to her feet beside him.

Expression closed, she was breathing as if she'd just run a marathon, but far from the heavy breathing of passion, he suspected it was panic. He frowned. He didn't take her for a woman who'd back off from anything, including passion. And it had been that for several minutes.

Overreaction?

Fear?

Jesus. Was she afraid of him? What the hell had happened to her to make her react this way?

Her hair was a sexy tangled mess from his fingers, her cheeks flushed. The peaks of her erect nipples showed clearly beneath the thin gray cotton of her T-shirt, which was hiked up beneath her breasts, the fabric twisted.

She looked down at him with dark, flashing eyes. "I told you. I appreciate your hospitality for letting me stay on board, but I won't pay you back with benefits."

She yanked the bottom of her shirt down over her midriff, but not before Logan saw the three-inch scar on the velvety, vulnerable skin just below her navel. His gut went cold. The thin red line was recent. Not as recent as yesterday, however. Had she been in a car accident? Surgery? Could be a burn, or a bad scrape . . .

He cupped the back of his head with both hands to keep himself from reaching for her. The temptation to haul her back into his arms, to cradle her, to stroke her and pet her, was ridiculous.

Like encouraging a porcupine to sit on his balls.

"Did you completely make up the story about the guy on the fancy ship mauling you," he asked conversationally, "or was that fact?" Because if it was fact, he was going to find the son of a bitch and swab the deck with his dick.

"There's always a mauler on a fancy ship to contend with," she said sweetly. "It wasn't that much of a stretch. Do you want Malcolm to stay with you, or can he come to bed with me?"

The dog made a low rumbling noise in his chest, as if to disagree with that name too. She glanced down. "Sorry, boy. Did I hurt you?"

"He's fine. To err is human, to forgive, canine." She didn't crack a smile. "Dog needs to take his evening constitutional. I'll bring him to your cabin when I turn in."

Logan saw no point in wasting time. He roused Jed before dawn and they took the chopper to Punta de Bombon, stopping briefly to refuel en route. Upon arrival, they chartered a boat and headed out to the site indicated by the emerald map. En route, he called Wes to tell him that the team could have an extra day of R&R in Lima. Jed overheard him and raised an eyebrow.

"You're getting soft."

Logan shrugged. "If this turns out to be the right place, they're not going ashore for a long time. May as well let them stay in Lima, instead of coming back to the *Wolf* to sift more sand."

It was Jed's turn to shrug. "We'll see. What about Annie?"

"What *about* Annie?"

"She's going to wake up and find us gone."

"I left her a note."

"But—"

"Are we there yet?" The subject was closed.

"Almost. Get out the fish."

The fish was actually a metal detector on a long line. Logan got it set up and they dragged it back and forth across the area, looking for hits. It was a painstaking process, but one they were both accustomed to; they knew how to wait. This time, it paid off. There was definitely something below them. A something large enough to be the *La Daniela* or one of the other gunships. The map had been off by several miles, but considering the location and the centuries of tides and winds that had passed, that was literally a drop in the ocean.

Logan called Piet and told him that the dive team was spending the extra day in Lima, and to get ready to move. No way that he was giving any details via a cell phone; the signal was too easy to intercept, something he'd learned the hard way. He resisted the urge to ask about Annie, said he'd be back that night, and rang off. Whereupon he had to deal with some uncomfortable facts.

Logan knew he'd never have found the frigate without the bowl. And never would've known what the bowl was telling him, without Annie.

And, he reluctantly acknowledged, her imbecile cousins.

When he returned that night, Logan holed up in his office, making calls and sorting out paperwork. He wanted every i dotted and t crossed. He still had a business to run.

Family first. His youngest brother Zane was planning an island wedding to Teal. No surprise. But they wanted to get married as soon as possible because Sam, Teal's father, was seriously ill.

Fortunately, Sam seemed to have a new lease on life since Teal had come back to Cutter Cay, and right now he was doing great. Zane and Teal wanted her father to walk her down the aisle. A fine sentiment, Logan thought. He liked both of them, and he was happy to see Zane relaxed and happy, and not trying so damned hard. Teal, well, Teal was practically his little sister anyway. She'd grown up among the Cutter boys, so he was glad to have her back in the family again.

Nick had landed himself a princess, and added a new brother to the mix. The whole dynamic of the family was about to change. Logan wasn't sure he liked it, but change, like shit, happened. He'd roll with it.

Speaking of shit happening, he put in a call to Nick to fill him in on the amusing message he'd gotten from the company's insurance agent, who'd heard about Nick blasting his own ship to hell. The man was only amused, Logan was sure, because his company didn't have to foot the bill for a new ship. The "friends" Nick had been helping had deep pockets, and they were the ones paying to replace the *Scorpion*. It was a good story, though.

Daniela woke up to the sound of Dog scratching at the door. She looked at him blearily for a moment, then realized that he needed to get out of the cabin.

"Give me a second, Dog."

She got up, let him out, and headed for the bathroom, stretching and yawning. She woke up in a hurry when she saw that a note had been taped to the bathroom mirror.

"What the—?"

It was from Logan. Short, to the point. He and Jed

were checking out the site, he'd be back by night, she was to relax.

Well, gee, thanks, buddy. And how the hell had he put that note in there without her knowing? She'd have a word with Dog later, the turncoat.

So, what was she going to do all day? It suddenly struck her that it had been entirely too long since she'd been able to answer that question with a firm "Nothing." Not only was she beyond Victor's reach for the moment, she didn't have to worry about keeping her guard up around Logan. Those blue eyes saw far too much, and she didn't mind having a break from being observed so closely.

She yawned again. She could even go back to bed. And the more she thought about it, and the more she relaxed (although part of her rebelled against following Logan's order to relax), the more tired she got. She'd been in constant motion for what seemed forever, and this was the first time she'd stood still long enough for everything to catch up with her. The bunk looked like heaven.

Six hours later, she woke up, went to the galley and got a bite to eat, and then sacked out again. As she drifted off to sleep, she decided she could get used to this life.

Logan stood at the rail near the dive platform, the noon-day sun hot on his shoulders, the cloudless sky a brilliant robin's egg blue reflecting in the gentle swell on the smooth surface of the water. A good dive day. Although he and his team considered just about every day a great dive day.

Yesterday would have been a good day for diving,

too, but they'd had to be patient as the *Sea Wolf* made its way down to the new site. After they'd gotten back from Lima, early in the morning, the crew had passed the time checking, cleaning, and fine-tuning their gear, getting ready for the next series of dives. To Logan's surprise, Annie had spent most of the day in her cabin, sleeping, coming out only for a light meal midday. The bruise on her forehead was healing, turning some fabulous colors, and he realized that her sudden exhaustion was most likely a delayed reaction to all of the trauma she'd been through. Just as well, he thought; one less distraction, and he had Dog's undivided attention again. Fickle beast.

Morale was high, anticipation thrumming through the entire ship, dive team and crew alike. Everyone eager to grab their piece of the pie.

He shaded his eyes and looked out over the water for signs of his nemesis, Rydell Case's *Sea Dragon,* and/or the mysterious redheaded owner of the *Sea Witch.* They were each, in their own way, a pain in his ass. All he saw in every direction was sparkling blue water with an occasional whitecap.

Sea Witch had put in her two cents in the last few months with both Nick and Zane. It was his turn next, he was sure. Logan was surprised the redhead hadn't already shown up on his dive. He suspected as soon as she found out he'd changed locations, she'd be on him like white on rice. Everyone on board knew to look out for her small, sleek black boat. Woman had sticky fingers, and a liking for the small and sparkly.

Although she'd made off with some prize museum-quality pieces over the years, she was more a yippy dog than a real menace. Still, over the years she'd swiped some valuable treasures from under his family's noses. If she became more of an issue, Logan would find a way to force her to back off.

Rydell Case, however, was a different matter. While not particularly confrontational, Logan would like it a hell of a lot more if he knew what the fuck Case's problem with him was. Unlike the Sea Bitch, who didn't play favorites with who she stole from, and who she annoyed, Case targeted the company, not each of the brothers specifically. If it was a Cutter Salvage dive, he muscled in to take what he wanted. And damn it to hell, the man wanted it all.

Not only had Case stolen multimillions of dollars, he'd interfered with investors and the public perception of Cutter Salvage. When he came poaching, he adhered to the one-mile rule—staying within the proximity of the legal limit, *barely*. It was his frequent challenges of Cutter's salvage rights and/or ownership rights that tangled them up in lengthy legal battles, tying up several locations, in some cases for years.

Over the last ten years, Cutter Salvage had spent a fortune in legal fees and exorbitant amounts of money paying publicists to keep shit out of the paper. The irony was, Case was so fucking clever, the stories he planted were mostly true, but so twisted, so diabolical, that even Logan sometimes had trouble sorting fact from thinly veiled fiction.

They'd taken Case to court five times. Cutter Salvage had won three, Case two. The legal fees alone were in the multimillions. Logan was throwing enough money at the South African lawyers to ensure he won that skirmish, too.

Case hated Cutter Salvage, and it seemed damned

personal to Logan and his brothers. And because of his actions over the years, Logan disliked him right back.

Logan had been raised on lies and chaos. Now he liked everything planned and organized, be that paperwork or people. Of course, life rarely cooperated, but he tried to foresee some of those bumps along the way like a good tactician or savvy chess player.

That Case would normally show up on this dive like a bad penny was a given. Logan expected it. Even more so, now that they were turned around and headed south. Too bad Case was tied up in the legal system a world away.

Not prone to flights of fancy, Logan still had a positive feeling about finding his treasure now. His heartbeat accelerated with anticipation, all his senses attuned to the water and the slap and slosh of the wavelets frothing against the hull. At his side, Dog yipped at a seagull wheeling overhead.

"She kick you out of the kitchen? Or did you get confused with all the names?"

Dog glanced at the dive platform, and back up at him.

"You don't give a shit what anyone calls you as long as you get to go in the water, right?" Dog's tail waved frantically. "Go get your vest then."

Dog bounded off in the direction of the platform, tail and tongue waving.

"Hey, Wolf?! You coming or not?" Jed yelled, already suited up and waiting below on the dive platform. He unhooked Dog's vest and lifeline from the equipment rack and started getting him set up to swim. Hard to do when Dog's entire body wagged with anticipation.

"Yeah. Give me a minute." He breathed in deeply of

the hot, salt-tangy air. Ahh. This was the life. Salt. Sun. Sea. The anticipation was almost—*almost*—as thrilling as the actual score. He wanted just a few more minutes to savor the thrill. For these few minutes he could picture the treasure waiting for them beneath the hull. He could almost feel the cool glide of the gold and silver against his skin.

That feeling never got old. He remembered having had the same sense of excitement when his father had taken all three of the boys out for their first salvage dive, years before. They were all sure they'd find something immediately; it was just a matter of who'd score first. That bond of joyful competition was still part of their lives; nothing beat going back to Cutter Cay with a hold full of treasure and a head full of stories to tell. For a moment, he was hit with a wave of missing his brothers. Maybe Jed was right; he was getting soft.

Zane and Nick seemed to have found their feet, and Logan would be glad to see the shadows chased from their eyes. He wanted them to be happy, to move away from who and what their dickhead of a father had been and realize that who they were had little to do with the man who'd fathered them.

His brothers were the most important people in his life. They always would be. He'd always wanted his brothers to find love, and peace, and a happiness that had never seemed attainable as they got older, no matter how fast they danced around it.

Logan was grateful he hadn't been destroyed on any level by his father's actions. His lie-dar had been fully operational from an early age. What you knew, however unpalatable, couldn't hurt you. His brothers hadn't known the half of it, and they'd both, in their own ways, been altered by the experiences.

Having a spare brother had come as no surprise to him. His father never had been able to keep his dick in his pants. Logan was fully prepared to accept Jonah, if the guy turned out to be telling the truth—that he'd only kept his identity hidden out of fear that the family wouldn't accept him. Of course, he'd still put Jonah through hell for the lies he'd perpetrated on a too-trusting Nick.

Seemed as though his zero-tolerance policy for liars was two for two.

"Jesus, that is one scary look on your face," Jed said, coming up beside him. He was clearly impatient to dive. "Someone piss you off?"

Logan took his dark glasses out of his front pocket and put them on. "Just thinking what kind of initiation I can put my newly acquired brother through before I welcome him to the family."

"Sounds like a decent enough guy." Jed looked out over the water, his too-long sun-streaked hair drifting around his shoulders in the breeze. "Are we diving soon, or are you going to stand here and solve the world's problems for the foreseeable future? Dog's getting hot in his vest."

Logan pushed off the rail, then gave his friend a look over the top of his sunglasses. "You aren't another long-lost brother, are you?"

Jed laughed. "If my mother had ever met your father, she would've clocked him with a cast-iron skillet while he wasn't looking. And my dad would've helped her bury his body."

"What I thought." Logan grinned. He enjoyed Jed's folks, and they'd traveled with them a dozen times over the years. "Let's go find ourselves a fortune in gold and emeralds, my man."

"God. I thought you'd never ask."

They jumped down the short ladder to reach the dive platform, and Jed waited while Logan suited up. Dog lay in a patch of shade, his paws bracketing his water bowl as if someone was going to confiscate it. The minute he saw that Logan was getting ready, his tail beat a tattoo on the deck. But he was smart enough to stay put, knowing he wasn't allowed in the water until he was attached to a line.

"Where's your mermaid this morning?"

His chef had reported earlier that Annie had shown up right after breakfast, ready to work. "Galley, helping Hipolito with lunch, apparently." Logan plunked his weight belt on the deck and stepped over it, then bent down, raising it to his hips and securing it.

"The woman looks like that and she can cook? Holy shit, Cutter. Marry her!"

Logan double-checked his tank valve, then strapped it to his buoyancy compensator and hooked his regulator to the tank without commenting on Jed's matrimonial advice. He'd long since realized that it was unlikely he'd ever marry. Wasn't as though he hadn't thought about it once in a while over the years. But . . . marriage wasn't a situation he wanted to deal with. The occasional attractive woman as a bed partner when it suited him, his fist when it didn't, and a contented life doing what he loved was enough. He liked no one rocking his boat. "I have no idea if she can boil water or not. We'll see."

Logan pulled up the BC, flipped it over his head,

and secured the straps into place over his chest. The others, as eager as he and Jed were, came out to hang out under the awning and wait their turn.

She'd been spooked the other night, and while he didn't think every woman he made a pass at should fall into his lap—although that was exactly what she'd done—Logan suspected Annie's issues went far deeper than an innocuous kiss.

He walked to the edge of the platform, Jed and Dog beside him. "Hey, Galt, keep an eye on Dog—we're going in." He turned to his friend. "Ready?"

Six

Much as she had needed that lengthy break, Daniela discovered she wasn't cut out for lazing around day after day. She was used to working long hours. The gallery kept her running from morning to late at night. The concept of leisure time had been appealing, until she found herself bored out of her mind. Worrying, fretting, and anticipating the worst should be a full-time job. But right now she needed to get her mind off what she couldn't fix.

Hipolito had put her to work when she introduced herself and reported for duty in the galley. A small Mexican man with a shock of black hair and a boxer's nose, Logan's chef welcomed another pair of hands—or so he said—and immediately gave her rapid-fire instructions.

He was almost as wide as he was tall, but he moved with the grace of a dancer, keeping time to the salsa music in the background as he moved about the state-of-the-art stainless steel kitchen, a spotless white apron tied around his ample middle. Humming tunelessly under his breath, he was constantly in motion.

Daniela felt her tension slip away in the well-ventilated kitchen, which was flooded with natural light. The pulsing music was a heartbeat to the activity of meal preparation. And anything that got her mind off the intensity she'd sensed in Logan Cutter's kiss was a good thing.

"This is Dell." Chef introduced a shy beanpole of a guy in his early twenties, with thinning white-blond hair, a bobbing Adam's apple, and lively brown eyes. "Chef's helper and steward," Hipolito told her. "We need to put some meat on his bones before his next shore leave."

"If he had his way, I'd be stuffed like a Thanksgiving turkey," Dell told her with a small smile, the tips of his ears going pink as he handed her a navy cotton apron. "You look much better than the last time I saw you, ma'am. How do you feel?"

"Call me Da-Annie. Surprisingly good, all things considered, thanks." She wound the long strings around her waist and tied them in front. Oops. She'd almost slipped up. He didn't appear to have noticed.

Daniela felt a giddy sense of excitement. Were they near *La Daniela?* She could feel the anticipation in the air. Of course, finding the shipwreck would bring with it another set of problems. But for now she'd had plenty of rest, and she was ready to *do* something. "Where do you want me?"

She might've been foisted on Cutter, but she didn't expect a free ride. She intended to work. Besides, she needed something to keep her mind off the what-ifs. This was perfect. In fact, this was the most relaxed she'd felt in months. Here, she didn't need to guard her every word or expression. Her lips twitched. All she needed to do was remember her name.

She allowed the light, the music, and the smells of the kitchen to saturate her senses, pushing out the worry and nervous tension relentlessly dogging her. She rarely cooked at home, preferring takeout, but this was nice. Who knew, she might need these skills in her future life. Placing her in front of a mountain of shrimp, Hipolito showed her how he wanted them prepared, and left her to it. Daniela wasn't a particularly adventurous cook, but she could follow a recipe and she was good with directions.

Yeah, well, if she hadn't been so damned good at following directions she would've realized early in her relationship with the senator from Maine that his directions and suggestions were actually *orders*.

There was nothing *benign* about Victor Stamps. His faults had turned out to be so numerous, Daniela was still trying to sort through them.

There'd been no indication of what he truly was in the beginning and she'd been swept off her feet by his charm. Victor was handsome, amusing, well educated, and well liked in Washington. He was on the fast track to becoming president. She'd been stupidly starry-eyed, taken in by the glamour and glitz of his world.

She'd had six months of a fairy-tale life before the gloss started wearing off and she was able to see beneath his shiny façade. And by then it was too late.

Security? Ha. That was a joke. He'd made her whole world crumble. Wealth? He'd stripped away her livelihood the moment he'd forced her to allow his illegal activities behind the scenes of her gallery.

Enough.

Breathe.

Victor wasn't anywhere near her. She had time to regroup. Time to wait while Special Agent Price brought things to a close and tied Victor up in a neat bow.

Daniela used the faucet over the stove to fill a large pot, threw in a handful of salt, then went back to deveining the shrimp while the water boiled.

Under Chef's benign dictatorship, and with Dell's

help, Daniela built enormous seafood salads and squeezed lemons for fresh lemonade. She might not be proficient wielding a paintbrush, but she had an artistic eye and discovered she could make a mean tomato rose.

The galley smelled of the hot yeasty rolls Hipolito slid from the oven. "You," he instructed Dell, pointing at the salads Daniela had built. "Put those in the fridge until they're ready. You," he indicated her, "go now and enjoy the sunshine." He shooed her out of his kitchen with a charming smile, and laughing black eyes.

He'd given her busywork and they both knew it. The gesture touched her, and foolish tears stung her lids. She put a hand on his arm. "Thanks."

"Dinner prep starts at five," he told her gruffly.

She smiled. "I'll be here."

Daniela's heart played ping-pong as she made her way down to the lower deck where the dive team apparently ate their meals together. A two-hour reprieve and she was back to hard decisions, and presenting a false façade.

Dell had gone to deliver a fresh tray of fruit to the dive team, and he met her in the hall as she left the kitchen, greeting her with the news that some of the men were getting ready to dive the new location. *Sea Wolf* had dropped anchor barely an hour earlier, and Logan was already diving? Excitement gripped her, until she realized that the sooner Logan found the treasure, the sooner the cousins would descend.

For Logan's sake she hoped he found what he was looking for. For her cousins' sake, she hoped they took whatever deal Logan Cutter offered them, because she suspected he'd only make one offer. And that offer only once.

And for herself, she hoped that nothing exciting, or attention-drawing, happened for the next two weeks and a day. She'd had enough high-octane cloak-and-dagger action in the last months to last her a lifetime. When she got home, she was going to make some drastic changes. What, she wasn't sure. But she'd never be that trusting ever again. Right now, she was forced to put all her faith in Price to resolve the Victor problem once and for all.

He was the only one who knew what had happened, and knew all the players. He'd arranged false papers so her parents could go on a monthlong cruise, stay out of danger, and not worry.

He'd offered her the same thing. In her case, fake passport and all, but Victor's people had found her in three days. She prayed nightly that her parents had fared better. She'd learned that an association with Victor had the unsavory side effect of shortening one's potential life span.

She rested her hand below her belly button, where the bullet had burned her. She wasn't dead and she planned on staying that way for as long as possible.

It was good to want things. Too bad life rarely unfolded the way people wanted it to.

She hadn't slept well after she'd left the library the other night. Falling into Cutter's lap had been clumsy and embarrassing. What man wouldn't presume the woman had done so intentionally? She hadn't, of course, but he'd taken the opportunity to kiss her anyway.

She remembered the feel and taste of him in pulsing Technicolor even now, days later. She'd braced her fall with her hand on his belly—and now her fingers flexed in memory of his muscles contracting as he'd kissed her. His skin had been hot and silky smooth to the touch. She wanted to kiss him there. The thought shocked the hell out of her.

The instant his mouth found hers, she'd felt a long-dead ember erupt into flame. Daniela was stunned at her response to his kiss. Stunned and shocked. She had honestly believed that Victor's actions had stripped her sexual feelings raw, then annihilated them completely. Yet she'd forgotten everything that had gone before and melted into the heat of Cutter's kiss.

She remembered the feel of his fingers spearing through her hair, the way her scalp tingled at his sensual touch. The brush of his hand against her cheek. The way her mouth opened beneath his and her tongue had met his. Her entire body had felt electrically charged, buzzing with currents that moved like fire through her veins.

Like her numb feet, her libido had reawakened with a pins-and-needles vengeance. Talk about bad timing.

Squinting against the sharp sunlight dancing off the water, she stepped out of the wide sliding door of the library/multipurpose room onto the aft deck. The divers were seated at the large table in the shade of the wide awning. As soon as they saw her, they all, with various levels of enthusiasm, started getting to their feet.

She'd never seen so many half-naked men in one place. They all wore swim trunks or shorts and not much else. In her borrowed jeans and T-shirt she felt almost overdressed. Except for the braless part of the program. It was fortunate that she wasn't a large-breasted woman, but she wasn't comfortable in front of all these strangers without wearing one. She hoped Wes had remembered it was on her short list.

She waved the men back into their seats. "Please. There's no need." Wes came around and pulled out a chair for her, and she gave him a smile as she sat down. "How was your trip into Lima?" she asked generally, studiously avoiding glancing at the dive platform, a small deck a level lower than where they sat. Since Logan wasn't at the table, she presumed he was diving.

She let the men's conversation flow around her, accepted a soda from Wes, and welcomed Dog as he leapt up the five-foot drop between the deck and platform and trotted, dripping, up to the table. He shook, spraying everyone, then stood still while Earl, who was closest, unhooked a long lead from his vest, then unbuckled the vest itself.

Earl patted Dog's rump, and barking, the animal took off, running as if the hounds of hell were after him, down the deck.

"Is he all right?" Daniela watched the dog scrabble around a corner, and nearly spin out on the deck as he sped out of sight.

"Excess energy," Wes told her, rubbing a hand over his crew cut as he stretched his legs out under the table. Daniela could see herself reflected in his sunglasses as he said, "He'll be back. I brought you some stuff. I'll bring it to your cabin later."

"Thanks, Wes, that's—" A loud noise overhead made her start and cover her ears. "What on earth . . . ?"

"Blower!" Cooper yelled, waving a hand in the general direction of the water. "Moves the sand around."

Wes touched her arm. "Good news," he shouted when she turned to face him. "That means they found something."

Too damned soon! The cousins would descend like ticks on a dog the second they knew Cutter had found their treasure. Daniela looked out over the sparkling water. No sign of the fishing trawler, just water as far as the eye could see. She relaxed just a little; she'd almost expected to see the stinking trawler tied up alongside Cutter's magnificently, pristinely white *Sea Wolf.*

She turned back to Wes, and mouthed, "How soon will we know?" How would *they* know?

With a wide grin, he shrugged his massive shoulders. The guys all lifted their soda cans and toasted across the table, grinning from ear to ear. Their excitement was palpable, their energy infectious.

Dog came running at full speed back from the direction he'd disappeared to. Tongue lolling, he flopped down under the table on Daniela's bare foot. He was wet, but she used her other foot to rub his back. The noise of the blower didn't seem to bother him as he put his head down on his paws, sighed, and closed his eyes.

The blower stopped. "They'll be down another half hour or so," Wes told her. "Wanna go up to your cabin and see what I scored for you in Lima?"

The blower started up again. Daniela nodded, and got to her feet. Dog got up with her.

Accompanied by the roar of the blower, they went up to the main deck where the divers' and owners' cabins were. Daniela waited out in the corridor while Wes went into his cabin for the bags. He came out wearing a tank top, which somehow made him appear more muscle-bound than he'd looked shirtless.

"Good grief, Wes! Does Logan know how much stuff you bought for me?" Daniela eyed the pile of bags he carried. "I'm only going to be here a little while, you know, not the next twenty years!"

He swung a handful of bags toward the other end of the corridor, waiting for her to precede him. "Logan won't mind, I promise."

"*I* mind." She used a key card to open her door. "He's already letting me stay on board, I don't want to outstay my welcome." Turning, she asked, "Are you coming in?"

"I got the impression when you arrived that I . . . I'm kinda intimidating . . ."

Yes. He was. And her body instinctively recoiled. But she couldn't spend the rest of her life tarring every man she met with Victor's brush. "It wasn't you." She pushed the door open and stepped inside. "Come in."

Wes followed her. "I told you I'm gay, right?"

"Believe me, that has no bearing on it. It's your sheer size, that has me—I—I had a really bad experience with a guy, and I'm still a little freaked out being in close proximity with large men. Especially in such tight quarters. I'll get over it." *Eventually.*

He dumped the bags on her bunk, and sat down on the end of the other one. Dog jumped up beside him, looking alert and ready to play. "Logan would never hurt you, Annie," Wes told her, gently rubbing Dog's ear. "I can swear to that."

She lifted an eyebrow. "Who was talking about Logan? But since we are—tell me who he is."

"Über intelligent, takes care of things, hates liars, loves his brothers, lone wolf, doesn't like crowds, loyal, can be ruthless, controlled, hardheaded, and stubborn."

"No vices?" she asked dryly, because those pretty much all sounded like vices to her.

"Not that I've seen in the six years I've sailed with him."

"You know the trouble with someone with no vices?

They usually have a lot of pretty annoying virtues. How come this cabin's empty?"

"His cabin's next door," he said, then told the dog to lie down. Dog did so and gave her a hopeful look. "He likes a buffer."

She shot a glance at Wes. "The dog or Logan?"

Wes cocked a brow.

"A buffer from *what?* Does he do primordial screaming in the dead of night?"

Wes grinned. "Never heard him. This cabin's a buffer."

Amused, Daniela shook her head. "Let's see what we have—Oh, my God, Wes," she laughed, holding up a short, slinky black dress. There was about an ounce of fabric. "Where would I wear this? To dinner on deck?"

"It'll look amazing on you. I got shoes, too."

"Lord, you really know how to shop, don't you?"

"It's part of my gay gene, I don't defy the stereotype. Plus my sisters trained me well. I loved my Barbies, what can I say? Underwear in that one."

"This isn't underwear, it's two pieces of black licorice!" She put the thong aside, and opened another bag; this one held a selection of T-shirts. "How many sisters?"

"Three. One older, two younger. Three brothers-in-law. Five nieces, one nephew. A mother and a father. Two dogs, five cats between them. All live in Akron, Ohio. We're really close. I miss them on long trips like this. But my folks sailed with us a couple of months ago when we left Cutter Cay for this salvage. They had a blast. Go into the head and try that on. I wanna see."

"I'm going to change into these shorts and this T-shirt, and—thank you, Fairy Godfather—put on this bra, thank you very much." She went into the head and shut the door.

"What do you think of Logan so far?" Wes raised his voice.

"I don't think about him." Unfortunately, another lie to add to the ever-growing list.

"He's one of the most decent men I've ever met, and that's saying a lot."

"Hmm."

"What you see is what you get. He's one of those strong silent types, steady as a rock."

"I've been dashed on those rocks one too many times. What do you think?" She came out of the bathroom wearing white shorts and a lime green T-shirt. The bra and bikini panties underneath fit perfectly. Armor in place, she felt ten times better already.

"Color looks amazing with your skin tone, and you have great legs." Wes paused, giving her a serious look. "Are we talking physical abuse, Annie?"

She dumped out all the bags on her bunk, then went to open what she figured was one of the closet doors. It was locked. "Do I need a key?" she asked over her shoulder.

"That's the door leading through Logan's closet on the other side. When we have family on board, he sacks in here and lets them have his cabin."

Lovely. Having him next door wasn't enough. There was a connecting door. The very thought gave Daniela goose bumps. She yanked on the other door, and it opened to reveal a small closet, with a bunch of empty hangers, and two drawers.

She gathered the hangers, and started hanging the items up. "Physical, psychological, and every way there was." It was a relief to share at least that much, knowing she didn't have to report dates and times in triplicate.

He sat forward, elbows on his knees. "If you ever want to talk about it—?"

"Thanks, Wes." She busily folded T-shirts. "It's a nonissue now, and I'm working through some things. I'll be good."

"Logan would never let anyone hurt you, you know."

"Wes—" Daniela opened a drawer, and carefully placed the folded shirts inside. "Logan doesn't even know me. I'm not his problem, and I'll be out of his hair soon enough." She straightened and went back to get the pile of flimsy underwear. The man was gay, but he'd outfitted her for a porn movie. She gave him a stern glance. "And stop playing matchmaker. That *is* what you're doing, isn't it?"

"Wouldn't dream of it. The man's a loner. We don't call him Wolf for nothing."

Daniela huffed out a rude laugh. "Overkill with a ship called *Sea Wolf* and a dog that *looks* like a wolf. Maybe he's trying to make a point?"

"They mate for life, you know."

Daniela punched him in the shoulder. It was like hitting a brick wall. "Stop."

"Just saying, if you're in trouble, Logan is a master at untangling knotty situations."

"I get it. He's a saint. I'll keep all his sterling qualities in mind. What are some of his bad qualities? Those would be more helpful."

Eyes twinkling, he scooted back to lean against the wood-paneled wall. Dog put his chin on Wes's thigh. "He thinks he's patient."

Ah. "You did say he was stubborn."

"He usually *is* right. He's sensible and to the point."

"And hardheaded," Daniela interpreted as she bunched up colorful bikini panties and stuck them in the drawer. What Logan was was immaterial to her.

Wes grinned. "He loves his family to distraction. He'll do anything for his brothers, Zane and Nick. Absolutely anything."

Wes had bought three more bras. Delicate confections of pastel lace and sheer fabric that made them almost more revealing than concealing. She tucked them in with her new underwear. "What a man."

"There's only one thing he hates—"

Daniela straightened, turning to shoot him an amused glance. "Anyone who doesn't toe the line?"

"*Liars.*" Wes sobered. "No joke. He's pretty much inflexible about people lying to him. He'd rather hear the unpalatable, unvarnished truth than people's lies. He's axed multibillion—that's *billion*—dollar deals because the investor shaved the truth a little."

A chill skittered up her back. "Wow, must be nice to be so perfect."

"He's not by a long shot. He hates failing. So not finding the *Nuestra Señora de Garza* treasure really fried his cookies. When's your birthday?"

"I'm sorry, this is relevant how? We went from listing all of Cutter's sterling attributes, to his pet peeve, to my birthday?"

"Logan is a Taurus."

"A bull? That figures. My birthday is November second."

"This should be interesting."

"Do Scorpios and Tauruses get along?" Not according to her friend Zazoo, who insisted on telling her what her moons and stars were doing all the time. And just look how accurate *those* cheerful horoscopes had been.

"*Absolutely*. His brother Nick is a Scorpio. Get on like bacon and eggs."

Daniela shook her head at his BS. "High in fat and bad for the heart. Got it." A bell chimed. "What's that? Lunch or a fire drill?" Either way, saved by the bell.

"Means Logan and Jed are out of the water. Let's go hear all about their find."

She stuck her key card into the front pocket of her shorts. "Maybe they didn't find anything at all."

Wes smiled. "Nah. Can't you feel the excitement on board? They found something. Let's go!"

She hesitated. "I'm not that hungry, I think I'll stay and put away m—"

He opened the door. "Cluck-cluck-cluck."

"Of what? *Cutter?!* Oh, please!"

His dive team could barely contain themselves. Logan thought about the countless salvages they'd done together, and he had rarely seen them this excited. The minute he and Jed had surfaced, he'd pulled off his mask, his gaze going to the table where everyone gathered. Most of the guys were there, but Annie was nowhere to be seen.

"My God, how long would we have searched the original area before we called it a day?" Jed asked, grinning from ear to ear as he shrugged off his tanks.

"Well?" Galt and Horner hung over the short railing near the ladder, as eager to be the first to hear the good news as two enthusiastic puppies.

Logan had been about ready to throw in the towel. And that was something he rarely did. So no matter the who or the why, he had his uninvited guest to thank for what might very well be the salvage of the decade, giving him a one-up on the current contest he had going with his brothers. "Couple more weeks at most," he told Jed as he, too, removed his equipment, taking his time. They had baskets of goodies to show the others. All in good time.

"You're killing us!" Cooper joined the other men at the top of the ladder, followed by Vanek. Missing was Wesley Roan. And Annie. And his damn dog, who'd switched allegiance as soon as he'd seen a pretty face.

"Lunch on the table?" Logan asked, stripping off his suit.

"Not yet," Galt said impatiently. "I can call Hip—"

Logan and Jed each grabbed a mesh basket and, one-handed, scaled the ladder up to the deck. "Good," Logan cut him off as he gained the deck ahead of Jed. The others backed up to give him room. "Because this'll take up all the real estate." He dumped his basket upside down on the table, as did Jed.

"Oh, man, is that pretty or what?" Cooper said reverently, staring at the pile of doubloons, several gold bars, and a mess of gold chains piled haphazardly on the table. It wasn't the value of what he and Jed had brought to the surface right now. It was the implication that there was plenty more where that came from.

"What'd we miss?" Wes slipped between Cooper and Horner, put out his arm, and eased Annie in front of him so she could see what was going on.

She looked pretty in a bright green T-shirt, her long legs displayed to perfection in well-fitting white shorts. But it was her shining eyes, turned up to meet his, that took Logan's breath. "The bowl was real." She sounded breathless, and almost as surprised as he was.

Suspecting this was the first time he was seeing the real Annie Ross, Logan felt a weirdly unfamiliar clutch to his chest. "Apparently," he told her mildly. "Hold out your hand."

The others shifted so he could get closer to her as she obeyed. He brought out the hand he was holding behind his back. "The treasure of *Nuestra Señora de Graza*." Trying not to fall into the amber pools of her eyes, he dropped a raw emerald the size of his fist into her waiting palm.

Seven

It had been a crazy day. *La Daniela* was already giving up a fortune, and they'd barely started. They worked in teams, hauling up baskets full of treasure. Logan spent his off-diving time filling plastic tubs and lugging them down to storage. Salt water was added to preserve their finds until they got everything back to the Counting House on Cutter Cay. There, resident bean counter Brian and his team would sort and catalogue to their hearts' content.

The *Sea Witch* showed up in the late afternoon, adhering to the one-mile-away rule. Her captain must have a homing device or a Vulcan tractor beam to always find a Cutter ship so quickly. It had barely been a day, and she was waiting in the wings like a bird of prey, ready to sneak in and swipe part of the treasure.

Logan indicated the small, sleek black shape hovering on the horizon to Jed and Cooper as the blower spurted out a muddy jet stream of sand and water over the bow.

Jed wanted to take the launch and go over right away. For years he'd been trying to get Logan to agree to a face-to-face with the redhead who was apparently the captain. "I'm telling you, talk to her, and she'll be on her merry way."

Listening to Jed gripe with ten percent of his brain, Logan cupped the back of his head as he watched the blower. He had a lot on his plate. He always did. Not only did he run his ship, but he ran the entire Cutter Cay Salvage business. On a daily basis he dealt with investors, public relations people, the press, their fleet of accountants, government regulators and departments governing discovered sites, and all the archaeologists who catalogued and cleaned the salvage of a dozen Cutter Salvage ships.

They donated some artifacts to museums, sold some to others, and while the nitty-gritty of micromanaging was left up to their department heads, it was Logan who held every string for their vast and far-reaching empire. Zane had his charm and now Teal, Nick had his secret life and his princess.

Logan had Cutter Salvage.

The irony was, none of them gave a rat's ass about the money. He wondered if the newly acquired brother, Jonah did.

"There's absolutely no use talking to you when you aren't listening to a word I'm saying," Jed pointed out, his volume decreasing as the blower shut off.

"Mano a mano," Logan repeated. "Sea Bitch. Merry way. If she wanted to jump your bones she would've done it the last time you threatened to tear her limb from limb," he told his friend dryly. "I guess your shtick just isn't good enough."

"*You're* the big boss. *You* should go."

"Ah, but you see, *I* don't give a shit." Logan dropped his hands and reached for a bottle of ice-cold water. "She only steals the lowest growing fruit, she doesn't take much, and she doesn't stay long." He chugged and shrugged at the same time. "She's a pest, but no threat to us."

"Aren't you even mildly curious as to *why* she dogs our every move?"

"Nope." She had her reasons, they were apparently important to her. She didn't steal enough to be a flyspeck in their lives.

"She's stunning, right?" Cooper asked, leaning his forearms on the table. He'd seen her ship dozens of times, but had never seen the woman on board.

"You've seen her," Jed said as he adjusted the binocs for a better view. "Mile-long screaming red hair, Jessica Rabbit body . . ."

"No, I haven't—"

"Not that Jed has the hots for her or anything." Logan's smile went unnoticed since the other two had their eyes glued to the *Sea Witch* in the distance. "Go over and ask her on a date."

"I'd plan something sexy and romantic if I had a mermaid on board and within easy reach," Jed told him, handing the binoculars to Cooper.

Logan stopped the water bottle halfway to his mouth. "Two issues with that. One, she's under my protection. Two, I don't know if you noticed, but she came wrapped in electrified barbed wire with a flashing neon sign stating KEEP OUT."

"Seriously? I don't see any of that. Maybe that's just in place to keep you out, maybe I sho—"

Logan set the water bottle down with enough force that some of it sloshed out onto the table top. "One back-off wasn't enough for you, Jones?"

"See, now that's just unreasonable. If you don't want

to play, doesn't mean you have the right to shut the toy box lid."

"Not only *shut* it, preferably with your fingers in the way, but *lock* it and *nail* it shut." Logan shoved his chair away from the table, got up and stalked inside, then stopped dead in the middle of the great room and shook his head. "What the hell?" There was only one explanation for his behavior.

He'd lost his damn mind.

With his hands stacked beneath his head, Logan lay naked on his wide bed staring out at the stars twinkling in the black sky beyond the open sliders. The doors to his small balcony stood open, letting in the faint briny scent of the ocean and the tung oil Dell used on the brightwork.

No lights were on in the cabin, but moonlight cast a milky wash across the polished wood floor, and made the white sheets around him glow in the darkness.

The *Sea Witch* was still anchored a mile away. The redhead hadn't made any moves to pilfer his treasure. Yet. She would soon enough.

A soft warm breeze tickled the hair on his body, sliding erotically like silk across his skin. Annie had avoided him all day. Not that hard on a ship the size of a small hotel. So be it. Tomorrow was another day.

He'd made a complete ass of himself this afternoon, and knew Jed well enough that it would be a while before he lived it down. A damn good thing that he could laugh at himself, Logan thought, staring out over the blackness beyond the open window where the long sheer drapes lifted and fell as if moved by the breath of some giant beast.

What *was* it about Annie he found so damned compelling? She wasn't the most beautiful woman he'd ever been attracted to. Nor the most witty. The sum of her parts was pretty damn ordinary. But taken all together . . . Something indiscernible about her made his heart race, made everything around him seem sharper. Better. He shook his head. He really *had* lost it.

The sound of the ocean, the gentle slap of wavelets against the hull, were his lullaby. No matter what happened in his life, the sea was always there. Lover and friend. Confidant in the cold, lonely hours before dawn when his ship slept and a new day had yet to unfold.

Yeah. The whole bowl thing had paid off. And paid off big. The story about the cousins almost rang true . . . Almost. He *knew* Annie was still lying to him. With nowhere to go, she might open up and tell him what was really going on. The fact that he was willing to give her that chance floored him, and he prodded the notion like a tongue to an aching tooth.

He wasn't an inquisitive guy. If a person wanted to hide something, he figured it was important to them, and he didn't pry. He walked away. *Sea Witch* being a case in point. Unless that omission directly impacted him or his family in a dangerous way, he left well enough alone.

Lies were a whole other issue.

His brothers told him repeatedly that his zero-tolerance policy made him a hard-ass. Logan didn't give a damn. People could take him or leave him, and what they thought of him didn't matter.

If someone chose to lie to him, he cut them off at the knees. Done. Done. And done. He wasn't curious enough to dig deeper. None of his business. He washed his hands and moved on.

It was the only aspect of his life where there was no gray.

Black or white. Lie or truth.

And then there was Annie—

Over the sound of the ocean and the ship settling for the night, he thought he heard Dog whine, and swung his legs over the mattress. Annie must've let him out of her cabin and shut the door. Sometimes Dog liked company when he went topside to do his business in the area designated Dog's dog-a-loo.

Logan pulled on shorts. He wouldn't mind a run around the decks himself. He snagged his running shoes as Dog howled. Damn, he'd wake everyone. As Logan neared the door, he heard a hard thump.

"Okay, okay, I'm hurryi—" He yanked open the door. Dog fell limply across his feet.

Logan scooped up the inert form, kicking the cabin door closed as he raced over to the bed. He laid the dog down on his side on the rumpled sheets. "What is it, boy? Ate something bad?" Really bad, since Dog was clearly unconscious. But not dead, thank God. The animal's chest moved with his breathing, which seemed strained.

Logan felt for a heartbeat and was relieved to find it slow, but steady. "Okay, Dog. What happened?" He extended the dog's head, and lifted his upper lip. The animal's gums were bright red, and although he was struggling slightly to breathe, he didn't appear to be in shock, which would've indicated internal bleeding.

Logan yelled, "Annie!" as he pulled Dog's tongue out to keep his airway open, elevated his hindquarters on his own pillow, and tucked the light blanket around him.

Logan strode to the connecting door, and banged on

it. She must be awake, Dog had only just left her cabin. When there was no answer, he frowned. She might've let Dog out, then just presumed he wouldn't be back, and gone to bed. He pounded on the door with his fist. "Wake up. Dog's sick. I need to know if you fed him anything." He pounded again.

Nobody could sleep through the racket. He unlocked the door from his side, hoping she hadn't locked it from hers. She hadn't and the door slid open soundlessly.

"Annie?" He didn't want to scare the crap out of her by suddenly materializing beside her bed out of the darkness, but he needed answers. The light from his cabin filtered through the darkness, and he could make out her form on the far bunk.

"Annie. It's Logan. Wake up." He spoke in a normal voice, but she didn't move.

"What the hell's going on?" He scooped her up in his arms, blanket and all, and carried her through to his cabin. Her head lolled against his shoulder as he moved swiftly to the bed. She was limp and unresponsive as he laid her out beside Dog.

Food poisoning? Jesus, what if other people on board had eaten the same thing? Except food poisoning wasn't likely to render a person unconscious. Unless the food had been deliberately poisoned.

Or there was some sort of gas leak on board. Possible . . .

Logan glanced over at his dog as he straightened Annie's limbs. The animal's eyes were open, and he looked confused and disoriented. Logan leaned over the woman to rub the dog's muzzle. "It's okay, boy. Everything's okay." But it wasn't.

He checked Annie's vitals. She was unconscious,

but her pulse and respiration seemed all right. Reaching for the phone with one hand, Logan tapped her cool cheek. "Annie, wake up."

He managed to hit the right buttons to sound the general alarm. All the lights throughout the ship automatically turned on as the first of a series of seven short rings followed by one long ring sounded. Deafening, as it should be in an emergency.

Annie's lashes fluttered, and she lifted her hand weakly to push at his chest. "Don't—"

Logan covered her fingers with his. "I'm not going to hurt you. I think we have a gas leak. I'm going to carry you out onto the balcony, all right?" He spoke calmly, but his mind was racing as, not waiting for an answer, he scooped her up again, and pushed his way through the billowing drapes. Gently he placed her on one of the chaises on the small curved balcony.

Giving him a dazed, helpless look, she swallowed convulsively and tried to swing her feet to the floor, but was too weak to manage it.

"Want to throw up?" he yelled over the sound of the alarms.

She shook her head no, but her panicked eyes told another story. Logan reached inside the cabin and grabbed the Murano glass shell from the small table beside the doors. He got it under her chin just in time, then braced her forehead in his palm as she hurled.

"Carbon monoxide. Great, just freaking great," Daniela told Dog. Somehow he'd managed to stretch his big body alongside hers on the chaise. They were like two drunks together. Disoriented and wobbly. The alarm bells had gone silent a few seconds before, but her ears were still ringing. Daniela wanted to get up and go help. But Logan, autocrat that he was, had instructed her not to leave the cabin. And frankly, the clear glass railing looked low enough to topple over in her shaky state.

"So we'll stay right here, and listen to that racket and wonder what's really going on." She had her fingers buried in Dog's ruff. "I'm sure Logan will figure out that it's my cousins. But I'm going to have to tell him myself. Oh yay. I can't wait to see his expression for *this* news."

She still felt a little sick to her stomach, and Logan had left the glass bowl for her. Her cheeks burned with embarrassment. She was dying for some water, but she wasn't sure her wobbly legs would carry her, so she stayed put.

"You know it was my slimy Apaza cousins, don't you?" She told the dog, who had his head across her lap, and his eyes closed. Poor thing was probably sick to his stomach as well.

"We'll be okay, Malcolm. Just breathe this nice fresh air and before you know it, we'll be feeling right as rain." *And I'll find my cousins and knock their fool heads together.* "I have no idea *how* they pulled this off, but I *know* they did it. This was no accident."

It was too much of a coincidence to believe that on the same day that Logan had placed a chunk of emerald in her hand, and then hauled up a mountain of gold coins and jewelry, that this wasn't Piero, Angel, and Hugo's way of scooping up the treasure and hotfooting it back to Lima before anyone was aware that the treasure had been stolen from under their very noses.

"I told you they were morons. Whatever they took was one day's haul. If they managed to get anything at all. *And* they could just as easily have *killed* us all!"

By contacting her cousins out of sheer desperation last week, she'd jumped from the frying pan into the fire. She'd run out of money, and out of options. Which of course had been Victor's objective when he'd sent his goons after her. She ran from one cheap hotel to the next, crisscrossing the country for almost a month.

She hadn't been able to access any of her bank accounts, and the cash Special Agent Price had given her, with several sets of fake papers, had run out a week after she arrived in Lima, despite how frugal and conservative she'd been.

She'd been desperate enough to contact her long-lost cousins, erroneously believing blood was thicker than water.

Her life had already been crazy scary. Adding her cousins to the mix had just taken crazy scary to a whole new level of danger.

She could hear indistinct voices carrying over the black water from the deck above. What was going on up there? Had they discovered that their day's treasure was gone? Had they caught Angel, Hugo, and Piero?

She shivered even though the air was quite warm and Dog was tucked next to her under a blanket. Her fingers flexed in the animal's thick pelt. Logan was going to be pissed. She shivered again, a full-body shudder of bone-deep fear.

"How does he show his anger?" she asked the dog, her voice thick. "Is he a hitter? A yeller?" The blood drained from her head, leaving her dizzy and even more sick to her stomach. "God—*worse*?"

If he came at her, she wouldn't hesitate to retaliate. She looked around for a weapon. This time, she would neither falter nor would she miss.

* * *

"This is what we have," Logan told the assembled group, his tone grim. Everyone was in the common room. The door and windows to the aft and side decks were wide open, letting in the freshening night breeze. "Several hose clamps were removed, hoses were rerouted from the engine exhaust systems in the generator exhaust system. Supposed to, I imagine, lead us into thinking this was an accident.

"We think Captain Vandyke interrupted them, because we found several canisters of CO hooked up to the ventilation system. We presume they meant to take those with them when they left." There'd be fingerprints on those, and Logan had them locked securely in Jed's cabin.

"Why didn't the alarms go off?" Cooper demanded.

"They circumvented the CO detectors in the vents." When disconnected or tampered with, that would cause a supervisory signal at the main annunciator. Which had been disabled on the bridge. "These people knew their way around a craft. They were in and out, and nobody saw them. The captain was taken from behind and knocked out. Two crew members, one in the engine room, the other returning to his quarters, were cold-cocked as well. All three are being transported via chopper to the hospital in Arequipa. Anyone else need to be checked out?"

He scanned the room. There was a swell of negatives. Relieved, Logan contacted Jed on his headset and told him he could take off.

"Thank God all of you are all right." He sat on the arm of one of the comfortable chairs scattered about the room. He heard the throb of the rotors overhead and was pissed. He felt violated. And worried as hell. Not that he'd let that show to the men who were all looking to him for answers.

"If Dog hadn't howled for help, we might be telling a different story right now." They were fortunate more people hadn't been hurt. Three people were bad enough, but they all had head injuries from being struck; they didn't have to be rushed into a hyperbaric chamber for treatment.

"Who did this?" Galt demanded. His bald head was shiny with perspiration. He still looked green around the gills, and ready to pass out. The carbon monoxide had affected everyone slightly differently. Logan hadn't been hurt at all because of his close proximity to the open door in his cabin.

Fortunately, Logan, Piet, and Jed had advanced medical training. But Piet had a serious head wound and would require a hell of a lot of stitches. The other two men had minor wounds. He and Jed had got everyone sorted out, then Jed had gotten the chopper ready. Logan wasn't taking any chances. They shouldn't have had to handle anything, damn it.

Once he'd established that everyone was back to normal, he'd dispatched them to search the ship in pairs if they were mobile. They'd gone from stem to stern looking for the culprit; but the only thing found were the redirected hoses and CO cylinders.

They all had drinks, either soft or alcoholic—God only knew they deserved a drink under the circumstances—and they were crowded into the room so that everyone was in the loop.

"Rydell Case," Logan told them grimly.

"Shit! Seriously?" Galt demanded.

"How did none of us see his ship?" Cooper demanded, pissed.

Earl Horner scowled as he got up to refill his glass. "Isn't he tied up in all that legal red tape in Cape Town?"

"Last we heard." Logan's tone was grim. Inside he was seething with fury. This time Case had gone too fucking far. The sight of Annie unconscious would haunt him. "Either he slithered out of that tangle, or possibly he sent someone else." Saying it aloud made Logan realize that didn't make sense, unless Case had changed his MO. He liked the hands-on approach.

"What about those cousins of Annie's?" Vanek demanded.

"Possibly. I'll make inquiries." Logan, who was drinking strong black coffee, paused with the mug to his lips. "We'll take it from there."

This time he refused to let their lawyers deal with Rydell Case. *This* time he'd deal with the son of a bitch himself.

"Who checked today's haul?" Izak Vanek straightened from his slouched position in one of the easy chairs scattered throughout the room.

"Relax," Cooper told him. "Horner and I checked there first. Everything is exactly like we left it earlier."

"*Nothing* touched?" Galt asked, surprised. "Are you serious? Maybe it was the Sea Witch? Easier to come aboard and take directly instead of diving for it."

"She's foolish enough to dive alone," Logan told the men. "But I doubt she'd be stupid enough to board our vessel alone. There are people wandering around at all hours. She would've been seen."

"Well, *someone* came on board, and that someone, or

someones, was *not* seen," Vanek pointed out, his fingers white around a beer bottle.

His guest's relatives, or Case? The bastard would've done the job himself. And gotten great satisfaction in doing so. Doing so and then getting away cleanly without leaving a clue behind. That was Case's MO. One phone call would tell Logan where the man was. This seemed more like a Case trick than something done by Annie's cousins. But he'd know who was where soon enough. Piet had already called the authorities.

Worried about Annie and Dog, Logan got to his feet. Everyone appeared to be fine. No one had the cherry-red–tinged skin indicating a high level of carbon monoxide, no one was still puking, or exhibiting signs of poisoning. "Clearly he wanted it to look like an accident."

"Question is," Jed said grimly meeting Logan's eyes, "did he mean to kill us, or was this a shot across our bow in retaliation for the South African lawsuit?"

"I don't know," Logan said grimly. "But I'm damn sure going to find out."

Eight

If not for Logan, she'd be dead.

Daniela had thought the *Sea Wolf* would be the safest place for her to wait. She'd been deluding herself. Her idiot cousins must've decided not to allow Logan to get all the treasure up before stealing it. Maybe tossing her in the ocean had been a prelude to their plans to kill her, and leave no witnesses. She hadn't believed they could pull something like this off.

How had they managed to sneak on board and target her cabin? Her mouth dried. Was it that specific? Maybe the entire ship was affected. What if someone else had been stuck in the cabin and was now seriously ill, or worse, dead? It was as bad as if . . .

Daniela went hot, then ice cold.

"Dear God." Not her cousins at all. *"Victor?"* Had he found her after all? Had her sense of triumph at outwitting him been nothing but an illusion?

Panic flooded her system.

Dog yelped, and she realized her fingers were digging into his ruff as if she were hanging on for dear life. "Sorry, boy. OhGod, ohGod, ohGod."

How had he tracked her down? Her mind unfroze, sending her thoughts spinning a mile a minute. "Calm down," she ordered in a voice thin with fear. "The chances of the cousins skulking aboard are much higher than Victor finding me." They were.

"I'm breathing," she assured the dog, who stared up at her with worried golden eyes.

The cousins were the more logical threat. They might be out of sight, but she knew they'd be keeping a close watch on the *Sea Wolf* to claim what they believed was theirs.

The last place Victor's people had seen her was Florida. A world away.

There was a third possibility. The gas leak had been an accident. Daniela let out a shuddering breath and crossed her fingers.

"Accidents happen every day, right, boy? Yes, they do." She needed more information, and if it looked as though the cousins were responsible, it was her duty to inform Logan.

She wasn't thinking beyond that. She couldn't.

Daniela staggered to her feet, then wobbled her way through Logan's dimly lit cabin. Guilt assailed her as she noticed her host's huge bed, covers pushed onto the floor. She'd disrupted his life, his ship, his dive. Daniela winced, wondering if he thought the finding of *La Daniela* was a worthy trade for the trouble that had come with the information.

The décor of his spacious cabin, much like the rest on board, was predominantly black and white, his appreciation for color evident in the two massive paintings. One hung over his bed, the other over a stunning ultramodern glass gas fireplace on the opposite wall. Daniela was familiar with both artists.

She'd had a gallery show for Rosslyn Klinger last

year. In fact, this very oil, of a deserted tropical beach, two pairs of wet footprints in the sand facing each other, and a discarded top of a blue bikini, had had pride of place in her gallery. It had sold to an anonymous buyer for a staggering amount. Logan Cutter. Wow. It was a strangely small world.

She went into her cabin, closed and locked the door, then went into the tiny bathroom and turned on the shower.

He'd chosen the bright young stars of the future, and he'd chosen very well. These two oversize pieces alone would be worth a fortune in a few years. He'd made sound investments. He was a very smart man.

The thought that the Klinger painting had once hung in her Washington, DC, gallery, and now, a year later, hung over Logan Cutter's massive bed a world away, was chilling. She didn't want the world to be this small. Especially while Victor was scouring the planet looking for her.

Still a little nauseous and dizzy, she forced herself to step into a cool shower until she regained her equilibrium.

Feeling considerably better, she dressed in record time, linen drawstring pants in an eye-popping pink and a white T-shirt. She called it good, then glanced in the mirror. Armor it wasn't, but now she at least had on a bra, which beat walking around half-dressed.

"I have to warn him," she said to her reflection.

Uncertainty flickered in the gaze staring back at her. "If what Wes said about him is true, I'll be lucky if he doesn't throw me overboard for the whoppers I've told him."

She gripped the counter and took a deep breath, closing her eyes. "I just need to keep putting one foot in front of the other." And it was true. The more she moved, the better she felt. Physically, anyway. After she drank several glasses of water, the nausea abated, and she was no longer light-headed. "Good. At least I won't fall over when I deliver the bad news to Cutter." Whatever was going on with the rest of the ship was her business, too. She padded back through Logan's cabin to check on Dog, even though she heard him snoring out on the balcony.

The animal lifted his head from his nest of blankets as she came outside and leaned over to rub between his ears. "It's okay, Doofus. Go back to sleep." The dog tilted his head as if trying to understand her, then snuffled, laid his nose on his paws, and closed his eyes.

Turning to the water, she curled her fingers around the smooth wood topping the Plexiglas half-wall, the wind lifting the damp strands of her hair around her neck and face. Lights from the various decks above and below reflected in the black water, and indistinct voices melted into the sound of the ocean slapping against the ship.

The tension was palpable, the air thick with ominous murmurs and whispered threats. Her paranoia was back with a vengeance. Damn it. Determined to make the best of a bad situation, she'd allowed herself to be lulled into a false sense of calm, believing that the cousins wouldn't make their move until Logan and his team had gotten all the treasure from the bottom of the ocean.

They'd barely waited forty-eight hours.

And to sabotage his ship?! Holy Mother of God. They

were *insane*. When they'd thrown her into the pitch-dark ocean with nothing more than a life vest to keep her afloat until—*if*—someone on board the *Sea Wolf* discovered her, that had only been criminal stupidity.

But if they'd come on board Logan Cutter's ship . . . She wrapped her arms around herself and rubbed the goose bumps on her bare skin.

The situation was escalating, and she wasn't sure what to do to stop it. Logan would most certainly ensure she was taken back to Lima, if she asked. She suspected he'd be more than happy to get rid of her, but that didn't resolve anything.

Her cousins would hound Logan until they had what they believed was rightfully theirs.

And without money or resources, she'd be in a world of hurt alone in Lima. She just had to stay alive for two weeks. But was her life worth more than Logan's, or his crew's?

Trapped. Damned if she did, and damned if she didn't.

She was as tense as a bowstring, and rotated her shoulders to try and ease her knotted muscles. Daniela shivered as the chill permeated her entire body. It was so damned illogical of those idiots to come charging in before they knew what Cutter had found. Or if he'd found anything at all! How could they know one way or the other?

She and Logan had been lucky, but other people on board might not have been swooped up and taken into the fresh air. God forbid, someone could have been seriously harmed, possibly have *died* tonight because of her family.

Logan could probably use another pair of hands. Doing what, she had no idea. But if nothing else, she could make coffee. She turned away from the never-ending expanse of midnight water, and went through the billowing drapes, back into the dimly lit cabin.

The wood floors felt cool and smooth beneath her bare feet as she walked the perimeter of the room, stepping onto one of several soft, thick area rugs dotted about the dark floor. She picked up a smooth piece of jade from a shelf, running her thumb over it as she rambled, delaying the inevitable even while she knew that the faster she told Logan, the faster it would be over.

She had no idea how *he* reacted to bad news. God . . . There was nowhere to run on a boat in the middle of the Pacific. She was at his mercy. Damn it, she was sick of being a victim. Sick to death of being afraid. Sick of running.

Five more minutes and she'd go and find him. She was still a little queasy. Daniela let her gaze pause every now and then on something interesting. There were a lot of fascinating artifacts from his travels scattered about in a very deliberate way. He must have hundreds of interesting stories.

Not that she'd be around to hear them.

Please, God, let this be over in a couple of weeks.

Over, leaving what in its wake? The gallery was closed. Her disappearance had been explained by her frantic-with-worry fiancé as "mysterious and troubling," her mental health put under a microscope. Victor was clever that way.

They'd never *been* engaged, and her disappearance had been far from mysterious. She'd fled the second she knew Victor would kill her before she testified. The fact that she was still very much alive, despite the hit man he'd sent to that cheap motel in Pensacola, must be very troubling for Senator Stamps. She hoped he'd be troubled right into prison.

And standing around delaying the inevitable wasn't helping anyone. Dragging in a deep breath, she left Logan's cabin, heading to the lower deck where she knew the men gathered in the evenings.

"Warn him and offer to leave." She rolled her shoulders again and kept moving. One thing at a time. She bumped into Wes and Galt going down the stairs.

"Annie." Wes touched a large hand to her shoulder, "Are you okay? Any nausea? Headache? Anything?"

"I'm perfectly fine. Was anyone else affected?"

"Not from the g—" Wes nudged Galt in the arm.

"Does Logan know you're wandering about?" Wes gave her a worried frown as they reached the lower landing and heard the sound of voices.

"I'm a big girl. Capable of wandering on my own for some time now," she told him dryly, giving his Hawaiian surf shorts an amused glance despite the tension roiling in her stomach. "Where's he meeting everyone?"

"In there," Galt told her, while he met Wes's eyes over her head. "Maybe you should wait in your cabin? I'm sure Logan will fill you in when he's got everybody's reports."

"I'm sure he will, but since I'm here." She smiled as she looked up and up and up. Steve Galt must be at least six eight or nine, and had to stoop to get between sections of the ship. "I'll save him some time." She couldn't wait, not for this.

They entered the room to find a group of men already

gathered. Logan and Jed stood near the open doors talking quietly. Cutter wore black shorts. That was it. Black shorts. The man didn't like clothes, apparently. And just as apparently it didn't matter how many times she saw him half naked; the sight made Daniela's mouth go dry and her heartbeat accelerate. The reaction had nothing to do with nerves.

As if he sensed her on the opposite side of the room, Logan's head swiveled and their eyes met. He scowled. *Oh. Not a happy camper.* Daniela mouthed, "I have to talk to you."

He shook his head even as he turned back to Jed and a crewman. They talked for several minutes, as more divers and crew came and went. The room hummed with a current that was palpable.

"I'll go help Hipolito with coffee, sandwiches maybe . . ." she trailed off as Wes pointed to the buffet table by the open slider. Nobody seemed to have touched anything. "Never mind." It had just been a delaying tactic, she knew.

"He's right in the middle of this, Annie. Can't it wait?" Wes said quietly. "Someone sabotaged *Sea Wolf,* and we're trying to put all the pieces together."

Wes was still talking, Daniela could see his lips moving, but all the sound in the room was muffled, as if she were hearing it underwater. Sabotage. So they *had* endangered everyone. It didn't make her feel any better having her suspicions confirmed.

"I have a missing piece to his puzzle," Daniela told him flatly, edging closer to Logan in the hope she could zip in and tell him what she had to tell him and then leave. She waited for him to finish talking to Cooper.

But then another of the crew stepped in, and spoke with his hands. Logan scowled.

He turned back to Horner and they exchanged a few more words before the diver strode off. Everyone was strung tight, which didn't help ease Daniela's feelings of anger and guilt for the role she played in this. What she had to tell him wasn't going to make him any happier, and after several minutes, she moved through the men clustered in the middle of the room. "Excuse me. Sorry. Thanks."

When she reached Logan, she laid her hand on his arm. Big mistake; it was like touching a live wire. She quickly dropped her hand when he whipped his head around as if he'd been poked by a cattle prod. "Unless you know something about the gas leak, whatever it is can wait," he said tightly. "I have a situation—"

"Of course it has a direct bearing," she assured him. "Why else would I bother you? He'll be right back," she told the two men he was talking to. "I just need thirty seconds of your time. Outside?"

"Make it ten." He indicated she precede him out onto the side deck. It was bright as day with all the lights on.

The breeze lifted her hair off her shoulders as she went to the rail. There was not much to see out there but white-tipped black water. She turned her back and leaned against the rail, drawing in a ragged breath.

Awareness sparked to life as he ran his turbulent ocean-colored eyes over her. His dark hair was rumpled as if he'd been shoving his fingers through it, his gaze shadowed. "I thought you'd be asleep."

"I wanted to talk to you before I—Logan, I'm sorry," she rushed into tumbled speech, her voice low. "It was the Apazas."

He frowned, adjusted his earpiece to give her his full attention. Even half his attention, she'd found, was too intense. "The Apazas?"

She heard a loud throb and whirring sound overhead. A helicopter? She hadn't seen one on board—maybe it was landing?

It sounded as if it was taking off. A few seconds later a small dragonfly with a helicopter's blinking lights flew overhead and away. "Jed," he told her absently. "What's this about the Apazas?"

"My cousins did—" she waved a vague hand. "Whatever. We all could've died. You should press charges."

A muscle in his jaw jerked, and he shoved his hands into the pockets of his shorts. "Are you saying you've been in contact with them since you've been on board my ship?"

"No. I—Of course not, how would I—"

"Then how do you know who tampered with the hoses?"

"Hoses?" she repeated blankly.

"*And* brought canisters of CO aboard. Carbon monoxide has been leaking into the interior spaces for who knows how long. If you haven't been in contact, how do you know it was them?"

She gripped the smooth rail until she thought she might snap it in two. "You brought up a fortune in treasure from the sea today," she pointed out, her voice tight. "Who else could it be?"

He came to stand beside her, then leaned his elbows on the rail, his big hands hanging over the smooth wood. He turned his head to look at her. He was very close. "Oh, believe me, plenty of people."

Daniela frowned. "*Plenty* of people?"

"This is a business where everyone feels entitled to take your pie before you've had a chance to pick up your fork. So yeah. Could've been your cousins, could've been someone sent by Case, could be your common garden-variety pirate."

"Trust me. My cousins are after what you brought to the surface today. This was their way of getting it on the extra easy plan."

"The exhaust hoses were cut and rerouted. Containers were found discharging the gas into the ventilation system. Overkill, to put it mildly."

"Hugo would probably know how to do that. He used to be a technician at a heating and air-conditioning company."

"This whole thing feels too sophisticated to have been them, from what you've told me. Still, they'll be picked up for questioning. It's a miracle that nobody was fatally injured. Alarm systems were deactivated. The captain was struck violently over the head while on the bridge. As were two crewmen as they went about their business," he told her, then jerked his chin to the helicopter's lights in the distance. "Jed's getting them to the hospital."

Her chest felt tight with strain. "Who else would possibly kill an entire ship of people for just a sample of your treasure? Who else is that stupid and shortsighted?"

He seemed closer to her, but maybe it was a trick of the light. "Who else?" His tone was mocking, his jaw tight. "Anyone who wanted to get their hands on a fortune in gold and emeralds. I can think of at least two other people with even stronger motives than your charming cousins."

The air left Daniela's constricted lungs. Relief flooded

her veins. Not the cousins. Maybe. She drew in a breath of relief. "Who?"

"Hell, we have an embarrassment of suspects right now." He rubbed the bristle on his jaw. "Could be either Rydell Case or the Sea Bitch, or both for all I know. From the little you've told me about your guys, I'm not sure they have all the skills they'd need. On the other hand, it's not as if you know everything about them on such short acquaintance."

He cupped her cheek, and she couldn't help but lean into his strength, as he said evenly, "Whoever boarded was familiar with this type of ship, and I'd hazard a guess, professional."

She tried to swallow, her throat too dry. Her legs felt rubbery and insubstantial. Locking her knees, she pressed a shaking hand to her throat. Her nausea and dizziness returned with a vengeance. She could barely push the words out as she stared at him blankly. "Professional . . . what?"

Victor's assassins?!

White-faced, Annie swayed on her bare feet as Logan responded, "Professional thiev—Whoa!" He lunged, grasping her upper arms as her knees sagged.

She blinked up at him as if swimming up through a fog. "Th—thieves?"

His fingers tightened around her upper arms as she wilted. He shouldn't have left her alone. Damn it, she should be in the chopper with the others. "I'll have Jed turn around and come get you—"

"No! No, it's nothing. Really. I don't have my sea legs, and I felt a little dizzy, that's all."

"Sure?" He realized she didn't seem to be aware that he was practically supporting her weight. Her skin felt cold beneath his hands.

"I—" She ran her tongue over her lips in an unconsciously provocative swipe that had Logan's body humming. "Yes. Positive." She tried to maneuver away, but Logan wasn't sure she was capable of standing just yet.

He ran his thumbs up the silky smooth skin over surprisingly firm biceps. She blinked a couple of times, but didn't jerk out of his hold. He stroked her arms again, and felt the fine tremor, hyperaware of her reaction to his touch. If she expressed even a shadow of fear, he'd make sure she was steady, and he'd let go. He checked her pupils to see if the carbon monoxide was still affecting her. Jesus. Who was he fooling? How would he know? Dilated could mean the low lighting, could mean damn-well anything at this point. "Damn it, you're shaking like a leaf. I'll call J—"

"No—"

"Hospital," they said in unison.

Logan swung her up in his arms. For a moment she stiffened, and her eyes went wide. "Put me down." Her fist skated off his bare shoulder as she tried to push him away.

He tightened his arms beneath her legs and around her back. "No." He figured she was so focused on either the conversation, or trying not to pass out, she didn't notice he was carrying her back inside. He gave Wes a small shake of his head and he started forward, a worried look on his face. "I won't drop you."

"I'll drop *you*," she said through clenched teeth. "I

don't like being manhandled." She arched her back, stiffening her legs. "Put. Me. Down."

It was like carrying a cat in a sack as she squirmed to get her legs free. "Pretend I'm the doctor." His hold was inextricable, but he was very aware that he had to be gentle with her. Didn't mean he was letting her go. Not right now. He took the stairs three at a time, reaching his deck in record time.

She gave him a slitted look that spoke volumes, as he maneuvered her so he could reach his key card in his front pocket. Annoyance pinked her cheeks. "I've never played doctor, and I don't intend to start now—"

He carried her inside, the door open so Dog could race out and disappear down the companionway. "He's obviously feeling better. I have a question for you."

"*I* didn't do it," she said flatly. "I can barely work my toaster."

As he continued across the cabin, turning off some of the lights as he went, she gave him a defiant look. Since her face was only a few inches away, he could read fear in her eyes. He cursed himself for putting it there.

"Planning on throwing me overboard?" He carried her out onto the patio and scooped up the soft throw he'd wrapped her in earlier. "Because there's always some guy who has a hero complex that'll dive in and save me."

He carried her back inside, and rounded the foot of the bed. "Were you raped, Annie?"

He sat down on the edge of the mattress, her across his lap.

"What a strange question. No."

"You swear?"

"Yes."

He got comfortable, one shoulder propped against the headboard. "Is that true?"

"You can believe anything you please. I wasn't raped. Shouldn't you tell someone to go after my cousins?"

"Already done." She wiggled on his lap, and he realized she wasn't pulling away, just getting comfortable. Something in his gut eased a little.

Her silky hair tumbled over the hand he had bracing her shoulders, and he tucked a strand of it behind her ear. He slid that hand up to cup the back of her head. Unable to resist touching her skin, he brushed the edge of his thumb across her cheek. Her breath caught in a sexy little intake, and this time he knew it was desire that made her pupils dilated.

He traced his thumb in a feather-soft caress across her cheekbone, and was rewarded as he felt warmth seep into her chilled skin. "I'm going to kiss you, Annie. Brace yourself."

She put her palm between their mouths, eyes narrowed to glittering slits over her fingers. "Don't even try it." The hard edge in her voice made something inside him crumple, and he gentled his hold even more. Interesting; she didn't make any attempt to get off his lap. She reclined in his arms, shooting daggers.

Daggers he could deal with. "Don't be afraid of me," his command was soft. "I'll never hurt you."

"If I had a quarter for every time a man said that . . ."

"Not this man."

For several slow, thudding heartbeats she said nothing. Logan could almost hear her mind processing the information. He felt a lie tremble through her body, then she pulled the rug out from under him when she said, "I wasn't raped, but I was . . . was traumatized," she told him baldly, barely above a raw whisper. "Seriously, badly traumatized. I don't like—"

He didn't ask who, and he didn't ask when. His suspicions were confirmed. She'd tell him, eventually, and he'd go after the son of a bitch. But for now, Logan didn't let his thoughts show. The cabin was dim and filled with shadows, his ship quiet; a cool breeze stirred the sheer drapes beside the open doors.

His throat tightened as he held her lithe body as gently as he would an injured baby bird. She didn't fly away. "I'll never do anything with you that you don't like."

She gave him a hostile look from bruised amber eyes. "I don't like *anything*."

He brushed the outer shell of her ear with the hand threaded through her hair, and felt her shiver. "Tough girl."

"Yes," she assured him, meeting his eyes head-on over the barricade of her fingers. "I am. I've had to be."

"I won't mess with you, then." He brushed his lips over the back of her hand. Her skin was cold and slightly clammy. God. Who'd done this to her? "How about this?" he murmured, stroking his lips across her knuckles. "Hate it? Love it? Don't care?"

"Don't care."

"Hmm. How about . . ." Logan turned the barricade between them gently, then pressed his lips to the center of her palm. "This?"

Her fingers curled defensively, brushing his cheek.

"Don't care," she told him tightly. Just a rim of brown showed around her pupils, but her gaze was steady.

She'd forgotten one simple thing. He was a treasure hunter. Going after the difficult was a piece of cake. Going after the impossible—that just took more time.

Nine

"The guys all set?" Jed asked as Logan came onto the bridge the next morning.

"Yeah." Early morning dew beaded the large windows without impeding the view. The ocean was a sheet of coral glass blending almost seamlessly with the sky. "They know their shit."

The guys in question were the six security men Jed had brought back from Arequipa half an hour before. "Good job at such short notice."

"Mpho worked on the systems last night—or this morning, rather, to get everything back to speed." The taciturn engineer, whose last name was even harder to pronounce than his first, had voiced his displeasure at people screwing with his ship. He and his crew were in the process of checking every nut, bolt, and screw in each piece of machinery and equipment on board. Twice, if Logan knew his engineer.

Annie had fallen asleep in his arms, something he was pretty sure she hadn't planned on doing at the start of the evening. He'd tugged the cashmere throw over her shoulders as the air chilled, then listened to her breathe, while wondering how bad things had been for her, and what the hell she was hiding. After half an hour, he'd reluctantly returned her to her cabin. He'd whistled low for Dog.

"Good boy." He pointed to a spot beside the bed. "Sit. Stay. Anyone so much as breathes the same air as her, bite 'em." Dog padded to the spot, planted his butt, ears pricked, eyes alert. He wouldn't lie down until Logan told him he was off duty. With the dog on guard, Logan went to meet with his men.

The dive team was forgoing today's dive to assist the security guys wherever was needed, starting with checking each piece of dive equipment. The crew was still scouring every cabin, every room, every square inch of *Sea Wolf* for signs of more tampering. Then those that could, switched places and went through everything again.

Logan was coldly furious. Everyone on board had the same sense of violation, and almost everyone wondered if there was something they could have—should have—done to stop the saboteurs. Piet and the two crewmen hadn't stood a chance, but they felt guilty as hell, even though Logan didn't blame them for being overwhelmed.

Piet walked in. The sandy-haired Dutchman had a bandage on the side of his head and a pissed-off glint in his eye. He was dressed in white shorts and a golf shirt with epaulets on the shoulders. He was rarely this formal. He was dressed for war. "Get off my bridge," he told them evenly. "I'm not dead, and a little headache won't prevent me from doing my job."

Jed shook his head. "You had a *concussion*."

"Well, I don't have it now," Piet told him sourly as he waved a hand to get them to move. "I have things to deal with, and you'll just be in my way."

"How many stitches?" Logan asked, scanning the older man's face to assess whether he really was fit enough to be back. Jed had called from the hospital and told him the captain and crewmen were insisting on being allowed to report back to the ship.

"Twelve or so."

"What did the doctors say?"

"To go back to work, and find out who sabotaged my ship."

Logan smiled. "We're all taking his advice." He updated the captain before leaving to corral his own crew and meet with their engineer. He stopped at the door to take one last look at Vandyke.

Piet turned his back, then glanced over his shoulder. "You two still here?"

Logan went downstairs with Jed. "Doctor really did say he checked out fine," Jed assured him as they took the stairs.

"I want these people caught and brought to justice," Logan said grimly. "This is unacceptable on every fucking level." And it made his belly clutch to think that Annie might have something to do with it. He was not a curious man. He researched his wrecks diligently, and knew what he was about as far as salvaging went. Unlike Zane or Nick, he didn't care who'd been on board a centuries-old ship, or why. He wasn't interested in the details of the past as much as he was fascinated by the present.

And he sure as hell had never been curious about a woman. Mystery schmystery. He didn't give a flying fuck if a woman wanted to keep her past blacker than night.

But Annie Ross . . . ? For some inexplicable reason, Logan wanted to ferret out all her secrets, wanted to know where she'd been when she was thirteen, and seventeen, and twenty. Seven days ago.

Maybe he'd get some of the answers today.

He heard the throbbing beat of salsa before he and Jed turned the corner into the galley. The room smelled deliciously of strong black coffee, bacon, and the yeasty fragrance of freshly baked bread. The sunrise was visible through the large windows, and bright white light suffused the spacious galley, glinting off spotless stainless steel appliances and white marble countertops. The place looked as sterile as an operating room to Logan. Not a thing out of place. Hipolito ruled his galley with an iron fist in a steel oven mitt.

"Breakfast is already set out," the chef told them as he poured, handing each man a large, steaming mug, then returned to his bread dough, prepping the next batch of rolls. "How is Miss Annie doing?" he asked, not glancing up from his task. He didn't like people in his galley, and made no bones about it. He'd made an exception for Annie, a big concession from him.

"She doesn't seem to have any ill effects," Logan answered. "How are you feeling this morning? Any problems here?"

"I always sleep with my window open, so I wasn't that affected." He shrugged his rounded shoulders, then punched into the soft dough. "Dell, *tiene un pequeño dolor de cabeza*. A *very* small headache, which he'll be pleased to tell you about, so don't ask him how he is when you see him! Six extra meals for how long?"

"Until we're sure we don't need the security," Logan told him flatly.

Hipolito thumped his dough with his fist. "*Excelente.*"

"Annie still sleeping?" Jed asked, as they went down to the common room to grab breakfast.

"How would I know one way or the other?" Logan asked mildly as they strolled into the empty room. Hipolito's handiwork had already been sampled, as was evidenced by the stack of used plates, and the hole right in the middle of the scrambled eggs. Wes's signature serving.

Jed shot him a knowing look. "Hello? Have you met my friend Logan Cutter, rescuer of fair maidens and slayer of dragons?"

"She's in my office, talking to Nick."

In the process of tonging bacon onto his plate, Jed looked at his watch, and gave him a raised brow. "At six A.M.? Interesting thing for the least curious man I know to do."

Jed was aware that Nick had the uncanny ability to identify exactly where someone was from just by listening to them speak. By the look on his friend's face, Jed knew what Logan was up to—speeding up the "getting answers" part of the process.

"If she wanted you to know, she'd tell you," Jed pointed out, scooping up fried potatoes from the heated serving dish. Logan topped off his coffee and grabbed an orange sweet roll, and they went outside to sit at the table under the awning. He shot a regretful glance at the dive platform that no one was using. All the equipment was up near the table because the guys had checked every valve and hose, and emptied and refilled all the tanks. Logan was leaving nothing to chance.

"In light of last night's events, I can't wait for full disclosure," he told Jed. "She thinks her cousins were responsible, but I have my doubts. Rydell is still on the other side of the world. Sea Bitch"—he used his mug to indicate the sleek ship, barely visible on the edge of the blushing horizon—"is a woman alone."

Jed shoveled eggs in his mouth. "So, not Rydell, or Sea Bitch. Could still be Annie's relatives, right? Considering they were ruthless enough to throw a woman overboard, this sounds right up their alley."

"Yeah. And we know they have no problems hitting people on the head." Logan finished his coffee and set the mug on the table. "I have someone in Lima getting their backstory for me. A quick Internet search pulled up their criminal records, and a few newspaper articles hidden on the back page. Not particularly interesting, petty shit. Nothing to indicate they could pull off a stealth mission involving tanks of CO."

Jed pushed his empty plate aside and reached for his mug. "Maybe they have partners in crime, people who know exactly how to stage an operation like that."

"Yeah. Maybe. They want the treasure from *La Daniela.* So why swoop in on day one when they have no idea what we have and how much more is below? Why not wait until we have everything in bins and then come and take it? It doesn't make sense. Not even for small-time operators like this."

"So what are you thinking? Pirates?" Jed drank. "They didn't *take* anything, right? Could be they were testing our security. Or lack thereof."

"Well, it's pumped up now," Logan said shortly. "And we'll all be more vigilant from now on."

Daniela had no idea why Logan had insisted she be the one to tell his brother what had happened the night before. It was the very crack of daybreak and the poor man must've been dragged out of bed for absolutely no reason. Nick was half a world away, and she was pretty sure he'd rather hear the story from Logan, but his older brother had brought her a cup of coffee—exactly the way she liked it—and disappeared to do "Important Things."

After talking to Nick Cutter for twenty minutes, she put the phone down and yawned. She'd woken at some godforsaken hour to Dog wanting to go out, and as she'd opened her door, Logan had been about to go into his cabin next door. There'd been a moment there when they'd just stared at one another, and her heart had skittered.

She didn't remember going back to her cabin after he'd teased and tormented her, and she didn't remember letting Dog in. Clearly Logan had done both. She'd woken to find herself in her bunk, Logan's cashmere blanket wrapped around her, Dog sprawled across her feet.

Despite the brevity, she'd slept, she realized, like a rock. The first time *that* had happened in months. Even during her two-day rest, she'd slept lightly.

Logan had fed her some story about his middle brother being worried, and asked her to give Nick the details. She didn't have many of those, but she gave it her best shot. His brother was charming, and funny, and surprisingly quite chatty.

Daniela placed the emerald bowl she'd been holding back on Logan's desk. It really was quite beautiful. And worth, she guessed, a large fortune on the open market. That side of the family had had the damn thing for hundreds of years. It stunned her that they hadn't sold it at some point.

Apparently each generation had believed that the *La Daniela* treasure was worth a lot more than a giant stone.

She was just about to get up and turn on the television to watch the news, when the door opened. She used her momentum to head for the door. She didn't want a face-to-face with Logan this early in the morning.

"All done?" he asked easily, stepping inside, but leaving the door open. He was alone. No Dog in sight. He'd changed into royal blue swim trunks and a red muscle shirt, and his feet were shoved into deck shoes, no socks. He'd shaved, and looked bright-eyed and delicious.

Daniela's heart skipped several beats. "I'm sure he wanted you to tell him. I told him what I knew, but he wants you to call him later."

"Yeah. I'll do that. We're still checking out your cousins.

"How about that guy you thought was in South Africa?"

"He's still in Cape Town. He could've sent someone else to do the job, but that's not Case's style. We've ruled him out for now. Want breakfast?" Apparently perfectly at ease, he was blocking the door.

No. She did not want to sit across a table from him and attempt to swallow. If it turned out that her cousins hadn't snuck on board last night, and it hadn't been the guy in South Africa, that could only mean one thing. Victor and his minions had found her. "I'll grab something later," she said with forced cheer. "Is anyone diving yet? I'd love to watch."

She had to leave. She'd come up with some reason, and just—leave. Logan knew to watch his back about her cousins. Bringing them to him was bad enough. But bringing the kind of trouble Victor favored? No. She couldn't do it.

"Nobody's going down today. Don't worry, the treasure will still be there tomorrow. It'll take weeks, if not months, to retrieve everything. We're checking all the equipment six ways from Sunday to ensure nothing else was tampered with."

"Of course." Weeks? Months? She'd be long gone, and hopefully, *alive*. On the other hand, *Logan* would be in danger with every gold bar and emerald he brought to the surface.

Daniela hadn't left and she was already worried for him.

"Ever dived?" he asked, propping a hip against his desk so that she had to turn around to look at him. She'd rather not. Everything about him was too . . . Big. His body. His personality. The brilliance of his eyes. He was too in her face. And that was when he was sitting six feet away from her.

She suppressed a shudder at the very thought of diving. She was in far more imminent danger from *him*. "I'm not crazy about putting my face in water."

"I'll take you down and teach you. Once you get used to it, you'll love it."

Yes, she'd heard that before. Just not in the same context. Daniela rubbed the goose bumps on her upper arms, and swallowed the jolt of fear that shot up from her tummy into her dry throat. "I think I'll grab a shower, then see if Hipolito needs help in the galley." And figure out what the hell she'd do on land with no money.

"Do you run?" His voice stopped her at the door.

She certainly had been ready to do just that a nanosecond ago. Daniela hesitated, her hand on the edge of the half-open door. She turned her head to glance back at him. "Run?" she asked warily. "Where?"

"A few laps around the upper deck. Dog needs a run

several times a day or he'll just lie around, eating bon-bons and snoozing in the sun. We do the treadmill if it gets too hot for him, but the deck makes a good track, and it's early yet. You game?"

His sparkling cobalt eyes said he wasn't talking about anything as mundane and safe as a jog around the deck.

Ah. She'd wondered about the purple running shoes Wes had brought back for her. Now all the pieces clicked into place. She didn't want to spend any more time with Logan than was absolutely necessary to be polite. But there was no good reason she could offer as to why she couldn't go with him. It wasn't as if she had something better to do. "Dozer doesn't really eat bonbons, does he?"

The corner of his mouth twitched. "Not sure what they are, but probably not. Hard to open the package without opposable thumbs, and I can't be with him twenty-four hours a day to watch his calorie count."

Was he . . . *joking* with her? It came so out of left field, Daniela wasn't quite sure how to react. "I—um, I have a bad knee," she said with faux regret.

"No problem," Logan said cheerfully. "We'll take it slow. Go put on your shoes. Meet us back here in five."

She kept him waiting an informative thirty-seven minutes.

His door was open, so she stepped inside. "Ready?" she asked sweetly. Dressed in lavender shorts, a purple-and-yellow striped tank top, and purple running shoes—all clearly courtesy of Wes—she looked like a luscious, lickable grape Popsicle.

He smelled the clean woman and grapefruit scent of

her skin all the way on the other side of the cabin, and was unsurprised by his body's instant response.

Damn logic, and to hell with general principles. He wanted this woman as he'd never wanted any other woman in his life.

Her thick, glossy dark hair was tied back in a high ponytail, which showed off her stubborn chin and the sweet curve of her cheek. Her legs looked a mile long, with strong, lean runner's muscles and mouthwatering definition.

Letting his eyes devour every inch of her from lips to toes and back again, Logan swung his feet off his desk and stood, Dog at his side. "I am." *I really, really am ready, sweetheart.*

With Nick's help, and the time she'd so generously allowed him to talk to his brother and make a few discreet phone calls, it hadn't been that hard to put the puzzle pieces together. Not *all* the pieces, he was sure, but the gist. And not all the pieces he had, fit.

He needed Miss Daniela Rosado of Washington, DC, to fill in the blanks.

They emerged onto the forward deck where one of the security men stood, arms akimbo, booted feet spread, facing the water. White-blond crew cut, muscled, and built like a brick house. Knife strapped to his ankle, gun at his shoulder. He looked ready for anything. "Sven, right?"

Logan frequently had security on the ship when they were hauling treasure, so he was used to heavily armed ex-military men strategically placed around his ship. They all were.

But Daniela gave him a startled glance as the guy said, "Yes, sir."

Logan rested his hand lightly on the small of her back, indicating she move to the foredeck. Her skin was cool beneath the thin fabric of her top, and she shivered slightly, shifting out of reach to walk beside him. "If whoever snuck on board wasn't one of your two prime suspects," she asked casually; "who do you think it was?"

Logan shrugged. "Could be almost anyone. People know that I have uncanny luck finding valuable wrecks. Don't worry about it. The local cops are on it."

"You don't think it was personal?"

"Conjecture is useless at this point. The cops haven't even had twelve hours to figure it out."

"Will they shoot to kill if an intruder comes on board?" she asked, glancing back at the security guy as she started to warm up.

"Would you prefer they shoot to *almost* kill?" he asked dryly, more interested in watching her warming up than anything else right then. She was poetry in motion.

Holy shit, Logan thought shaking his head at his own folly. The woman was a lie machine, and had some heavy-hitting friends in very high places, according to Nick.

"We have forty-six people on board," he told her, shoving the disjointed bits and pieces of his hasty investigation aside to be worked on by his subconscious. "And the bad guys didn't hesitate to pump my ship full of lethal gas. Hell yeah, they're ordered to shoot to kill. If anyone harms what's mine, they'd better be prepared for the consequences."

He stretched his arms over his head. He schooled his features to blandness, when what he wanted to do was rip into the assholes with his bare hands. "Worried your cousins will get hurt?"

She stopped stretching. "Frankly, I'd be stunned if they *aren't* hurt at some point during all this. I don't want them dead, they are blood after all, but I wouldn't mind if they were—suitably bruised."

"I can assure you, for hitting you, and for chucking you into the water at night? They'll get a little more than suitably bruised. Yes, boy. We see you," he told a prancing, butt-wagging, tongue-lolling Dog. "Ready?" Logan asked Daniela.

Because right or wrong, fact or fiction, he was more than ready.

They did a steady circuit around the entire ship, keeping a good slow jogging pace. Clearly she was a runner. "Again?" he asked, amused when she took off without answering.

"Race you," she yelled into the wind, Dog at her heels as they took a left turn at the aft deck, picking up the speed to a balls-out run. Logan dropped back a few steps to admire the view, then loped ahead.

"Sure," he yelled over his shoulder. "Twenty laps equals about a mile. How many do you usually do?" He liked a good hard five-mile run first thing. Of course, he preferred hot and heavy sex first thing, but that wasn't usually to be on a months-long salvage. Fist. Run. Fifty-fifty.

"Ten."

"Laps?"

She made a rude noise. *"Miles."*

Logan laughed. "Liar." And he didn't give a shit.

The longer she ran, the more mussed she became, as her thick, shiny hair slithered from its mooring, to stick to the sweat on her skin. Her olive skin became flushed, her eyes shone. It was almost as if running was liberating her from her cage of fear. Logan wished he could give her that when she was still.

Dog stopped at the four-mile mark, flopping down in the shade, and watching their every circuit. They stopped at six. A good run, a perfect day, and the shocking, sheer pleasure of running with a partner when he'd always preferred running alone. But for the rare occasion, Logan didn't even run with Jed.

His heartbeat and respiration were elevated, and he was hotter than hell. Hot because the morning temps were rising, and hot because his mermaid had her hands braced on her knees, head down, butt up. It was a fine look.

Grabbing two bottles of iced water from a plastic bucket Harris had left out for them, he opened one, draining half before he came up for air.

If he'd been alone, Logan would've taken a dive off the railing to cool off. Looking at her, with the thin cotton of her top clinging to her damp skin, and her eyes glowing as she stood up to face him, made him even hotter.

He cracked the other cap, unscrewed it, then handed it to her, ensuring their fingers brushed. Her eyes widened at the contact before she muttered, "Thanks," and rubbed the frosted bottle across her flushed cheeks, then around the back of her neck.

Her hair had fallen completely out of the rubber band, and hung in glossy damp strands around her shoulders. She shoved it off her face as she chugged the water. For a moment he indulged his new hobby—*her,* watching her throat work as she drank.

"Come with me," he told her silkily, heading around the corner. He had to get his hands on her. Now.

"Where're we going?" she asked, falling into step beside him.

"Right here." Right in the shade of the upper deck, where there wasn't another living soul. For the moment anyway. Logan leaned against the rail, extending his arms on either side of his hips. He curled his fingers around the warm, polished wood and held on for the ride, which was sure to be bumpy, he thought with inner amusement.

Her amber-brown eyes narrowed to lick over him with cool suspicion. "What are you doing?"

He gave her a surprised look. "Standing still so you can kiss me."

She huffed out a laugh. "Why would I want to do that?"

"To the untrained eye, I'm considered quite handsome."

The lines of strain eased around her eyes a little. "To the trained eye, you appear to be delusional," she tossed back smartly. But she didn't walk away. Progress. "I'm hot and sweaty and I need another shower."

"Kiss me first. Look, no hands." He wiggled his fingers on the railing. He'd positioned himself in the least threatening, least aggressive stance.

She raised a beautifully arched dark eyebrow. "You kiss with your hands?"

"Not on a first date," he told her piously, itching to grab her, hold her, and show her precisely what his hands could do. His fingers flexed against the unyielding wood on either side of him, but he kept them there with admirable control.

She rolled her eyes. A stray shaft of sunlight tipped her lashes gold, and highlighted her fine-grained, damp skin. Lust surged through him like a vortex, pulling him under. "One kiss," his voice was light, but he felt the hard thud of his heart. "My reward for letting you win."

She shook her head, biting her lower lip. Something that Logan very much wanted to do himself. Her eyes sparkled up at him, and his thudding, crazy heart did a triple axel.

"You didn't 'let' me win, Cutter. I beat you fair and square."

"And you did it with that bum knee. Remarkable." He smiled, holding out his hand. "Come over here and kiss me, or I'll think you're chicken."

Amusement faded from her features as she said flatly, "I *am* chicken."

"You are the least chicken woman I know," he told her seriously. But I still double-dare you." He beckoned with one finger. "One kiss. The security guys will be sweeping this area in seconds. I can't give you much longer than that."

"You are so full of yourself." She narrowed her eyes. "Put that hand back on the rail."

Triumph pinwheeled inside Logan as he clamped the offending hand on the rail beside him.

She stepped closer. "This is just so anyone watching doesn't think *I* think you're . . . repulsive."

The whisper of her breath fanned his chin as she moved an inch closer. Maddening woman. All she had to do was tilt her face a little . . . "That's a relief," he whispered, flexing his fingers on the rail, and imagining his fingers cupping the soft lobes of her breasts instead.

"I do have my reputation to upho—"

Her soft lips brushed his, and he felt the shock of contact right down to his toes, and in happy pulse points through his body like little starbursts.

She hesitated a moment, then closed her eyes and leaned closer. Logan smelled the clean, grapefruit-tinted perspiration on her skin, and then she swept her tongue into his mouth, and he couldn't breathe, and wasn't thinking of anything but the little sound she made as she kissed him.

The world went away.

Ten

Logan's body radiated heat. Daniela inched closer, the animal part of her brain reacting to the scent of virile male. She wanted to climb inside him and pull him over her like a blanket.

Kissing him was sure to be a mistake, but her good sense was overwhelmed by his hot, lean strength. Consequences and regrets teased the edge of rational thought. She slowly brought her mouth to his. The time for timid tastes was past. She wanted a real kiss.

He tasted of coffee and expectation. Nerves fluttered in her belly, and moisture pooled between her thighs although they touched nowhere but their lips.

"Don't go," he murmured as she lifted her head.

Her heart was pounding and prickles of nerves danced across Daniela's skin at the heat in his eyes. The breeze chilled the moisture on her lips. "This is—"

Dangerous.

"Elemental," he finished, voice husky, gaze steady as he met hers. His knuckles shone white as he gripped the railing, but he didn't reach for her. "We're in public. I'm not going to ravish you beneath the sky, surrounded by sparkling water," he said softly. "Just a kiss, Dani, it's just a kiss. Come back."

It wasn't just a kiss, that was the problem. Her mind stalled for a nanosecond. Had he called her Dani? She blinked back reason. Of course not. The man was addling her brain. He'd said "ravish" and she *wanted* to be ravished. She wanted to be naked with Logan Cutter on that big bed upstairs, wanted to feel his rough skin against her smooth skin.

She wanted . . . she squeezed the thoughts away, eyes closed, because he saw too much. Wanted too much.

And in doing so, made her want too much, too. Damn him.

Helpless to resist, she rested her palms on his chest. He went still at her touch, but his heart beat a rapid tattoo beneath her fingers. The hair on his chest tickled her palms. She went hot and then cold and then hot again as she brushed his lips with hers again. Once. Twice.

She'd already proven her judgment in men was flawed. But at least with Logan she was already aware of the danger. She'd be gone soon. She'd take this memory with her.

His pectoral muscles went hard as his entire body tensed. Daniela realized she was flexing her short nails against his skin like a cat. He growled low in his throat, and changed the angle of his mouth, taking control.

Everything around her faded. The sun. The shining water. The sounds and smells of the ship filled with people. It all went mute. All she heard was their syncopated heartbeats. All her senses were focused on this man. Here. Now.

Logan slid his hand around the back of her neck, then cupped the back of her head, his fingers tangling urgently in her hair as he kissed her with heat and passion, using his tongue and teeth to drive her crazy. His other hand, sure and insistent, skimmed over her hip to rest firmly at the base of her spine.

He lifted her into the hard jut of his erection, and Daniela's insides went into a meltdown as liquid heat sped in a dizzying race through her veins. Wrapping her arms around his neck, she kissed him back with everything she had.

Logan made a harsh sound in the back of his throat, his arms tightening around her with steely strength as he gave her the real kiss she craved. Hot, devouring, all-encompassing, and more kiss than Daniela had ever known or imagined.

Intoxicated by his insatiable sexual energy, she kissed him back, tapping into stores of sensuality she hadn't known existed.

She loved the smell of his skin. She loved the feel of him, she loved his taste. Eager. Bold. Delicious.

Addictive.

They were pressed together so tightly there was nothing between them but sweaty skin to sweaty skin. Her softness to his steel. Her heartbeat duplicated the rapid thundering of his. The sound filled her, spiking like small explosions of heat and light throughout her entire body.

Daniela shifted against him to relieve the ache in her breasts. The large splayed hand on her butt pressed her more tightly against his erection. He was strong, vital, powerful. She wanted all of that and more.

"Hey, Logan, I need—Oh, shit! Sorry!"

Logan broke the seal of their lips and it was like being doused with ice water. Disoriented, she blinked the world back into focus.

"What?" he demanded tersely of someone behind her. His fingers tightened in her hair, and he eased her face to rest against his shoulder. His skin was satin smooth, and hot under her mouth. She slicked her tongue over his collarbone and thrilled when he shuddered. She did it again, and his fingers flexed in her hair.

"We've done a thorough sweep of the ship," the guy spoke rapidly. "I think we can let everyone stand down."

"If you think that, Jedidiah, then fucking-well make an executive decision and implement it."

Jed said something, which Daniela didn't hear as Logan tilted her face up. His blue eyes were navy and smoldering. The interruption had barely fazed him. "Where were we?"

Daniela went up on her toes, tightening her arms around his neck. "Right. Here."

They had dive time after all. After sweeping the ship one last time, they'd unearthed nothing new. By early afternoon, the dive team was suiting up and sinking beneath the water to explore *La Daniela*.

Armed with baskets to load small items, and the blower to move the sand out of their way, Logan and Vanek went down first. They swam into the silky water, and for Logan it was like returning to the womb. Serene and peaceful.

Too bad he felt anything but peaceful after the call he'd just received.

While Vanek filled his basket with gold bars from a stash they'd discovered yesterday, Logan swam along the torn hull of *La Daniela*.

The storm had dashed her against the only reef this far-off land for fifty miles. She lay on her side, her hull ripped open from stem to stern. Her cannon had scattered a distance from where they'd been positioned. Time and the tides had untidily rearranged her so there was a debris field a mile long.

They'd already found gold bars, a few good-sized emeralds, and hundreds of gold chains. The big prize was the uncut emeralds the captain of the *Nuestra Señora de Garza* had meticulously noted on his manifest. Those, they hadn't found. Yet.

Logan and his brothers had an ongoing bet. Whoever found the biggest haul had the privilege of running Cutter Salvage for the year, and a ten-grand cash prize. A drop in the bucket when one considered the sheer magnitude of their finds, but it made for an interesting competition.

It was fortunate that he'd always gotten the biggest haul, because Logan had no intention of giving up control of Cutter Salvage. The plus of that was, Nick and Zane would hate doing what he loved to do. It was a win-win. Still, he'd be happy to take ten grand from each of them—*again*—when he went home to see what the hell his brothers had managed to get themselves into.

Vanek pointed, and Logan shifted the blower where he indicated, keeping it steady as sand and small debris swirled around them.

He and Dani's kiss had shaken him to the nth degree, but the call that followed had splintered that euphoria and brought him down to earth with a solid thud.

If her story about her family's connection to the emerald bowl held true, he didn't doubt Daniela had been named for the ship. But there was also a possibility that she wasn't who she claimed to be. Daniela Rosado might not even be her real name.

Damn, how much more convoluted could this be?

Logan liked simple. Straightforward. *Nothing* about his mermaid was uncomplicated. But hell, he'd known *that* before Nick offered him an interesting set of facts and left him to connect the dots.

Her mother had been born and raised in a small farming town south of Lima, father in South Dakota. His brother had offered specific place names of towns, but Logan was more interested in Daniela's immediate past than her heritage.

"Okay, think that'll do it. Turn her off." Vanek spoke over the noise. His voice came through the mic in Logan's headset as if he was speaking directly into his brain. Logan snapped back to his surroundings and shut his musings off for the time being. They waited for the crap in the water to settle before checking to see what, if anything, they'd unearthed.

His brother had given Logan a number to call if he wanted discreet inquiries made. Surprised at himself, Logan had called the number without a second's thought. The call had clearly been rerouted several times, and he was told the nameless man would call him right back. The guy had called him five minutes later. And then again a couple of hours ago.

Daniela Rosado owned a successful art gallery in DC. Her passion was for talented new artists. In a small shop inside the gallery, she sold one-of-a-kind, locally made Peruvian artifacts. She was fiscally solvent. Owned the building housing her gallery and shop in an upscale neighborhood, and drove both an SUV and a Mercedes. Paid her taxes on time, and had a healthy balance in her bank account.

She was engaged to Senator Victor Stamps.

Man probably kissed hands and shook babies and

looked charming doing it. Fine upstanding fucking citizen and shoo-in for president.

While he wasn't happy with what he'd learned, Logan couldn't see anything in that charmed life that gave him any insight into the real question: Who had put the wariness and fear in those big brown eyes? Her father? The senator? Her cousins? And why in fucking hell was a woman in line for First Lady dumped overboard in the middle of nowhere, left to die?

For a man who didn't normally give a shit about answers, he sure as hell had a lot of questions.

His brother Zane asked a million questions of everyone. He was interested.

Nick could wear a T-shirt that stated, No Questions Answered Here.

And Logan's motto was, Don't Know. Don't Care.

"Hey, man," Vanek gave Logan a worried look through his mask. "You okay?"

Logan gave him a thumbs-up.

The senator from Massachusetts was at the end of his six-year term, and it was rumored he'd be running for president in the next election. The groundswell of support said he had a damn good chance of winning. He was young, handsome, charming, and wealthy.

Logan loathed his guts sight unseen.

Damn it to hell, Daniela would make an amazing First Lady.

Vanek touched his arm to get his attention; apparently yelling in his ear hadn't done the trick. "Buddy, you look like crap. Let's send the next team down to check that out. Go have a breather."

"Sorry, just thinking." Which at this depth, and in this environment, was not only stupid, but dangerous.

Not just for himself, but for his partner. Logan shoved his speculation and opinions of the unknown senator out of his head. "I'm good. Let's see what we have."

Five fat bass lazily swam between them as chunks of vegetation and coral swirled in the water like a slo-mo whirlwind. Logan and Vanek angled down into the crater made by the blower, where items from *La Daniela* had scattered four hundred years ago.

The Czech grabbed his arm, and pointed. "Oh, man, lookit!"

Logan had already seen. Normally his heart would've sped up in anticipation. The area was ripe with a variety of treasure. The cannons were a given, but they'd leave those on the seabed. The rest were the spoils of the *Sea Wolf*. Scattered gold coins glinted in whatever light caught them, but it was the pile of tangled chains that drew the two divers over for a closer look.

The large box in which the jewels had been encased had long since been mostly devoured by toledo worms, but the overall shape of the container remained, making it look as though the chains and coins were encased in an invisible container.

He and Vanek hauled several baskets onto the dive platform, then gave Jed and Cooper their turn. At a rough estimate, the haul from this dive alone was worth a quarter mil on today's market.

A good day for everyone.

He'd called her *Dani*.

Maybe she'd misheard.

No. He'd *definitely* called her Dani.

Daniela glanced through the window of the great room to where the guys were gathered, as they usually were, at the table near the dive platform. It was dusk; warm, and fragrant with the savory smell of the steaks Galt was cooking on the grill. Her tummy rumbled. It had been months since she'd felt anything as normal as hunger. Either kind.

She'd wanted to leave right after their run. Then it had been after lunch. Then it had been getting dark and she hadn't wanted anyone to take her to shore so late.

She'd leave first thing in the morning.

The television was on low. She didn't need sound. The control was in her hand so that if anyone strolled in, she could switch to *Sleepless in Seattle* instead of CNN.

Victor wasn't getting any airtime. Good.

How had Logan discovered her real name? She knew damn well she hadn't dropped any clues.

He really was a dangerous man.

The dangerous man walked past the window outside and stepped through the door. "Dinner's ready."

Daniela unwound her legs and got to her feet. "Good," she said a little too brightly. "I'm starving. Where's Auggie?"

Logan's smile was easy as he stuck his fingertips into the front pockets of his jeans. His hair was slicked back, still wet from a recent shower. His face was smooth from a recent shave. Lickable.

Only a couple of table lamps were lit, and his eyes looked like sapphires, dancing with humor. "I'm presuming you're referring to the animal formally known as Dog? He's been sent to his room for stealing your steak."

She walked around the arm of the sofa, waiting for him to shift out of the way so she could get to the open door. He stayed planted. She stared him down. "Who said it was *my* steak?"

"Everyone whose steak it wasn't." He held out his hand, palm up. "Come on, I'll share."

Daniela hesitated. He seemed perfectly at ease and relaxed, but there was . . . an edge to him tonight. She didn't mean to, but she looked at her hand resting on his palm. The difference between their hands was startling. Hers was much smaller and paler of course, but it wasn't just the size difference. His was stunningly masculine, his palm broad, and his fingers long. It had the calluses and small scars of a man who worked with his hands.

Daniela felt almost dizzy with the need to have those hands touch her bare skin.

Crazy.

His fingers closed around hers, and he tugged her forward. His expression said he knew exactly what she was thinking, and he wanted the same thing. She didn't resist. In fact, she had to resist acting as though her body were jet-propelled and leaping into his arms.

She braced her palm on his chest. His skin was hot through the fabric of his T-shirt, and she could feel the steady beat of his heart beneath her fingers. *Insane.*

"Whatever it is," he murmured quietly, "is fixable."

"But—" Her eyes stung sharply, as her throat closed. Mutely, she shook her head. Victor was *not* fixable. Not until he was in a federal prison. Not until evidence was gathered, and—

Logan cupped her chin, so that she had to meet his penetrating gaze. "I swear to you on my life. *Whatever* it is. *Whoever* it is. We'll make it disappear."

"Logan, I—"

He bent his head to brush his lips over hers. "I never make promises I don't keep. Now come outside and eat half a delicious steak before it gets cold. The guys are waiting."

She sighed and followed him outside, where the men were handing around bowls heaped high with corn, baked potatoes, and a spinach salad she'd made with Hipolito's careful instruction an hour ago. The night sky was a dark entity beyond the glow of the ship's lights. Logan had decreed that the lights in all public spaces be left burning all night to deter any more pirates.

The men welcomed her and immediately launched into excited discussion of what they'd salvaged that afternoon. It fascinated her that they all appeared to be more interested in what they'd found rather than the monetary value. But that could be because they hadn't hit the mother lode yet. The treasure that should've been on board the *Nuestra Señora de Garza*.

It was a beautiful night, with just a light warm breeze that made her hair tickle the back of her neck. It brought with it the outdoorsy fragrance of Logan's soap, and the smell that was uniquely his, which made all of Daniela's girl parts sit up and take notice.

There were plenty of steaks to go around and she chose the smallest one, which was big enough to feed a small army and all their dependents. A few minutes later, Dog ambled outside and settled under the table on her foot.

She ate her dinner slowly, enjoying a glass of wine with her meal, fascinated by the camaraderie and deep friendship of the team. These men were family to Logan, she could tell. They were all friends, especially he and Jed, but one thing was abundantly clear: Logan Cutter was the alpha wolf of this pack.

After dinner, some of the men went off to watch a movie in the media room on the deck above, while the rest went to the galley to play poker with Hipolito, who they claimed owed them a month's wages they wanted to win back. Jed clicked his fingers and Dog got to his feet and followed him inside.

"That was . . . abrupt," Daniela told Logan, who was sitting beside her drinking a cup of coffee. "Did you tell everyone to leave?"

He glanced around. "Didn't someone mention fleecing the chef?"

"You know what I mean. They'll think we—"

He made a "so?" gesture with his hand. "We are."

"Logan—" Daniela shook her head.

He shoved his chair back, and rose to his feet. "Wanna watch the news?"

Now *that* was abrupt. It was nice sitting out there with the soft quiet all around them, and the gentle sounds of the ship as it rocked on the black water. But they'd had enough togetherness today. Being with him was too seductive. No matter his assurances that everything would be okay. He didn't know how *not* okay her life was. The *Sea Wolf* and Logan Cutter were no more than a pit stop, a momentary respite from the chaos that had dogged her since meeting Victor Stamps. She got to her feet, too. "I think I'll just turn in."

"Nah." He reached out and grabbed her hand, leading her through the door. "We'll watch a movie neither of us wants to see." He scooped up a throw from the back of a chair, and maneuvered her toward the long sofa facing the big-screen TV. "Sit."

"For—Why?"

"Because standing will be awkward, not to mention uncomfortable. Sit." He tugged her down beside him, and picked up the remote, pointing it at the TV. "Ah. This is a good one."

She glanced at the giant scene. "It was his worst movie!"

"Perfect, sit right here and close your eyes. I'll turn off the sound."

"What am I missing?"

"The lights are on, anyone can walk in at any time. We're going to neck like teenagers until we disintegrate, and when we recover, we'll start again. We'll go from there."

All the lights were on inside the room and out on deck. One of the security guys passed right outside the window, looked in, and lifted a hand in greeting. "You are out of your mind, you know that. And what's the blanket for? It must be eighty degrees."

He gave her an incredulous look. "Have you never necked in the living room while your parents were upstairs?"

"Of course not. My dad would've stormed in and made sure we were ten feet apart."

"Fortunately, he isn't here right now. But in the event we're doing things that we don't want other people to see . . ." He held up the thin throw.

"I have no *intention* of doing anything I wouldn't want anyone to s—"

Logan wrapped both arms around her and carried her down to the sofa cushions, then he kissed her senseless.

A minute or hour later, he lifted his head, and bit out, "What?" to someone out of her line of sight.

Face hot, she blinked, thrown by the forgotten bright lights and the fact that someone had indeed walked in, and she'd been blissfully unaware. Her mouth buzzed with the delicious pressure of his. Her T-shirt was twisted, and his hand was on her breast. "What?" she asked, trying to regroup mentally.

"Three men just boarded," a diffident male voice said smoothly. "We have them in custody."

"Do we have a brig?" Logan demanded, eyes fixed on her face. "Throw them in there for a year or two."

"No brig, sir." The guy's voice had a thread of amusement in it. "We have them in the kitchen storeroom."

Logan swooped in to brush his mouth against hers, then tugged her shirt back over her tummy as he rolled off her and got to his feet. "Hold my place. I hope these are your Three Stooges paying us a visit. All answers will be questioned."

Daniela sat up on her elbows. "Do you want me to come w—"

"In the worst possible way," he told her sincerely, his eyes hot. "However, I don't want you there when I talk to them. Our laundry facilities are not adept at getting blood out of women's clothing. Stay put. I'll be right back."

She flopped back onto the soft cushions and laughed. If not, she'd burst into tears.

Eleven

"You stuck them in the *pantry?*" Logan asked mildly as he walked into the galley where a game of poker had clearly been interrupted. Chips and beer bottles decorated the butcher block table off to the side, and several chairs were missing. "You know there are heavy projectiles in there, right?" He looked at Jed, who carried a large, wicked knife.

Jed nodded. "We considered sticking them in the freezer, but figured they'd taint the food, which would mean another trip to Arequipa. Inconvenience on top of inconvenience. We thought you'd understand."

"I spotted their rowboat a hundred yards off our bow," Piet said, ignoring Jed's teasing. "Talked to the security guys and they grabbed them as soon as they boarded. Our uninvited guests are tied up and not going anywhere."

The galley was large, but with Logan, Piet, Wes, two security guys, Hipolito, and Galt, there wasn't much room to move, let alone swing a cat.

"Before they got up to mischief. Good man. I hope they aren't too badly damaged," Logan told the group, voice grim. "I'd like a word with them myself."

"We didn't—" One of the security guys, dressed in a western shirt and jeans started to assure him.

Wes put a hand on the guy's shoulder. "They threw

Annie in the ocean. At night. Logan would like to formally introduce himself."

The man stepped back, and extended his hand toward the locked door in a formal invitation.

"Should I take a gun in with me?" Logan eyed the weapons in the shoulder holsters of the two security guys. "Probably not. Unfair advantage, right?" He wouldn't shoot them when they were secured and unarmed, and it would be too damned *quick*.

He strode over to the steel door, glancing at the men over his shoulder. "If you hear anyone crying like a girl, don't bother coming in. In fact, don't bother coming in unless it's *my* blood flowing under the door."

"How will we know?" Jed asked, his brow cocked as Logan unlocked the heavy door.

"Dog can ID me."

"He's in there with them," Cooper told him, a wicked glint in his eyes.

"An excellent idea." Logan stepped inside, shutting the door firmly behind him before flipping on the light.

The long narrow room had shelves stacked on either side holding canned goods and paper supplies. It smelled of coffee, flour . . . and pee.

The three cousins were an unpleasant looking lot, and Logan waited until they stopped fighting the electrical tape binding them and noticed he was in the room with them. His crew had done a bang-up job securing the prisoners.

Their mouths were covered with heavy electrical tape, and they'd been—slightly overdoing the tape, in Logan's opinion—taped to three straight-backed chairs borrowed from the poker table. Their legs were secured to the chair legs, their wrists to the arms, and then for good measure tape had been wound around their middles, strapping them firmly to the chair backs.

Three sets of wild eyes swiveled his way.

Dog stood by the door, hackles up, teeth bared. His body vibrated from the almost inaudible low throaty growl. It was quite effective, since one of the guys had already peed his pants.

Logan glanced at the dog. "I know you're hungry, White Fang. You forgot to eat dinner." He let his eyes drift over the men. His jaw tightened as he gave them an all-encompassing cold look. "Who wants to talk first? Blink. Nobody? Well, that's just fucking rude."

He stepped around Dog and grabbed the tape at the corner of the closest guy's beard. "How about you and me have a chat, *primo*." He ripped off the electrical tape, and half the guy's bushy beard with it. The guy shrieked as Logan dropped the hairy tape on the floor.

"Now let's not pretend that you don't speak English. I can just as easily interrogate you in Spanish, and cut to the chase. What's your name?"

He gave Logan a hostile look. Spoiled because his beard looked as if he had mange. "Apaza."

"Curly, Mo, or Stupid?"

"Hugo."

"I think it's *stupid*." Logan's voice went steely, and he bent down in the guy's face. "You hit a woman—a relative—who depended on you for protection. You threw her overboard with an ill-fitting life vest. How do murder charges sound?"

"She refused to talk to you!"

Logan turned to look at Dog. "Hear that?" He swung around, accidentally hitting the guy in the eye with his elbow. Hard. "I understand her sentiment," he said, having to raise his voice over the guy's cries of pain. "Perhaps she figured as men, you'd want to come and talk to me yourselves. Make some sort of business arrangement . . . No?"

Hugo's eyes streamed. Pretty soon the left one would be swollen shut.

He went to the next cousin, whom they'd placed slightly behind his brother. As Logan leaned over to pull the tape off his mouth, he stumbled, his fall broken by the knee he slammed between cousin number two's spread legs. Since he hadn't quite managed to remove the tape, cousin number two's scream of agony was somewhat muffled. Unable to double over with the pain, he writhed in his seat until the chair crashed to the floor where he screamed uselessly through the electrical tape. Logan stepped over him.

The third guy's eyes were like saucers over the tape. "Ready to have a little conversation, man to man? I seem to be a little accident-prone this evening."

The guy nodded. He was about fifty, with wild, bushy black hair, and close-set, terrified eyes. He was the pee-er.

Logan pulled the tape off slowly. "Which one are you?"

"Angel, señor."

"Ah." Logan glanced over his shoulder. "Could you stop thrashing?" He eyed the guy on his side on the floor, who was noisily flopping around like a beached fish. "We're trying to have a convo here. What was the plan for tonight, *viscacha*?" he asked the third brother. The word in the local Quechua language either meant small rodent, or turd. Logan wasn't going to put a fine point on semantics.

The man's mouth opened and closed. Making sure he was well away from the pee-zone, Logan leaned against the shelves and folded his arms over his chest. "You came to steal what treasure we'd salvaged?" He waited for the guy to decide which way to go with his answer. "Or you came to visit your cousin?" He watched the guy's eyes. He waited as the man licked his thick lips, but said nothing.

"Both, huh? Well, here's the sad and sorry truth. I'll make sure that you never see either. And I'll make sure that you never see either from behind bars."

"We did nothing wrong!" the man sputtered indignantly. "We *gave* you the emerald. It is worth a lot of m—"

Dog suddenly body slammed the metal door and began barking wildly. Logan's words were cut off by a series of loud gunshots as the door sprang open, Cooper framed in the opening.

"Lock them in," he ordered Cooper. "Where's Annie?" he yelled at one of the security guys who had his gun drawn and was just about to run from the galley. Another shot rang out, followed by a barrage of semi-auto fire. What the fuck was going on now?

The guy hesitated, then spoke into a lip mic. "In her cabin. Sven standing guard outside. We have more intruders. Can I—?"

"Go!" Logan yanked open the door to the pantry, and yelled, "Did you idiots bring backup?"

"No, señor!"

Logan slammed the door. "Lock it!" he repeated. He met Jed's eyes. "I'm not using a bread knife to hold off armed intruders."

"Agreed." Jed looked as grim as Logan felt. "Your office is closest."

Logan's safe held four handguns. Pirates were always an issue in this business. And apparently the ones who'd just arrived had tossed the rule book. Time to even the playing field.

"Let's go. No heroics, people. He who has the biggest gun wins, got it?! Wes, Galt, stay close. Piet, radio this in. You two." He indicated the chef and Cooper. "Secure those guys, then get the hell out of Dodge. Haul ass."

They separated and ran.

When he and Jed arrived outside his office, Logan instructed his friend to get the guns and ammo. Then he jogged down the corridor to speak to the guy guarding Daniela's cabin, weapon drawn.

"She okay?" Logan demanded. No more shots were being fired; he didn't know if that was a good thing or a bad thing. But it pissed him off that his ship had turned into a fucking collection point for bad guys.

"Yes sir. I brought her up right away."

"Good man. Don't let anyone in or out of there until I get back."

"The dog's with her. He kinda insisted."

"Logan?" Daniela called through the door. "What's happening?"

"Not sure. But keep this door locked until I get back."

"Don't—" He heard her struggle not to beg him to stay. "Hurry back. I'll keep Diesel safe."

He pressed his palm to the door. "You do that." He dropped his hand and backed up. Making eye contact with the security guy, he said grimly, "Not one fucking hair on her head, got it?"

Daniela went into Logan's cabin because it was bigger and she needed to pace. Dog paced with her. Over the course of the next fifteen minutes there were a few more gunshots. Shouts, the sound of running feet, followed by the sound of bodies hitting the water. All of it coiling in her gut, making her nauseous. She ran to the closed door and peered out to see the lights disappear in the distance. "What the hell was *that* about?"

Dog, leaning against her legs, looked up at her. "Not everything is Victor, okay? Not every damn thing." But she was deathly afraid that this time Victor had found her, and she was a sitting duck.

She heard her cabin door slam open, then Logan yelling. "I told you keep her in—"

"Logan. In here."

The outer door slammed, she heard the lock snick, then Logan appeared in his cabin. His face was drained of color, and his jaw tight as he looked at her through eyes dark with fear. "I thought—"

Daniela ran to him, wrapping her arms around his waist as she buried her face against his chest. "I'm okay, I'm okay." She couldn't tell which of them was shaking, but her teeth chattered as if she were in the Arctic.

"What's going on?"

"Someone must've placed an ad for bad guys to show up tonight," he said dryly. "First your cousins decided to show their faces, wanting to see the treasure for themselves, no doubt. No sooner were *they* secured, than we had another batch of visitors. These were a hell of a lot better organized. No fucking idea what the hell they wanted. By the time we went topside, the security people had apparently scared them off."

Victor. It had to be Victor. She shouldn't have decided to wait until morning. She should've left the moment she'd put the pieces together.

Logan gently gripped her upper arms and pulled her away from the safe harbor of his body to scan her features. "Want something to drink?" He walked to a small fridge in the built-in bookshelf by the fireplace.

"Am I going to need it?"

He pulled out two bottles of water, and closed the door with his knee.

Things couldn't be *too* bad if they were going to drink water. "Do you have anything stronger?"

"No. Let's sit down." His tone brooked no argument as he indicated she sit in the big easy chair by the door leading out to the balcony. He sat on the foot of the bed, leaning over to hand her the bottle after he snapped the top. "What's going on, Daniela? Who's after you?"

He *had* called her Dani this afternoon. Her mouth was dry, but she was incapable of lifting the water to her lips. She looked at him, mute. Her heart felt as if it weighed twenty pounds as it thudded in uneven, heavy strokes. It hurt her chest to breathe. "How do you know my name?"

He gave her a cool look. "Do you honestly think that I would welcome a stranger on board my ship, and endanger my friends and crew, without putting out feelers? You fed me one preposterous lie after the other. It's my job to protect the people I care about."

She took a shuddering breath. "I know."

"Who are you running from, and why?"

Daniela felt relieved to finally share the truth. "Senator Victor Stamps."

"Your fiancé?" he prompted, frowning darkly. "Why?"

"How did you—never mind. I own an art gallery in DC. He's been using it to move cocaine from South America for distribution in the U.S."

Logan's brow arched. "Senator Stamps was responsible for getting the Ultralight Aircraft Smuggling Prevention Act of 2011 passed, right?"

"And the Habitual Offender Bill. Victor is big on drug prevention," she said bitterly. "Just not *his* drugs."

"Give me the Cliff's notes."

"My family is so normal, we're abnormal. My parents have been married for almost thirty years. And they *love* each other and show it. We've always been close. Really tight. I used to talk to my mom every day . . . Then I met Victor seven months ago . . .

"At first it was magical. Like something out of a fantasy. He was the up-and-coming young senator being groomed for the presidency, people loved him, they loved us as a couple. We went to the White House for dinner, were invited everywhere. I wore designer gowns given to me by the designers.

"Victor and his people thought I looked Mexican enough to get him the Latino votes. Then they decided I looked a little *too* ethnic. His advisors suggested I go blond. I figured blondes had more fun. I liked being a blonde. For the first six months, I was on cloud nine. He, and my life, were everything I could wish for."

"What changed?"

"One night after I'd locked up, I remembered that I'd

left my phone in the storeroom when I'd been helping my manager unpack our latest shipment." She and Victor had attended a formal dinner at the home of a fellow senator, and she'd gone home to her own condo after—after Victor had then insisted she accompany him to his house.

She'd been wearing a red Badgley Mischka, and should've felt like a million bucks. Instead she'd felt worn out, on her last nerve, and terrified. It had been a long and stressful day. But she needed the alarm on her phone to wake her for an early morning appointment the next day.

"I went back downstairs." She had to swallow before she continued. "Cut a long story short, my manager and Victor were in cahoots, and Victor had been using my shipments of Peruvian and South American artifacts to smuggle drugs into the country. As soon as I saw all those bags of white powder, I raced back upstairs and locked all my doors." The visceral memory of her fear that night still had the ability to make her shiver.

Logan rose and scooped her up, then sat down in the chair, wrapping his arms around her. He rested his chin on her head. "Get it all out."

No. *That* she *couldn't* do. "It was one in the morning, but I called the DEA right then. I was shaking so hard I dropped the phone a couple of times. The man I spoke to was Special Agent Steven Price. Over the next month, he was the only thing that kept me sane. There was no one else I could talk to, certainly not my parents.

"He tracked down Victor's contacts and wanted to wait until the next shipment came in to close the trap he'd set. Because of who Victor is, he had to be sure all his i's were dotted and his t's crossed. I didn't want to stick around while he did that, Victor was getting more and more—" She rubbed her face with both hands, and Logan's strong arms tightened around her.

"I thought he was getting suspicious. It was harder and harder to act naturally. It just seemed to take forever for Price to get what he needed to secure a conviction." And the drug issue hadn't been the only thing going on at the time.

"So you ran, and now you're waiting for Price to arrest him?"

Not quite, but close enough. "I went on a 'business trip.'" Logan's hand rubbed a soothing pattern on her back, but she was too keyed up to find comfort in it.

"So he knew you knew about the drugs?"

"I thought he was acting weird." *Weirder than usual.* "He'd always been *possessive,* but suddenly he was questioning me on everything. Where I'd been, who I talked to. He went through my e-mails, and my phone . . . I wanted to get as far away as possible. Victor sent his men after me. I eluded them in San Francisco, and kept moving. Price tried to help me. He wired me money and false papers so I could travel."

Logan frowned. "Why the hell didn't he put you in a safe house?"

"I *was* in a safe house in San Francisco. That's where Victor's people found me the first time."

He shook his head as he pulled her closer into him. "Jesus, Daniela . . ."

"I moved around. Cheap motels, expensive resort hotels, buses, trains, ferries—whatever. I was in Pensacola at this nasty little motor lodge, feeling safe for the first time in—well, I had a false sense of security. I hadn't seen or heard from any of Victor's men in a couple of weeks. I thought I was home free. On TV that night, I saw Victor at my parents' house in New Mexico, pleading with my kidnappers to bring me home. He got a lot of coverage on that one."

Logan snorted, his disgust clear.

"I called Price and begged him to get my parents out of the country until everything was resolved. He promised he'd give them new passports—papers to get out of the country without detection. He rigged it so it looked as though they'd won the trip."

"Then they're safely out of harm's way, right? So you don't have to worry about them. Finish up your story so we can go to bed. It's been a long night."

Go to bed? "I—I called my parents to make sure they were okay. Told them Victor and I had had a big fight and I didn't want him to know where I was. They told me about the trip they'd won, and we agreed to meet when they got back. Price promised me it would all be over in thirty days."

"And?"

"While I was in Pensacola trying to figure out where to go next, two men burst into my hotel room. I climbed out the bathroom window and ran like hell." She'd slammed into a Dumpster in the parking lot and gone head over heels. "One of them shot at me."

"Christ. Were you hit?"

She lifted her T-shirt to show him the bullet burn on her lower abdomen. "I got away. Stole a car and drove as far as the gas took me, then took a Greyhound bus, and a train . . ." She'd slept in places, eaten things, done things she didn't want to think about. "I found my cousins. They didn't know me from Adam. I told them my name was Annie Ross, and that I was their long-lost cousin from America, here on vacation. The rest..." She waved a hand.

Logan rose, carrying her to the bed. "That's enough for now. We'll deal with all of it in the morning."

She was too tired to move, and too needy to protest as he lay down beside her. "Nobody will ever hurt you again. *No one.*"

She did not ask if he included himself in that promise. Because if he said yes, God help her, Daniela knew she'd believe him.

Twelve

Logan pressed his lips to the warm, satin smooth skin of Daniela's belly. Lightly kissed the obscene, strawberry-colored scar just beneath the shadowy indentation of her navel. He squeezed his eyes shut, the only external show of emotion he allowed himself. He didn't want Daniela to see how deeply her story affected him. He had to keep his own emotions out of this.

Impotent anger surged through him, and he wanted—no, fuck it—needed to retaliate. Let Stamps know that there was a new player in his twisted game. He controlled his fury; that was for later.

Right now Daniela deserved his understanding, his patience. His gentle touch.

That he could do. Tonight.

His brain said slow and tender, his body urged hard and fast. "They'll have to go through me to get to you." It was a vow from his gut. To this woman, who'd endured so much, *and* to the man responsible.

Daniela let out a shuddering breath, but didn't say anything, and he didn't press for an answer. Yet he could practically hear the wheels turning in her brain. This wasn't the time for her to think, or worry, or be afraid. He could give her that.

A bullet wound, for God's sake. What kind of man

would shoot at a woman? No wonder she'd lied. She had been, and still was, afraid for her life.

She didn't know him well enough, yet, to understand that lies weren't something he tolerated. Under most circumstances, anyway. Though Daniela had lied to him, repeatedly, he now understood why.

He'd fix Stamps and there would never be another reason for her to lie to him again.

She was exhausted. It had been an action-packed day for her. She lay exactly as he'd placed her, making no protests as he'd unbuttoned her pants, slowing pulling down the zipper, then brushed his lips gently over the scar again. The cabin was quiet, the lights dim, the slider door partially open to let in the cool evening breeze.

He slowly inched her pants down over her hips leaving her bare to the touch. With infinite tenderness he stroked his fingers down the supple skin of her thigh and at the same time drew a damp trail down her other thigh with his mouth. His fingers explored the shapely muscles of her calves, strong from running, and sweetly curved.

Logan drew the bunched fabric of her pants off one slender foot, then the other, then cast the clothing aside. Trailing his mouth down her slender ankle, he paused over the delicate medial malleolus, and discovered that her anklebone was sensitive to his touch when he licked the small knob and felt her shudder. He then did the same to her other ankle.

Daniela made a small inarticulate murmur that turned him on even more. She came up on one elbow. "Oh, um—I don't think—"

"Good. Don't. Lie back. I'll show you how beautiful

you are." She had pretty feet, long and elegant with perfectly symmetrical toes, except her baby toes, which lay flat against their mates. He ran his tongue over the top of her toes, then backtracked to draw the baby toe into his mouth. She moaned as he sucked, swirling his tongue around the small digit until she squirmed and fell back onto his pillow.

The high arch was sensitive, her toes curling as he ran his tongue along it. Logan delicately kissed his way back up her leg, his fingers lightly leading the way, gauging what she liked from her movements. He glided his palms up the back of her leg, into the warm hollow behind her knee. Learning the shape of the muscles that flexed in her thigh as he brought his mouth back to the scar.

Sea Wolf's chopper had taken off while Daniela had been talking. Wes and Jed were taking her cousins, and one dead intruder, into Arequipa for the authorities to deal with. The ship was quiet. Security tight and in place. He breathed in the scent of her skin, and felt the soft brush of her fingers as she combed them through his hair.

"I can hear you worrying. Stop it. I'm fine," she told him quietly.

God. Was she comforting *him?* "Yes," he tasted her skin as he slid his hand under her, cupping the taut globe of her ass in his palm. "You are." He smelled her arousal, warm and earthy, and his body, already painfully turned on, ratcheted up another notch.

But this wasn't about him.

He pressed his open mouth to the damp seam of her sex, hummed his appreciation of her wet heat. Her fingers flexed in his hair, and her voice broke as she said his name.

Logan drew out each caress, gauging her response by her slightest movements, and every hitch in her breathing.

He slid his free hand up the inside of her thigh where her skin was impossibly soft, and gently parted her with his fingers.

She hissed in a breath as he stroked, dipping his fingers into her honeyed heat. "You don't have to be careful with me." Her voice was thick and her fingers tightened in his hair. "I won't break."

"This time it's all about you. Relax and enjoy the ride."

"It's impossible to relax," she said breathlessly, "and I'd rather—oh, my! Ride together."

"And we will, I promise." He slid a finger inside her, then two, reveling in her response. "But for now . . . sweet and slow. Then we'll go for hard and fast. Then we'll—"

Her broken laugh shimmied down her body. "I didn't realize you had an entire agenda planned. I'll just lie here and think of—what's on the menu."

"Oh, I have an entire *smorgasbord* to choose from. This will take a while."

Even as she laughed, Logan felt her internal muscles gather around the spear of his fingers. He added a third into the creamy channel. Her breathing became more and more rapid as she shifted restlessly against his hand. He pressed his palm on her clit and she arched off the bed, her fingers gripping his shoulders for purchase as she shouted his name.

He put his mouth to her and a long climax wrenched through her, jerking breathless little sobs of pleasure from her throat.

He pressed his smiling face against her damp, fragrant mound, breathing in the musky mélange of her scents, womanly, earthy, a hint of soap, and a hint of the sea, and beneath it all, the heady fragrance that was hers alone.

"I want you inside me." Daniela's voice was thick and husky as her nails scored his shoulders, urging him to shift where she wanted him.

Logan slid his body up her torso, careful to brace his weight on his elbows. He kissed a damp path from the gentle dip of her navel, stroked his tongue along the sensitive skin of her belly, then rose to lavish his attention on the impossibly soft underside of each breast. She felt so delicate beneath him, yet he knew she had a will of steel and a backbone to match.

Her knees rose on either side of his hips, and she slid her heels over the small of his back. Her fingers sifted through his hair and she gave a little tug. "Now would be good."

"Shh. I'm distracted." He ran his tongue around the ruched peak of her nipple, and she arched against him. "Later," he murmured, closing his lips around the tight bud, sucking lightly, then using his teeth and his tongue to make her arch off the bed again.

Daniela hummed her pleasure low in her throat. Cupping the back of his head she pressed his face against her breast, and demanded, "Harder."

Logan felt a surge of . . . What the hell was it? Euphoria? Joy? Something damned unfamiliar, but certainly addictive, that he'd never felt with any other woman.

He moved up her body and entered her in one hard, powerful thrust that had her hips pushing beneath him like a sail bent full by the wind. With every stroke, she shouted, "Yes!" It was so obviously a parody that it made Logan laugh. A first when he was in the middle of sex. But that quickly changed as his strokes intensified, leaving her too breathless for speech, and incapable of thinking about anything else at all.

It was all about Daniela's pleasure, but each urgent movement of her body, each moan, made his control slip until he was the one with none left. He kissed her deeply as they peaked at the same time, and came together. He loved that she was noisy and vocal.

"You okay?" he asked, smoothing her damp hair off her glowing face a few minutes later, when he was capable of moving.

Her skin was deliciously flushed, her eyes slumberous and glittering. "Better than," she murmured languidly, lifting her arms to wrap around his neck. "But usually one works their way up to that from a kiss."

His eyes devoured her face. He'd never seen her this relaxed, this beautiful. "I kissed you," he said with mock indignation.

He felt her laugh gurgle up through her chest, a sensation that filled him too. "Yes," she told him with mock severity. "And very thoroughly too. However, there are some important parts that were completely ignored."

He grinned at her serious expression. "I wasn't done."

"Well, no. I hope not. While you're catching your breath—" She lifted his hand and placed it on her breast.

He made up for the omission by rolling them onto their sides, bending his head to lavish her sensitive breasts with all the care and attention she craved. Sensations raced through her nerve endings like hot lava as he curled his tongue around her areola and sucked the nipple deep into the heated cavern of his mouth. Daniela dug her nails into his broad shoulders as his breath fanned the moisture his mouth left in its wake.

With every brush of his lips, with every gentle caress, she felt beautiful, desirable, and safe. "Don't stop—" she begged, barely able to catch her breath as the heat and need climbed with every brush of his fingers, every hot wet lick of his clever tongue. The shadowy cabin was filled with pleading moans. His. Hers.

She couldn't take it anymore. With the flat of her hand on his chest, Daniela shoved him onto his back—it wasn't difficult, he was apparently putty in her hands. Sliding her knee over his hips, her own back arched, fingers curled into the hair on his chest, as she impaled herself. The sensation of him filling her made her shudder with the unbearable sweetness of it.

His large hands clamped on her hips, his thumbs tracing the path to where their bodies were joined as they moved together in a dance as old as time, and as new as tomorrow.

The orgasm, hard, quick, and unbearably sharp, made her shatter into a million pieces. She shocked herself by bursting into tears. She pressed a fist against her mouth.

"God. Don't cry."

"I'm not." Salty tears leaked down her cheeks and pooled in the sweaty hollow of her throat.

"Did I hurt you?"

"Of course not."

He wrapped his arms around her and drew her down onto his chest. His hands slipped up her body. "It was beautiful. Memorable. You're beautiful."

His face was very close to hers, and she saw all the shades of blue making up the extraordinary color of his eyes. Azure and navy, robin's egg and sky, all there in a kaleidoscope of color that shimmered beyond her foolish tears. A sob ripped out of her throat, and he rubbed between her shoulder blades wordlessly, his touch speaking for him.

Though he'd shaved earlier, his dark beard had grown enough to shadow his cheeks and chin. The stubble was soft under her hand.

The arm behind her back tightened and he drew her to him as he bent his head and his mouth closed over hers in a kiss so sweet, so gentle, her throat closed and tears welled once more. For several minutes or hours he did nothing more than smooth long strokes down her back, and drop tender kisses on her face.

She was almost asleep, still joined to him, when he brushed away the hair stuck to her cheek. "Sleep on your back or belly?"

She breathed out a sleepy breath. "Tummy."

Gently, he scooped her up and turned her, and she immediately burrowed her face in the pillow and breathed a contented sigh low in her throat, one eye open.

He smiled as he reached out to pull the sheet over them. His hand stilled, then he bunched the sheet out of his way and his eyes flared with another kind of heat.

Oh God. How had she forgotten for even a second? She reached back to draw the sheet up over her ass, her heart pounding now for another reason. Through one eye she saw him reach out to touch . . . His fingers curled into a fist inches from her skin.

"What the hell—" His voice was raw and laced with fury as he demanded. "Is this a . . . *brand*?"

He sat up, swinging his legs over the side of the mattress, not touching her. "No more lies and half-truths, Daniela. I need to hear everything."

Throat aching, chest impossibly tight, the harsh tone of his voice much more painful now that he'd been so tender with her, Daniela rolled over and sat up, bunching the sheet to cover herself. It wasn't enough.

"I have to get dressed first." She slipped off the bed on the opposite side of Logan, and picked up her scattered clothing from the floor. She didn't try to hide her nakedness, he'd seen everything, after all. It was the memories she wanted to armor herself against.

Her hands were clumsy as she yanked on the linen pants, not bothering with underwear. "I don't even know where to start—"

"The senator." His voice was very calm. The kind of calm that had tightly leashed rage behind it. "The son of a bitch branded you on the ass with his fucking initials?! Jesus, Dani—"

Personally. With relish. She pulled the T-shirt, inside out, over her head, tugging it down. "It took two of his aides to hold m—" She swallowed bile. "To hold me down. I prayed I'd pass out. I didn't. Do you know what burning human flesh smells like? Not unlike a nice barbecue pork rib. Sweet . . . sweet and acrid and a hundred times more nauseating. I *tasted* that smell, and did for weeks afterward."

And just talking about it brought back a rush of Technicolor memories and smells that stuck in her throat. Her skin prickled with cold sweat as she drew in a deep, shuddering breath and walked to the door leading to the balcony.

"Do you want a drink? All I have is water or beer."

"Beer."

He got up and went to the mini fridge. She heard him pop the cap, and seconds later, the pop and fizz as he poured the beer into a glass. She watched his reflection as he padded, strong and naked, back to the bed carrying a glass and the bottle. He sat down heavily on the edge of the bed. "Finish it."

"If only—" Staring blindly at her own reflection in the night-dark glass of the doors, she let the air out of her lungs slowly. "As the branding iron burned through the nerves it—it eventually stopped hurting."

Logan's jaw was ridged and locked as he too was reflected in the dark glass, the beers in his hands forgotten. "Why would anyone do such a thing?" he demanded rhetorically.

He had no idea. He was too good. She breathed deeply through her nose, hands clenched, heart tripping. She turned to face him. She couldn't make eye contact. "Have you heard of autoerotic asphyxiation?"

"Choking one's partner to heighten sexual pleasure."

"I'd never heard of it. Never imagined it." Her face felt hot, and she placed her icy hands on it to cool the heat. Embarrassment. Humiliation. Shame. And all-encompassing anger. "He came in one night while I was in the bath, and held my head under the water." She dropped her hands and clasped them tightly at her waist. She needed a moment more to push the words through her constricted throat. "It was only a few seconds, but it was a few seconds when I panicked, and freaked out. He said it was a joke and laughed it off—" She recoiled from the icy fury in Logan's midnight-blue eyes.

"Don't," he murmured hoarsely, his eyes glittering now with something dark and nameless. "I'd cut off my own arm before I'd ever hurt you. And this was not your fault. Any of it. Autoerotic drowning—*Jesus*. Was this before or after you discovered he was moving drugs through the gallery?"

"A month before. The next time he held me under I threatened to press charges."

"You should have."

"I know." It was her biggest shame that she hadn't. She'd wanted to believe him when he apologized with utmost sincerity. She'd thought she loved him. He loved her to distraction. He'd teased her for overreacting, and eventually she was convinced she had.

"I walked in on him in the bathroom a week later. He wasn't alone. He and his publicist and a hooker were in the tub together. His bodyguards were holding them under the water as they had sex. Sick, I tried to run, but he'd told his people—They held me and forced me to watch. After that I left for good."

The glass in Logan's hand shattered. The yeasty smell of spilled beer permeated the room. He didn't seem to notice that his hand was bleeding as he carefully placed the bottle and broken shards of glass on the bedside table.

Daniela, grateful for something to do, went into the bathroom and came out with a hand towel. Sitting beside him on the bed, she gently cupped her hand under his to inspect the inch-long gash. After wrapping the towel around it, she lifted his hand to her cheek.

"Finish it, for God's sake. No," he said when she started to get up. "Stay right here."

"I called the police and charged him with assault. He was like this"—she held up twined fingers—"with the police commissioner, and the complaint was never filed. I told him I never wanted to see him again, and if he ever came near me, or the gallery, I'd go to the newspaper. If the police wouldn't do anything, I figured the press would."

He brushed hair out of her eyes with a tender finger, then traced the curve of her cheek, his eyes intent and only inches from hers. "You didn't hire a hit man?" he muttered, probably not joking. The savagery in his voice was in direct counterpoint to the gentleness of his touch. Daniela's throat and chest ached, and her eyelids burned. "I didn't think about it. *Then.* He begged me to come back, told me how much he loved me."

"I hope you kicked him in the balls."

"I probably would have if our conversations had been face-to-face at that point. But I'd had my locks changed, and refused to see him."

"What about your family and friends?"

"I was too embarrassed to tell my friends, and of course I never told my parents. Oh, my God . . ."

Wrapping her arms around her body, she got up and padded back to the doors to look out over the dark water. The silence grew thick as she swallowed, struggling to formulate an explanation of what had happened. How she'd *allowed* it to happen. Logan just sat there, still as a statue.

"I know it had nothing to do with me. But I have to admit, I wondered. If I'd done some of what he wanted . . ." Rubbing her bare arms didn't get rid of the bone-deep chill. The events had been hideous enough, but to tell Logan what had happened was humiliating. She sounded like an idiot for staying as long as she had.

She'd had resources—and a powerful boyfriend who'd already blocked her attempts at getting a restraining order. The press loved Senator Victor Stamps, and he played them like a Stradivarius. "He called incessantly, sent his aide, then his campaign manager to reason with me. They made it sound as if what he was doing was normal, and I was a prude."

"You're not."

"I refused to see him. The press speculated about our breakup. He was afraid that without me, he'd lose all those Latino votes come election time, and his calls became more threatening and wild. He inundated me with flowers and expensive jewelry. The press had fun with it, championing his romantic cause."

Logan watched her, unjudging.

"I finally agreed to see him one last time. So he could 'apologize properly,' as long as my manager and a few employees were present at all times. He came to the gallery and cried, begged—. I told him emphatically no more and I meant it. That night, after the gallery closed, and I went upstairs, I—I found Pyewacket—my cat—floating in a bucket of water in the middle of my living room."

She buried her face in her hands for a moment until she could stop shaking. More anger now than fear. That filthy bastard, she wanted to annihilate him, to wipe him off the face of the earth. She'd settle for the less dramatic and more practical route of putting him in prison for the rest of his natural life.

"I called the police." She turned to face Logan, who still sat, hands dangling between his spread knees, his face a mask. His eyes were like burning coals in his set expression.

"There wasn't a shred of proof that Victor was

responsible. We hadn't fought that afternoon. In fact, my manager Adam told them we'd made up and it was nothing more than a lover's quarrel."

"Let me guess. You signed this dick's paycheck, but Adam worked for Stamps."

"I found *that* out much later. This time the police questioned Victor, and his aide, and the security guy. For all the good that did, since they all had the same story." Daniela scooped her hair up off her neck and held it on top of her head with one hand, then let it drop.

"I woke up the next morning to find Victor and three men standing over my bed." *Don't relive it,* she warned herself, nausea churning in her stomach, and chills racing up and down her spine. *Just tell the story.* She blew out a long low breath, trying to control the panic seeping back into her bones. "He was livid. They held me down, and—they—basically the men waterboarded me while he watched. And then he brought out the branding iron, and gave me this so I would know who I belonged to."

She couldn't look at him.

"I knew I couldn't just run, unprepared. So I started planning. In the couple of weeks it took for me to pretend that everything was all right, that I was back to being the perfect ethnic arm candy, he made me watch him with other women every day. His bodyguards stayed in the bathroom, and made sure I didn't leave. Every night was a different woman in the water with him."

She'd only thrown up the first time he'd forced her to watch. After that her fear and fury kept her focused on how and when she'd make her move. It was the only thing that prevented her from falling apart.

She turned to face Logan. "I was forcibly restrained in the bathroom by his bodyguards. They'd take me home afterward. I stayed at the gallery later and later after work, avoided our social calendar by threatening to go public. It all came to a head when I went down to get my phone and discovered the drugs in the shipping crate. Everything sped up after that. I called the FBI, they referred me to Special Agent Steve Price at the DEA, and he helped me get away." Her words tumbled one over the other in her haste to get everything said and out in the open. "I had to leave everything behind. And as well as I covered my tracks, Victor's men still found me."

"And lost you," he pointed out, voice flat.

"And lost me, yes. And now, found me again." She shuddered, cold to her marrow. "The harder I try to knit up my life, the more I feel like he's behind me, unraveling and unpicking like hell. I was once an asset, now I'm a loose end he can't afford. He's going to kill me, Logan." He opened his mouth, and she shook her head. "Yes, he is, and he'll go to any length to do so."

Thirteen

The wind danced like a skipping stone across the water, whisking the waves into peaks frothy as whipped cream. The early morning air, with the windchill factor, was crisp. Scudding clouds smudged the pale blue sky, and a crimson streak across the horizon heralded an approaching summer storm.

Sea Witch perched on the horizon like a small dark bird of prey. She hadn't started diving yet, but she would, and soon, as they brought more and more artifacts and coins to the surface. She was just one more complication to take into account when the shit hit the fan.

Logan didn't know the redheaded captain, nor did he give a flying fuck what happened to her when she was out of sight. But he felt a sense of misplaced responsibility for her when she was anchored off his bow. She was a nuisance, but he didn't want her blood on his hands if this thing turned deadly.

A situation he had to address, and add to his checklist, before the day was over.

He'd convinced Daniela not to leave. Not until he knew exactly who all the players were, and what to do about them. He'd taken steps to protect her right here on board. For now, normalcy was the name of the game.

Dog, who'd twirled in circles while wagging his tail the instant they'd emerged from Logan's cabin earlier, as if giving his approval on their mated status, now slept with contented dog snores beneath Daniela's chair.

Wrapped in the soft black throw from his cabin, she rested her chin on her knees. Fear remained etched around her eyes, which were dark, and shadowed by concern. "If you'd just listen to reason—"

"Hipolito doesn't need your help right now. He's cleaning up last night's mess. Let him do his job uninterrupted."

Daniela wanted to go and help Chef in the galley. Logan didn't want her out of his sight. Not now. Not ever. Perhaps it wasn't realistic, but then what she'd been through had been a hellish nightmare and he wanted to make sure that bastard Stamps never got a chance to breathe the same air as her again. They were seated on the aft deck while Galt and Cooper suited up for a reconnaissance dive before breakfast. Business as usual. Or as close to as usual as made sense.

She slipped her hand from beneath the throw, reaching for her steaming coffee mug and taking a cautious sip. Logan noticed how her lashes were spiked from her morning shower, and her eyes, in this light, were more cocoa than aged whiskey. She swallowed and met his gaze over the rim of her cup. "I hope you pressed charges."

Against her cousins. "Yes." But the senator? For what he'd done? Prison wasn't bad enough. And no term could be long enough. Logan, who was usually too busy moving forward to bother with paybacks for people who crossed him, wanted time to formulate a punishment fitting and cruel enough for Victor Stamps, after what he'd done to her.

She put the mug down so she could hold back dark

strands as the wind whipped her hair around her head. She looked so beautiful. Logan's chest ached with pride. Courage and determination were as much a part of her as her broken nose, her brow, or her soft mouth.

While she'd slept with tears on her cheeks, or, he suspected, had fallen unconscious *resisting* sleep, he'd contacted Wes and Jed in Arequipa and ordered them to bring back more security. He considered, and rejected, abandoning the salvage.

A *brand* for fuck sake. A goddamn *brand*. He couldn't wrap his brain around it. A one-inch-across oval, with the initials VS inside, marred one smooth, creamy ass cheek.

He wanted to rip the senator's fucking nuts up through his nostrils, roast them slowly over a blowtorch, and then make him eat them.

Stamps knew where Daniela was. If he'd managed to track her here, he would track her anywhere. She knew too much for him to let her go.

"While we were dealing with the Apazas, another group of men—and I have to assume they were sent by Stamps—boarded the ship. We think they came from one of the boats that was lurking at the one-mile limit. Our best guess is that they used individual underwater propulsion devices to get from there to here undetected. When our guys chased them off, they went straight for the dive platform and vanished. Probably had their gear tied up there for a fast exit. Anyway, the whole thing was short, over almost before it had begun. One of my security people shot and killed one of them—Jed took the body to the authorities for ID. Two of my guys were shot as well."

"Oh, God, Logan. Are they—are they dead?"

"They didn't even need medical attention," he assured her. "There were various injuries that everyone is now claiming were no big deal." But then they were professionals. To the security men, getting shot at was part of the paycheck.

"Men! Did anyone actually go and see a real doctor?"

"It wasn't your fault."

She gave him an incredulous look. "*All* of this is my fault! If not for me—"

"If not for you I wouldn't have had the best sex of my life an hour ago."

"I'm serious."

He smiled. "So am I. Look, we figure that last night was reconnaissance to see what they were dealing with. Now they think they know. My security guys tell me there were ten or twelve of them. They didn't expect to encounter armed men on board the *Sea Wolf*."

He drank his coffee while she mulled that over. But Logan sensed that if Daniela had been seen, it would've been a snatch and grab. He wasn't letting her out of his sight for a nanosecond. He didn't realize how long he'd been silent until she nudged him with her foot under the table.

"Why don't you tell me what's going on in your head instead of glowering at my coffee mug?" Daniela suggested sweetly.

Because I don't want you to discover that I'm a brutal son of a bitch just like your sick-fuck ex. He'd never been violent before he'd met her. But shit changed when a man—*shit changed.* "Just working through some logistical problems."

"I can solve those logistical problems for you. Let me go somewhere else so you and your people are safe. I'll call Special Agent Price. He'll send someone to get me. We can try protective custody again . . ."

"The operative word there is 'try.' He tried, and failed," Logan reminded her, with barely leashed fury. He cradled his now cold mug, and considered her for several hard beats of his heart as he weighed his options. Places *he* could stash Daniela where no one would find her.

Even with his ship crawling with armed security men, in the middle of the damn ocean, he still had a prickle on the back of his neck, a heavy feeling of impending trouble in his gut that he just couldn't shake.

"It's counterproductive talking to yourself when I'm right here. Just say what you're thinking out loud, and we can discuss my future like rational humans."

"I don't feel very rational right now."

"No, I can see by that scary black look on your face that you don't. If you keep gritting your teeth like that you'll wear them down to unattractive nubs. Right now, right *this* second, the two of us are sitting here enjoying the sun coming up, and the breeze in our hair, and a cup of coffee. And I for one am still all hot and bothered and tingly after this morning. So let's discuss what's making your brain hurt, and then get on with our day."

"Pollyanna." He felt a smile crack.

"Don't buy trouble. I know it's hot on my heels, and I'm so sorry I've brought it to your door. But can we please live *in* this moment? Just *for* this moment? Let's discuss what has you worrying, and try to come up with a workable plan, then implement it, and enjoy all this. Can we do that? Please?" She plucked blowing strands of hair from her mouth.

"Stamps found you in the middle of the Pacific, despite you having no connection to myself or the *Sea Wolf.* If I send you to my home on Cutter Cay . . . Stamps could find you there just as well as he found you here." And who would protect her? He considered sending a veritable army with her, plus Zane. Plus Nick . . .

"I'm a sitting duck on an island. Eventually, I'd have to leave."

"Yeah." He'd already realized that, as tempting as it might be to know she'd always be there waiting—God, had he lost his mind? "You're right." Logan wouldn't allow this to continue, with them—*her* looking over her shoulder for the rest of her life. He had to put an end to it once and for all.

There wasn't anyone he trusted more than himself to keep her safe. On *Sea Wolf* they had a three-sixty view. No one could approach the ship without being seen. Not again. They hadn't known what the fuck they were dealing with yesterday. Today, everyone was on the same page.

"The solution to that is simple. I don't *want* to stay on board," Daniela told him, her expression mutinous. "I have cabin fever, *and* I'm seasick. Lima has a zillion people. I assure you, I can disappear there."

He knew she wasn't seasick, and his ship was too damned big to give anyone cabin fever, and she sure as hell wasn't going to disappear in Lima where *he* couldn't retrieve or protect her.

"No," he told her unsympathetically, as the ship's helicopter hovered overhead, frothing up the water before landing with a loud, wind-driven thud, on the upper deck.

Reinforcements had arrived.

He softened his voice. "Look, I know you're scared, and I know you don't want to bring him here. But it's already a done deal. Frankly, whether you're here, or we manage to stash you away, he'll send his people back. I'm not letting you out of sight until this is over. Which means, I'd go with you. And since I can't be in two places at once, that would leave my ship unprotected. So you stay here. With me." His ship had a full complement of crew, his armed dive team, and professional security guys; it wasn't exactly unprotected. But the buck stopped with him. If the bad guys boarded, he had to be there to protect what was his.

She rested her forearms on the table and gave him a heated look, eyes shadowed, mouth firm with determination. "It's not in your control for it to be over, Logan. You can't *will* Victor to leave me alone."

"When Price calls us back, we'll see where we stand. In the meantime, don't fight me on this." As soon as they'd woken about an hour ago, Logan had insisted on calling the DEA agent in Washington, DC. He was very interested to hear what Price had to say about this situation. Logan figured he'd be relatively polite until this was concluded, then he'd pay Special Agent Steven Price a visit to ask him some pertinent questions. Like why the fuck he couldn't protect one lone woman with enough proof to put the senator away for a long, long time.

But first things first.

"You're putting everyone on board in danger! People who don't *know* me, or give a damn about me. Why can't you get it through your thick head that I don't want people to *die* because I happened to show up? None of you owe me the time of day. Don't you see that? He's ruthless and vicious and he—" her voice rose. "Damn it. He's scary powerful, and he *knows* people!"

"Good. So do I." Logan assured her. "And I'm going to introduce my people to his people, if and when they show up again."

She threw her hands up in the air. "And what am I supposed to do? Sit out here like a tethered goat?"

That, of course, was a big fucking issue, but he said lightly, "You're a very *pretty* goat."

"If Jed would just take me to Lima, I could disappear . . ."

"No, Daniela. That's not going to happen. First off, nobody but me is taking you *anywhere*. If Stamps wants you, he'll have to come to me. And to get to you, he'll have to go *through* me, *and* my security people *and* my crew. And you and that Glock—"

"Hey." He cut himself off to greet Jed and Wes as they came outside. "Thanks for doing the garbage run. Everything work out?"

"Yeah." Jed flopped down next to Daniela and reached over to pour himself a mug of steaming coffee. He held up the thermal carafe, and Daniela picked up Logan's mug and her own, holding them out for Jed to pour. The breeze swirled steam and the scent of freshly roasted beans. A smell Logan usually appreciated but his gut was too twisted up right now to enjoy simple pleasures.

His antennae were vibrating with anticipation of the unpleasant kind, no matter how much he tried to shake the feeling. It was going to be a gorgeous day, warm and with calm seas. They'd dive, and they'd have to decide whether to start salvaging what they found, or leave it where it had lain for four hundred years, until this clusterfuck was resolved.

"We brought four guys back with us," Jed told him. "We'll have a dozen more in about an hour."

"Any excitement while we were gone?" Wes asked, reaching over to pour himself a cup of coffee and grab a sweet roll from the platter in the center of the table.

Daniela's sparkling eyes met Logan's, and she hid her smile behind her cup, murmuring, "Nothing worth mentioning."

Logan choked on a mouthful of coffee, gave her a look, and said, "I've contacted Nick as well." Nick had some very interesting friends. His younger brother assured him his friends would mobilize and be there ASAP. Logan didn't ask questions. If Nick said they could take on Stamps, he believed it. "And anyone on board who wants to be armed, *is* armed."

Logan had gathered everyone on board at first light, explained the bones of the situation, and offered them an out if they wanted to get off the ship. None had.

Jed shot a look at Daniela with a raised brow.

"Yes, she's armed, too," Logan told him flatly. "Because this dick wants her. And she has to know that every precaution is being taken all the way down the line to ensure that will not happen."

Jed put up his hands. "Hey, far be it from me to complain. I think a woman packing is hot."

"Then it'll make your day to go warn *Sea Witch* that hanging around here could get seriously dangerous. Tell her to bug off, and go follow Zane or Nick for a while."

Jed grinned. "She'll be touched you care."

"I don't give a damn. But I don't want anyone around who doesn't need to be around to muddy the waters. It'll be business as usual. Get rid of the redhead, and the rest of the audience out there, and get your ass back. We have a treasure to find." Logan met Jed's eyes. *And a ship to secure.*

Jed pushed away from the table. "Excuse me, I have to see a lady about an eviction notice." He started to whistle as he strolled off, then stopped dead in his tracks, shading his eyes as he looked over the starboard rail. "Wolf—"

"Yeah. I see it," Logan responded to Jed's sharp observation. Even from this distance, the whop-whop-whop of the rotors sounded powerful, and he'd heard the sound ten minutes before. "Wes, grab a couple of security guys, take Daniela to my cabin, and stay with her. I'll be right there."

Glock in hand, he walked to the rail. "Stamps has brass balls doing this in broad daylight." The large, black military-style helicopter was visible for miles as it approached.

"We'll show him just how fucking wrong he is." Jed joined him to stand at his shoulder.

"Hang on," Logan touched the earpiece as it beeped. "Yeah, Piet?"

"The Huey is friendly," his captain said evenly. "They just made radio contact. Nick's counterterrorist friends. They claim your brother requested their assistance on your behalf."

"Yeah, he mentioned it." Logan had no idea his brother's friends were *this* responsive to his call. He was impressed. "How—they'll figure out how to get on board, I'm sure." *Sea Wolf* wasn't equipped to handle a helicopter of that size.

"I'll alert our people to stay at the ready, but to stand down. For now."

"Leaning more toward stay at the ready."

"I hear you." Piet clicked off.

Logan indicated the chopper with his gun. "Nick's buddies. I'll be appreciative *after* I've seen the whites of their eyes." He didn't trust anyone. For all he knew, these were Stamps's people. How they knew about Nick and his connections was immaterial. Logan wasn't taking a chance on a single hair on Daniela's head.

He glanced back at the table, and raised a brow to see her still seated there, her steaming mug cradled between her palms and supported by her updrawn knees. She gave him a steady, unsmiling look. "You aren't the boss of me, *Wolf.* And those are your brother's friends, not my enemies."

"So they say; we'll see. Come with me," he ordered Jed, and to Wes, "Get six guys out here now. I'm going topside." Within minutes, the helicopter was overhead, casting a giant shadow and frothing up the water around the ship as the noise of the rotors blocked out any other sounds. Almost immediately ropes were dropped, and men started rappelling down like black dew on a half a dozen spiderwebs.

The first man down looked straight at Logan, and approached, hand extended. "Derek Wright," he yelled. "T-FLAC."

Logan shook hands. "Logan Cutter." But somehow this guy had already known who he was. There was no point attempting a conversation since he couldn't hear himself think.

He stood beside Wright as half a dozen black-garbed men, armed to the teeth, dropped lightly onto the deck.

As soon as the last man's booted feet touched down, the ropes started receding and the helicopter flew off.

"We've been given a brief overview of the situation," Wright told him. He removed a picture from his pack. "This is the latest image we have of Senator Stamps, taken yesterday. He's campaigning in Arizona, but paid a visit to Los Chaves, New Mexico. Anything you want to add?"

Los Chaves was where Daniela's parents lived. Logan told him what he knew of Stamps, and added the visit by Daniela's cousins. "I have security people on board. These are all men I've used before to guard valuable salvage. They're adept at discouraging pirates. But this is a whole different ball game."

"No problem. We brought our own jerseys." Wright's smile was sharklike as he jerked his head toward the others. "I'll take over security and we can brief all the men at the same time. You got a problem with that?"

Hell, yeah. Logan didn't relinquish control to anyone. But once he knocked his ego down, he acknowledged that Wright and his men were professionals. It wouldn't even be a fair pissing contest. The T-FLAC guys pissed harder and farther.

"I'm in charge of the ship, you've got the guns. I want Daniela protected at all costs."

"Roger that. Let me get the men squared away, then I want to meet with you and your lady."

* * *

"Wright's reconnoitering the ship with his men, and assigning posts to our guys," Logan told Jed. They'd moved inside while the men in black swarmed all over the ship. There was no mistaking who the counterterrorist operatives were. And it had nothing to do with their all-black outfits, reminiscent of wet suits, or the fact that they were all heavily armed. Logan's brother's friends were taciturn, steely-eyed, and the only instructions they needed were the basics.

Protect her at all costs.

Seeing so many trained people surrounding her, with the express purpose of keeping Victor away, brought home to Daniela just how powerful Logan and the others thought Victor was. They were absolutely right not to underestimate him.

Victor had a snake-oil salesman's charm, the wiles of a fox, and sick Machiavellian proclivities. There was a very good chance that if the authorities didn't put an end to him one way or the other, Victor Stamps could be the United States of America's next president. The thought brought acid to the back of her throat.

"All set." The tall, dark-haired guy Logan had spoken to outside earlier stepped into the common room. He was ridiculously good-looking, with serious dark blue eyes and a confident attitude. Daniela was more impressed that he wore a big black gun in a shoulder holster, and a lethal-looking knife stuck into a sheath above his ankle.

"Derek Wright," he shook her hand briefly. "The senator is in New Mexico making inquiries about your parents."

The very thought of Victor being anywhere near her

parents' home chilled Daniela to the marrow. Logan stepped up behind her, wrapping the warmth and strength of his arms around her.

"They're on a Mediterranean cruise," she said, leaning against Logan's hard chest, and wrapping her hands around his muscled forearms. "Special Agent Price gave us all fake IDs . . . They'll be back in a couple of weeks."

"Then they're safe where they are. You're our priority, Miss Rosado. I'd suggest you continue on as normal, and pretend we aren't here."

Daniela had to smile at that. "I think everyone on board will notice all of you—everywhere."

"You'd be surprised how well we can disappear." He addressed Logan. "If you give me your comm, I'll program in the channel we're all on."

Logan unhooked his headset from behind his ear and handed it over, then returned his arm to hug her close.

"If I need you fast," Wright said, handing it back to him, "I'll beep once. I don't expect them to hit in broad daylight, and don't expect them to show up tonight. We have a location for them, but we want them here so we have more control over the situation. They saw what kind of firepower you had last night, and they'll expect you to be ready should they strike again. They'll wait a day or two and hope the element of surprise is on their side."

"It'll be a pleasure to turn the tables. I have some work to do in my office. We'll be there if you need us." Logan slid his hand around hers and Daniela accompanied him upstairs.

It was a very, very long day for her. Interesting though,

because she spent the entire day glued to Logan's side. She and Dog accompanied him to his office where he spent several hours on the phone talking to various investors, two museums, one in Holland, and one in Germany, and at length to an insurance adjuster who, despite Logan's assurances that his company did *not* have to pay for Nick's ship, complained about his brother blowing up his own ship, and the value of the diamonds lost.

An interesting story, Daniela was sure, but Logan kept going. Dell brought them lunch, which Logan ate while he worked on his laptop, and Daniela, followed closely by Dog, wandered aimlessly around his office, pulling out books, reading a few pages and putting them back.

Logan glanced up and watched her padding around his office. "Bored out of your mind?" he asked politely.

"I hate people who claim boredom," she admitted, curling both hands over the back of a leather visitor chair. "But I'm like a fish out of water here. I don't have my own stuff—I don't have anything to occupy myself, and that, coupled with waiting for the other shoe to drop, is frazzling my nerves. Sorry. I'll find a book and stay out of your way."

"Why don't I take you to the storeroom? You can take a look at some of my artwork and artifacts, and see if there's anything there you'd like to hang. Would that help?"

"God, yes!" She could've leapt across his desk and kissed him. In fact . . . Before she thought it through, Daniela planted her butt on the edge of his desk, swung her legs over to his side, scooted a bit, and slid into his lap.

She wasn't sure who was most surprised as his eyes widened slightly, and his lips curved.

"Hi," she said softly, wrapping her arms around his neck. She could tell how happy he was to have an armful of willing woman by the hard length of his instant erection pressing right where she needed it.

His mouth found hers and he kissed her as if they'd been apart for a year. He lifted his head and skimmed his hands under her T-shirt, pulling it up and over her head, then captured her mouth again.

Daniela reciprocated, feeling the heat of his satin smooth skin as she skimmed the fabric up, then feeling the tickle of his chest hair. She paused to bend her head and kiss a path between his nipples, then lingered to stroke her tongue over the small nub. Logan made an inarticulate growl and yanked his shirt off the rest of the way, tossing it somewhere on the floor.

Somehow her bra disappeared, leaving them bare from the waist up.

"You know we have on far too many clothes?"

"It's certainly a conundrum." She smiled against his mouth, feeling as light as if she was filled with helium.

He put his hands on her waist and lifted her onto the edge of his desk, her bare legs dangling beside his hips. She propped her feet on his chair. "And this helps . . . How?"

"Move your—Thanks." He pulled open a small drawer, and took out a pair of scissors, then proceeded to cut off her shorts and pink lace thong. Daniela combed his hair back with her fingers as he worked industriously cutting her clothes away.

"You know, a simple 'would you mind standing here and stripping' would have worked just as well."

Glancing up, his eyes met hers, as he took his time sliding the strips of fabric between her legs, and then tossing them to the floor. His smile was wicked, and caused her blood to race. "But not nearly as much fun."

"Can I take the scissors to your clothes too?" The glossy wood of the desk felt cool under her bare bottom as she reached for the scissors.

With a laugh and a shake of his head he got to his feet, and pulled off his shorts. Standing between her spread knees, Logan grasped her hips in his broad palms and slid her to the edge of his desk. There was no preliminary exploration; he surged inside her like a heat-seeking missile, hot and hard and powered by need.

Daniela gripped his shoulders and wrapped her ankles around his waist as his hips pistoned as he pounded inside her.

The gathering orgasm rolled through her, driving her along.

Limp and replete, she dropped her head to his chest as they both fought for their next breath. "My first ever desk sex. I think we need a plaque."

He smiled. "I'm impressed, not even a pen flung to the floor. You didn't disturb anything on the desk. Except me," he said, laughing as he glanced over her shoulder. "Did you by any chance lock the—"

The door burst open, and Wes walked in all smiles and excitement. "Hey. You *gotta* come and see what Cooper and Jed just fou—Oh my God!" Red-faced, he backed out. The door slammed shut.

Her own face flaming, Daniela rested her forehead on Logan's broad chest. "Dear God," she said half amused, half mortified. "He'll be scarred for life. *I'll* be scarred for life."

"All he saw was you sitting on the desk," Logan pointed out reasonably.

"Hello? *Naked*."

Fourteen

Daniela sat on the couch in the common room, Wes attached to her hip. She was flipping through the channels; reception in the middle of the Pacific was iffy, and she paused whenever a relatively clear program came on. As much as she didn't want to know, burying her head wasn't going to prepare her for Victor's next move. At least if she saw him on the news, she'd know where he was.

Four T-FLAC men faced the windows, forming a blockade of wall-to-wall muscle. There was nothing out there but water as far as the eye could see. What a boring job. She prayed it *stayed* boring. Unfortunately, she felt as though a nest of spiders was crawling inside her clothes. Or Victor's other Italian Testoni dress shoe was just about to drop.

Logan had reluctantly left her to dive. His team had found something "unbelievable and amazing" that he *had* to see. He'd only agreed to go because there were plenty of people to keep watch over her—more than half of them highly-trained special ops personnel with more firepower than an army—and she'd insisted.

"You don't have to hang around," she told Wes, not quite able to meet his eyes yet. Dear God, she'd never been so embarrassed in her life. And while he hadn't seen more than her naked back, she knew that *he* knew what was going on behind Logan's desk.

His head rested on the back of the sofa, his feet up on the table, hands folded on his belly. The very picture of relaxed. Except that energy pulsed off him in waves, and his eyes kept slewing to the window where the rest of the team was gathered.

"I'd rather be in here with you, watching infomercials for—what *is* that stuff? Bacon grease?"

"Face-lift in a Jar." She kicked his thigh as she changed channels. "Liar. *Go.* I've got all these—" She stopped short with a small intake of breath.

Wes jerked upright at the sound. "What?!"

Transfixed, Daniela turned up the sound. ". . . with Stamps's standing falling as other candidates surge—" Victor's face filled the screen, and her hearing went dull. ". . . was a candidate in serious contention for a nomination," the pretty blond anchor said as they flashed a picture of Victor and herself at a White House Christmas party. "May be jeopardized by his search for his fiancée, DC gallery owner, twenty-seven-year-old Daniela Rosado, who has been missing for sixty-three days. No ransom demands have been made, but Senator Stamps holds out hope that she is still alive. Anyone knowing—"

Daniela knew if she moved, she'd vomit on Logan's nice wool area rug. She pressed a fist to the churning acid in her stomach, squeezing her eyes shut, taking measured breaths in through her nose and out through her mouth to quell the nausea.

She felt a familiar hand on the back of her head, and heard Logan say calmly, "Put your head between your knees. There you go. I have you." Something cold dripped down her cheek. She buried her face against her knees, trembling as if she stood in a high wind.

"—four front-runners and seven switches in the lead seen in Gallup polling since May. He falls short of the—"

"Turn that crap off," Logan instructed, and she felt someone—Wes?—take the TV remote from her lax fingers. Then there was blessed silence. Her pulse throbbed in her ears. Cold, clammy sweat sheened her skin.

The sofa cushions beside her dipped, throwing her sideways against Logan's body. The fabric of his wet suit felt rubbery and slick against her bare arms, and it was still wet. Hot and cold prickles raced along her skin like fire ants swarming on honey. Nausea pushed up the back of her throat, and she swallowed convulsively as her mouth filled with saliva.

Daniela buried her face against the hard plane of Logan's chest, and he wrapped his arms tightly around her. "Talk to me," he said quietly.

"His poll numbers are down," her voice was muffled by his chest.

"He can't get to you, sweetheart."

Logan got it. Victor was already determined to find her, and with his poll numbers down, he had to find her even *faster.* Either to march back to DC with her on his arm as a prize, or with the news of her tragic death. Either would shoot up his numbers. Right now it appeared as if public opinion was divided between sympathy and suspicion.

She shifted her head to bury her face against his warm neck. He smelled of the sea. "I'm screwed."

He touched her hair with his lips. "Only by me." For several minutes they stayed that way, her face pressed to his warm, Logan-scented neck, his arms around her.

He dropped a kiss on her temple. "Want to see what the guys discovered?"

Still slightly sick to her stomach with nerves, she lifted her head and said brightly, "I'd love to." Anything to distract her from the hideous reality clutching at her throat.

He got to his feet and held out his hand. Wes had disappeared, and the guys standing around ignored them as they went outside. It was surreal to see that the sun was shining, that clouds danced across the sky on the wind, and that the ocean around them maintained its same brilliant blue. It all looked so normal, so totally and utterly normal. She felt like a fake standing on deck with Logan making small talk when she wanted to race down to his cabin, triple-lock the doors, and hide under the bed.

"You look very sexy in that getup," she told him, eyeing the close-fitting black wet suit. "You can't hide a thing in that, can you?" she asked wickedly. It was a little forced as she struggled to regain her equilibrium.

"We can turn right around and go down to my office," he said. "I have something big and important to show you there as well."

"Where's the latest and greatest?" She glanced at the table and down onto the dive platform where the guys were gathered. Dog jumped off the edge with a happy bark. He was wearing a life vest and his neon red harness.

"Do you want to learn how to dive?" Logan raised his voice over the dog's excited barking as he swam in circles, trying to bite the water, his paws and tail thrashing happily.

"Not really. I used to love to swim when I was a kid." She bit her lip, then met his eyes. Tone dry, she said, "Now I'm not that fond of having my head under the water."

He nodded in acknowledgment of what she'd left unspoken.

"Different animal altogether, I promise. It's magical down there. Quiet enough to think, and beautiful enough to make you forget what's going on up here."

She stood on her toes to whisper in his ear. "We could see something magical in your cabin too."

Logan slid his arm around her waist. "We'll go there later. Come down and see my world. I want to share it with you."

Daniela could only nod. Logan called Wes and two of the black-clad men to accompany her to and from her cabin where she changed into the bikini Wes had bought for her in Lima. She wrapped a towel around her body before going back into the hallway where the three men waited.

"You know this suit is for a malnourished eight-year-old, right? Didn't they have grownup swimsuits at that store?"

"Logan won't think you look like a malnourished eight-year-old in it, I can assure you," Wes told her. "It's not too small, it's your size. And you'll be covered by a wet suit, so don't worry about it." They took the stairs down.

When they got to the landing, Wes took her arm. "I've salvaged with Logan for eight years, and in all that time, I've never seen him show affection for a woman in public."

"He has a protective streak a mile wide, I know."

"Yeah. He does that." Wes grabbed an apple from the buffet Hipolito had set up and held it out. Daniela shook her head. After seeing Victor's face, coupled with the prospect of her first dive, her stomach didn't need any more assaults.

"I see the way he looks at you. Hell, I see the way you look at him."

Daniela figured their heated glances were pretty obvious to everyone. And the fact that they couldn't be in the same room without touching was a big tip-off. "I get it. You're watching out for your friend's interests. I like him. A lot. But when this is all over"—*and if I'm still alive*—"I'll go back to my life in Washington, and he, if he thinks of me at all, will remember this as a . . . holiday fling."

"I don't th—"

"There you two are." Logan was halfway up the ladder from the dive platform. "Ready?" he asked, his eyes level with her thighs. She felt that look straight to her core, and was surprised the ladder didn't melt in his fingers.

She eyed his hands, tightly fisted on the top rung. "As I'll ever be."

He climbed back down, and then stood at the bottom and assisted her. By gliding his hands up her legs from ankle to knee, and knee to thigh. She made a grab for the towel, but that was a lost cause as he slid his hands onto her hips, and then closed his fingers around her waist to lift her down the last few feet.

"I need to give Wes a raise." His voice was husky as she turned around in his arms and he got the full impact of her in the lipstick-red bikini. There wasn't much to it. The solar flares in his midnight eyes were enough to heat Daniela's skin and make her forget her inhibitions. She could lose herself in the infinite depth of that look, and never come back to the surface. Nobody else existed in the world. "I had no idea he had such great taste."

"Am I going to wear one of those?" She indicated his wet suit, but she didn't move away.

"Eventually."

She ran her palms up his forearms, feeling the strength of his muscles. "You know that we have a large, fascinated audience, don't you?"

"They're looking for bad guys. Let's get you suited up while I go over the basics."

While Logan explained each piece of equipment and then helped her put on all the paraphernalia, he used every gesture to stroke and touch. To tease and torment. He explained how to use the regulator, but she was already breathless because she was so aroused by his touches.

When she was outfitted from head to flipper, he held out his hand. Daniela placed her fingers in his. It was awkward moving around with the unfamiliar clothing and tanks as they stepped to the edge of the platform.

"There's a mic right here." He showed her the control on the side of her mask, then put it on her, lifting her fingers to the control. "Turn it on to talk like this. You can talk normally. If you want to come to the surface for any reason, just say so. Ready?"

Nodding, she followed his lead, stepping off into the endless blue unknown.

"You're breathing too fast," Logan cautioned as they sank beneath the surface. Her bubbles rose erratically. "Just relax and breathe normally."

"Easy for you to say."

"We're going for a quick tour of your namesake, then I'll show you her treasure; it'll blow your mind." He took her hand, and together they descended into a blue-washed world. "Okay?"

"It's like flying," she said with wonder, letting go of his hand to spread her arms and legs and float. Then with a smile she did a flip before darting as gracefully as a mermaid. She was poetry in motion.

Logan didn't let her get too far from him. He caught up, indicating where the hull of *La Daniela* lay on her side.

Logan pointed as they swam along the broken hull. *La Daniela* had sunk aft end down, so she stood upright like a crumbled wooden pillar, broken masts parallel to the seabed. "See there? One mast was still intact when it crashed against the reef. The other two broke off, and are there, and there." He pointed, although he doubted she saw them in the gloomy blueness. "She was a *fragata*, what we'd call a frigate. Built for speed and maneuverability, unlike the more cumbersome *Nuestra Señora de Garza*, which was why they unloaded the treasure and sent her home. She carried ninety guns—we've already found most of them—and weighed around three hundred tons."

He put his hand on her arm. "Stay still. Look." A shoal of *anchoveta* curled in a silver ribbon between them and the shattered hull of *La Daniela*. Thousands upon thousands of fish in a tight stream. The fish didn't seem concerned by the visitors in their midst and for several minutes they stayed suspended in fish territory. Logan kept them afloat, as Daniela seemed hypnotized.

"That was amazing. What were they?"

"Similar to anchovies."

"First time I've seen an anchovy that I *like*." She grinned through her mask.

"Come on. I'll show you something you'll *love*."

"Hope it's not a brussels sprout."

"You don't like sprouts?" He shook his head. "Well, what I have to show you *is* green. But you can't eat it. This way. Jed and Galt are fanning the area now. Hear that? That's what the blower sounds like down here." The dull roar was muted under the water.

Logan announced their presence to the others and Galt turned it off. "Daniela wants a look at what you discovered."

Jed waved an arm at the floor of the ocean. Scattered for several hundred feet on the sandy bottom were chunks of emerald, gold bars, gold coins, and snakes of gold chain. Even in the less than optimal lighting, pieces glinted as one moved, and everything was easy to see.

He heard her quick intake of breath on the mic. "Oh, my Lord. Look at the size of this! May I?" She glanced at Logan.

"Sure."

He let her swoop down the six feet to scoop it up from the soft sand. She held up an emerald the size of her fist. "Are we going to pick everything up and take it back with us?"

"There's more than the four of us can carry back in one trip." More than his whole dive team could carry back to the surface in thirty or forty trips. He was going to win the ten-grand bet with his brothers with ease. "For now we're leaving everything where it is."

"Oh, but—Oh. Until the other thing is resolved."

* * *

It was raining when they surfaced, a gentle, persistent shower. It pitted the dark blue of the water with white dots, and made everything look ethereal and other-worldly. There was no demarcation between sea and sky. The inclement weather didn't seem to bother the security guys, who patrolled or stood guard as if water wasn't dripping down their faces.

Dog, still wearing his vest and harness, barked, happy to see them, then clambered up on the diving platform via a ramp, where he waited as they climbed on board. Just as they neared, he shook violently, spraying them with Dog water.

Daniela smiled, and bent to rub his ears. "You love the water, don't you, Flipper?"

"Haven't hit on just the right name yet?" Logan asked, handing the tanks to Cooper for a rinse off before taking them to get refilled. Dog lay down, his nose over the edge of the platform as if eager to go swimming again.

Logan scraped his dripping wet hair off his face, exposing the starkly masculine lines and angles of his face, the dark stubble on his strong jaw, the blade of his nose. He unzipped the front of his suit, then tugged it over his shoulders and peeled it off his chest and arms to hang around his waist.

No fair, Daniela thought as her eyes feasted on the present he'd just unwrapped for her. Excitement pulsed in the pit of her stomach, tightening every muscle in her body. His bronzed skin gleamed in the fractured sunlight shining through the rain. His stark male beauty made her breath snag in her throat.

She loved the clearly defined muscles of his shoulders

and arms, the hard six-pack that made his skin look like tightly stretched bronze satin. His flat brown nipples were tight, and she didn't think it was from the cold air.

Droplets of water sparkled like diamonds in the dark hair on his chest, then converged, suspended for a moment before gathering to trickle lazily down his rock-hard abs, to pool briefly in the shadowy indentation of his navel, then trail across his flat belly and follow the narrow path of dark hair to disappear beneath the folded-down suit.

She reminded herself to breathe as he stalked toward her, lifting her eyes to his as he got closer. She could tell by the glint there that he knew exactly what she was thinking. "Need help with that?" he murmured, his voice soft, but raised just above the sound of the waves slapping against the platform at their feet.

She frowned. "With what?"

"Getting the wet suit off; it can be tricky."

"Sure." Wet suit or body armor, nothing would protect her from his heated gaze. He reached between her breasts and tugged down the zipper. A wash of cool air hit her damp skin. She shivered. But it wasn't the cold that made her skin pebble, and turned her nipples painfully hard.

The deliberate brush of his fingers sent a delicious shiver through her. He helped her remove the mask from where she'd shoved it on top of her head, turned to place it neatly in the plastic tub of fresh rinse water. He then slid his warm hands against her cool skin inside her suit to peel it off her shoulders. Every touch sent an erotic message down her nerve endings. Her body was having a party, as everything came alive and surged with heat.

"I still have—"

He peeled her suit down just below her breasts, then carefully readjusted the top of her bikini to cover her, blocking her body from view from above. She gave the crown of his dark head a speaking look, which he missed completely, because he was looking down and gliding his cupped hand inside the flimsy red fabric almost covering her breast, shifting not the fabric, but the weight of her breast.

"Plenty more to try out," she added, getting breathless. "Fluffy's going to love one of them."

"Or just be happy to be called to dinner," Logan teased, running his thumb over her distended nipple. "And you are not calling any dog of mine Fluffy."

Daniela's feet were planted firmly on the deck, but her upper body swayed toward him as if drawn by a powerful magnet. Her nipples peaked and a different moisture pooled between her legs. She wanted him to touch her, but he stayed where he was, a couple feet of rain-washed deck between them. She wanted him. Now.

"Ho—how about Killer?"

Logan finished adjusting her top, then dropped his hand, shifting away a few inches, locking his eyes with hers.

She licked her dry lips, tasting salty seawater, and saw his eyes flare as they tracked the movement. "Rocky?"

His eyes, dark with knowledge, met hers as he hooked his thumbs into his wet suit and slowly peeled it the rest of the way, the backs of his hands brushing hers as he tugged it down his strongly muscled legs, hairy, and shiny with moisture, over his feet. "Ready for a hot shower?"

"Would you mind helping me get this off? It seems to be stuck r-i-gh-t here." She pointed to her hip.

Eyes level with the hard throbbing pulse at the base of his throat, she was surprised that the rain spattering their bodies and trickling down their faces and hair wasn't turning to steam. She pressed her open hand over his heart, feeling the hard thump-thump-thump that matched the timpani of her own.

"Tricky suckers to get off. Takes practice. No time to get it off now." He grabbed her hand and started tugging her toward the ladder. "We have to hurry."

"Why? Does someone else want to wear i—" She let out a little scream of surprise as he put his hand under her butt and boosted her halfway up the ladder. "Okay. Okay. I'm moving."

Daniela didn't doubt for a moment that he'd catch her if she tumbled backward, but she curled her fingers around the rail and hauled herself up on deck in record time, even hampered by the wet suit dangling around her hips.

She wasn't steady on her feet yet, when Logan grabbed her about the waist and hustled her inside. Through the common room, up two flights of stairs, he pulled her along as if there were a three-alarm fire. Her heart beat so fast she couldn't hear their wet feet slapping against the teak floors. "Logan, slow down—what on eart—"

Her back thumped against a closed door, as he pressed her hips between his erection and the wood at her back. His fingers speared into her hair, the small pain turning her on even more. He shoved the bikini bra up, his large hands urgent on her sensitized skin. Her breasts were cupped in warm, hard male hands that knew what they were doing.

"Ahh," she sighed as he kissed her ravenously.

His fingers gripped her ass, pulling her up onto her toes so his hardness fit perfectly. She fought to get a hand between their bodies to fumble with the waistband of his trunks. Wrong angle; his body was too close. She whimpered and tried to tug them down, wanting the prize hidden behind the thin fabric.

"Everyone knows what we ran up here to do." She bit his chin, then lifted her face. Sweat and rain dewed her skin, and it felt as though she was on fire from the inside out. Her skin burned. Her entire body vibrated. She needed to feel his hard hot length buried inside her to the hilt. She had to have his mouth, his hands, his—anything, everything, on her naked breasts. *Now. Now. Now.*

"Don't give a damn." Logan's mouth crushed down on hers again, his tongue a hot spear. She met it with her own, a duel that both won. He shifted to change the angle of her head, and she wound one leg around his, to get closer contact. A small, reptilian part of her brain, the part used for self-preservation, reminded her that they were standing in the hallway outside his cabin and she was still half in and half out of a wet suit. Any minute some security guy or a crew member was going to get an eyeful of her bare breasts, as Logan had somehow managed to maintain his hold, kiss her, *and* yank her bikini top off. Devilishly clever man, Logan Cutter.

The euphoria she'd felt under the water increased tenfold with Logan's touch, coursing through her body, making her feel invincible. She used the wall at her back for leverage and practically climbed his body, her legs spread around his narrow waist. Winding her arms around his neck, she pressed her aching breasts hard against his chest. The bulk of the half-on, half-off wet suit clumped around her waist. "Clothes! Off. Now!"

The hand in her hair left and she heard a vaguely familiar ding right before the door opened behind her, causing them to practically fall into the room. Still kissing her, he walked her inside, then kicked the door closed, shutting them into the cool dimness.

He crowded her until her back slammed against the wall just inside the door. Daniela slid down his body, both hands going to his shorts, dragging the fabric down his legs. She pressed her way back up his body, kissing everything in her path until she got back to his lips. She kissed him with everything she had, using one bare foot to push his shorts the rest of the way to the floor.

His hands skimmed the wet suit farther down her hips, then went to the ties at her hips. "Too damn slow!" she urged, trying to strip her wet suit off while one hand was in his hair, and her mouth was making love to his. Between them, they seemed to have too many limbs as they tangled and clashed, each trying to perform the same tasks. A giggle burst up through her chest, and she had to tear her mouth from under his to laugh and breathe at the same time.

"Five hundred men know exactly what we're doing in here right now," she told him breathlessly as he walked her backward toward the bed.

"And every one of them is jealous." He scooped her up in his arms. Laughing, Daniela wrapped her arms around his neck for the short trek across the cabin. The wet suit hung off one ankle, and her bikini bottom was undone only on one side. Her laughter died away. On fire for him, she pulled his head down and gave him a full-on French kiss guaranteed to blow his mind.

It was like a boomerang as a bonfire of lust and need burst through her. She was barely aware of being dropped onto the mattress, and then Logan was there between her spread thighs. She pulled his head down to kiss him. His hand closed around her breast.

Heat licked her skin, and desire liquefied her insides. She was on fire for him.

His tongue pushed into her mouth, and she met it with her own, welcoming, hungry for more.

Even as his mouth came down on hers, he was caressing her breast. He pushed his knee high up against the juncture of her thighs and she whimpered with need.

His mouth silenced her as he crushed his lips on hers. His tongue swept into her mouth, hot and slick, greedy. Fingers raking through his hair, Daniela kissed him back. He tasted of coffee, he tasted of lust. He tasted of desire.

His large hands slid around her hips to cup her ass, pulling her tightly against him. He was hard, and long, and her body jerked in response.

As she framed his face with her hands, they devoured each other. She felt the rough tug as the damp fabric of her bikini bottom was slowly threaded from between her legs.

His hand skimmed down her body, savoring the silky texture of her skin, shaping his hand to the curves and indentations that flowed from one to the other, the swell of her breasts to the flat of her stomach, the flare of her hips, the notch between her legs.

She moaned softly, rubbing her nose back and forth in his chest hair. He nudged her face up, taking her mouth like a pirate plundering a treasure ship. No holds barred. Winner takes all.

Logan flexed his hips and surged inside her. Arching her back, she gave a soundless cry. His arms bracketed her shoulders, his biceps and triceps bulging as he hammered his hips in a pounding rhythm that had her heartbeat manic, and her head thrashing on the pillow. Her hips came up in counterpoint to meet his every thrust.

But it was more than heat, more than raw lust between them, making her heart rage. Every touch of his hands, every press of him against her made her feel treasured beyond words. Made her feel safe. And no man had given her that gift before.

If this is what Logan meant by diving, she'd gladly dive every morning, noon, and night to be in his arms.

Fifteen

Two nights later, Logan untangled his body from Daniela's, missing her warmth as he left the bed. After making love, he'd insisted she dress. She had donned shorts and a tank top, and fallen face-first back onto the sex-rumpled sheets. Asleep before her head hit the pillow.

His body was well satiated, but his mind buzzed with details. How to keep her safe, how to protect the treasure as well as his crew.

With Wes awake and on guard in Daniela's cabin next door to his, a man on the balcony outside, and two men posted outside his door, Logan had stolen half an hour to himself while Daniela pretended to sleep. Maybe without him there to distract her, that would become a reality. She was strung tighter than a bow.

He locked the door behind him, jogged to the top deck for midnight tai chi. The moon hung high in the sky, surrounded by twinkling stars. The sound of the waves slapping against the hull was more comforting than the dozens of strangers occupying his boat, but even the waves held an angry undercurrent.

Slower breaths calmed his racing mind as he performed the tai chi forms by rote, concentrating on the steady beat of his heart and feeling the stretch of his muscles as he moved. The teak deck beneath his bare feet retained a hint of the sun's warmth, physically grounding him so he could sort out his chaotic thoughts. It had been forty-eight hours since the counterterrorists had arrived. Forty-eight hours since his world was turned upside down, and yet the moon still shone, the ocean gently rocked his ship, the men slept and ate and dove as if nothing had actually changed at all.

It went against the grain to unearth the treasure he'd been anticipating, and then leave it where it was, a hundred and fifty feet under the ocean. But with the next days or weeks of uncertainty, he didn't want to add a boatload of a haul, valued in multimillions of dollars, into the mix of potential craziness. It was safer where it had been for four hundred years. Things were complicated enough without having the treasure on board.

He agreed with Wright's strategy. Bringing the senator's people on board rather than going after them would confine them, making corralling and neutralizing them easier. Yeah. He got that intellectually. But he'd much rather go to where the bastards were holed up and take them out. Now. At least that way he'd have a say in the when and the where.

If Stamps's men were thwarted, the senator would get desperate enough to launch a more personal offensive.

Now it was a waiting game.

Logan didn't like waiting. But he was damned good at it. He'd had enough practice over the years. Waiting for his father to come home. Waiting for his brothers to grow up. Waiting for a woman like Daniela who tilted his well-ordered world sideways.

So he waited.

But not with his usual sangfroid.

Moonlight tai chi usually brought his mind and body peace, but tonight the precise, languid movements didn't bring him what he sought. A Glock lay incongruously beside the towel he'd tossed over the table. Breathing in again, striving to block the negative, he closed his eyes as he identified each separate smell on the still night air.

The scent of ozone, of brine, of the men patrolling the decks around him like shadows, of gun oil. Barbecued bass they'd enjoyed for dinner. But it was the spicy musky fragrance of Daniela clinging to his hair and skin that overrode everything else.

The air was muggy and close, sticky against his bare legs and chest. The ocean looked and sounded as irritable as he felt, the whitecaps' agitation captured by the lights from the ship.

Sea Wolf was crawling with security. The men he'd hired, and the T-FLAC operatives who never seemed to rest. Stamps hadn't made a move for forty-eight hours, but none of them had let their guard down for a minute, and the tension could be felt like a heavy, electrical net over all their activities.

The fast-moving clouds rolled in, blocking the moonlight and the stars, but there was plenty of illumination. Lights on board, interior and exterior, burned 24/7. No shadows. Nowhere to hide.

The ship wasn't quiet. The usual noises were somewhat obliterated by the sound of booted footfalls on the decks and corridors as security patrolled. There was barely an inch of space on board not occupied by a heavily armed professional. The senator was now campaigning in Colorado. According to Derek Wright, the senator's hired thugs were holed up in a cheap hotel in

Punta de Bombon, a town five hundred miles south of Lima, and a mere seventy miles from where the *Sea Wolf* lay at anchor.

He wasn't the only one too wired to sleep. His dive team had decided after dinner that they'd move a couple of hundred bins holding small artifacts and coins down to the storeroom in the hold.

It wasn't necessary, just busywork. But the hope was that it would tire them out, giving them something else to think about.

Logan executed a Chen Four step, then paused as a thump broke the stillness of the night. He nodded in greeting to one of the security guys as he passed by on patrol, then went to the rail to peer down as he yelled, "Guys? Need a hand?"

"We're good." The voice was distorted, probably from the weight of the bin being carried.

"Be with you in ten," he shouted back at the sound of another thump.

Jed had gotten rid of the *Sea Witch*. Logan hadn't had a chance to talk to him in the general organized chaos that had ensued yesterday. Quadrupling the people on board made it a logistical feat to ensure that everyone had a place to get some shut-eye. Meals had to be served around the clock to accommodate this many people. Hipolito was in his element, and was busy enough to welcome Daniela's assistance, killing two birds with one stone.

As he moved, Logan observed the lights from some of the distant ships. There was no way to keep everyone away. The second it had been sent out over the radio by one of the observers that *Sea Wolf* had found *La Daniela*, and that they'd already discovered a wealth of jewelry and artifacts, people had come from all over to see. There were perhaps half a dozen boats adhering to the one-mile limit, who just wanted to observe, and get a glimpse of the treasure.

Several of the T-FLAC operatives had taken the tender and gone out to interrogate every one. Most, just day-trippers curious about the process, had hightailed it out of there, not wanting trouble. A couple of boats, potential pirates Logan suspected, lingered. The extra security ensured they stayed away at the legal one-mile limit.

"Logan!"

"Be there in a minute," he yelled back. The voice had come from the lower deck where the guys were handing up the bins from the dive platform. He heard a muffled groan, and grinned. Those bins weighed upward of fifty pounds, and moving them was a bitch, no matter what the value of their contents. He had a warm willing woman waiting for him in his cabin. But he'd give the guys a hand for an hour.

Sticking the gun in his waistband at the small of his back, he wiped his face with a towel, and jogged to the stairs heading to the next deck, passing two more black-clad operatives as he took the outside stairs three at a time.

"Okay," he shouted as he hit the lower deck where his guys were. "Serious muscle has arrived. Step aside, my man."

A sweep of his gaze stopped Logan in his tracks.

A man's legs protruded from the open slider exiting the common room. "Shit!" Logan ran.

First thought, the worst. Stamps's men had somehow managed to sneak aboard. But since that was highly unlikely, considering how many good guys patrolled the ship, and how well lit everything was, his next thought was heart attack. Light from inside shone on Galt's bald head. *Damn.* He started to crouch beside him, then saw the shiny red blood on his friend's face and head.

"Behind you!" Cooper yelled, tearing around the corner at a dead run, two shadowy figures behind him. Without pausing, he thrust out his hand and vaulted over the rail into the water. The kid hit the water with a loud splash. Smart move.

Logan swung around, narrowly missing being hit in the face as a burly guy in a wet suit swung an air tank two-fisted at his head. He hadn't seen him, just felt the rush of displaced air.

Putting his head down, Logan rammed into the bad guy's soft gut, felt the blunt force shimmy down his spine. They both grunted on impact. The heavy dive tank clattered to the deck, then rolled, hitting the rail with a resounding clang that was almost lost in the cacophony surrounding them.

Now Logan heard the sound of gunshots and the grunts and exclamations of men in hand-to-hand combat.

Gasping, the guy countered, swinging his beefy arm in a tight arc. Light reflected off the short blade of the knife clutched in his fist as the glint jerked up toward Logan's unprotected belly. He danced back, felt the white-hot streak as the tip skimmed his ribs. Adrenaline wiped out any pain. Slamming his forearm on the man's wrist, he enjoyed the sound of bone cracking, and the guy's scream of agony. The knife wheeled out of his grip and clattered as it skittered across the deck.

The man clutched his broken wrist against his belly, fumbling for his weapon. It was clearly his nondominant hand; the gun was awkwardly positioned for a quick draw.

Logan reached for the Glock tucked in the back of his shorts. Nothing. Fuck. The man was joined by a twin in a black wet suit—still dripping water, murder in his eyes.

Jed came out behind the second man, grabbing him with his arm across the man's throat and grappling with him, while Logan scanned the deck for his gun, dropped in the scuffle.

He saw the Glock at his opponent's feet. Damn it to hell. He dived across the deck, sliding into base. Grabbed up the Glock and rolled. The bad guy fumbled his gun into his meaty fist, trying to awkwardly adjust for a different angle.

"You snooze, you lose." Logan rotated up on his shoulder, braced one hand under the other and fired. He wasn't sure who was more fucking surprised, himself or the guy with a dark wet blotch on the front of his wet suit. The man's eyes went wide, then he toppled to the deck, already slick with water and blood.

Nausea welled in the back of Logan's throat. Jesus. He'd done that. Willfully, and without a second's hesitation, taken a man's life. How the fuck had he come to this? He'd never killed before. But he didn't have time to think about it now as he jumped to his feet.

Pirates, or Stamps's men? Whoever they were, bad guys were pouring over the rail like ants at a picnic. Where had they come from? His people were everywhere, watching, waiting. *Professionals*. How the fuck had they been caught unaware? And where the hell was everyone, on a fucking coffee break?

The clothing was so similar to that worn by the

T-FLAC operatives that it was almost impossible to differentiate the good guys from the bad, even in the bright lighting that made the scene surreal.

Worse, the army who'd boarded seemed just as skilled, just as motivated as the men he had on board. And there appeared to be three times as many of them.

All around him was utter chaos and pandemonium. Earsplitting hails of shots were being fired from every direction.

These guys had serious firepower to counteract *Sea Wolf*'s serious firepower. They were clearly well-funded and extremely motivated.

Someone came up behind him, grabbed him around the throat with his forearm. Logan bent, throwing the man over his head. Well, over the *rail*. He cartwheeled over the side with a scream and a splash.

Another man was right behind him. They were like fucking Weebles. Knock one down, and six more popped up. Logan didn't wait to ask questions, but spun, slamming the Glock at the guy's nose. Crunch, grunt; the guy hit out blindly and got him with a painful jolt on his arm, which went numb from wrist to shoulder. Logan shot up his knee, hard, hit the man straight in the balls. He winced as the guy doubled over and fell to the deck screaming.

Fuck empathy pain; more were coming without end. He danced back to parry a man with a long-bladed knife, red with someone else's blood. The man showed yellowed teeth. Close enough for Logan to get a whiff of chain-smoker. Logan's feet shot out from under him as he slipped in God only knew what on the deck, and flew backward on his ass.

The guy jumped him while he was still sliding, sitting on his chest. Logan grunted as his good arm was pinned beneath both their weights. They were equal in strength, but the man was thirty pounds heavier, better trained, and sitting on him.

These bastards favored knives, and one was raised now, descending as if in slo-mo. Logan grabbed the guy's wrist in his still numb hand, fought to bend the arm back. The knife got closer to his throat. He wrenched it back a few inches, repelling it with more determination than brute strength as he twisted and bucked.

Fuck it, he had no leverage.

He couldn't drag in a breath because of the weight crushing his chest. He arched his back, hoping to get the guy off balance, or just—hell—*off*. Instead he ended up with a face full of crotch. That left his legs free. He tilted up, let his heels climb the guy's back. The man twisted, slashed at his legs, but Logan wrapped his legs around the guy's head, locking his ankles over his nose. And squeezed. Squeeze. Twist. Twist. Squeeze. The guy was gurgling, flailing. Logan wasn't done. They twisted and rolled.

Someone fell over them with a curse, someone else stumbled, his boot striking Logan in the kidneys. They rolled like lovers until they came to a jarring halt, Logan's spine hitting the rail with a *thwack* that jarred every bone in his body.

Grabbing the guy by the hair, he pounded the bastard's head on the deck until he went slack. Chest heaving, Logan staggered to his feet, gripping the rail until he was sure he was steady enough to move. There were men everywhere. Fighting. Some dead. Some wounded badly enough that they lay where they'd fallen.

He helped up one of Wright's men, with a quick yank

on the hand he held up. "Thanks, man." Then watched as the same man shot two men point-blank, on the run, without pausing.

Holy fuck.

The faint smell of cordite was joined by the metallic stink of blood and other body fluids. Men yelled, cursed, and grunted as fists and weapons slammed into bare flesh. Wood ripped and splintered. A liquid splash as someone else went overboard. Shit crashed and clanged in surround sound.

Pandemonium was all around him, but all Logan could think was *Daniela.*

He picked up his gun and ran, ignoring the crack and splinter of more wood breaking, glass shattering, shouts, and the pop of gunfire.

Galt was gone from the doorway, leaving behind a large bloody pool on the teak floor. Logan ran like his life depended on speed. *Her* life depended on his speed. He raced through the common room in seconds.

A man ran at him and Logan hit him in the face with his elbow, barely slowing down. He shot a second man who was squeezing the trigger on a semiauto. The guy's face exploded in a spray of red. Logan didn't hang around to see him drop.

He ignored the upturned furniture and shattered debris, ignored clumps of men at each other's throats, ignored the wanton destruction all around him.

Daniela. Jesus . . .

Daniela couldn't sleep. Even less so after Logan left the cabin. A lamp burned on the bedside table, and she was fully dressed, shorts, T-shirt, running shoes, *bra.* It made sense if Victor's men came back. "But wearing shoes to bed isn't exactly conducive to sleeping," she told Dog, who lay snoring on her feet.

She was curled on her side on Logan's big bed, her fingers under the pillow, but not gripping the butt of the loaded Glock she'd been sleeping with for the past several nights. Logan had given her a crash course in firing it for a couple of days on the helipad on the top deck. It would be impossible to hit anyone with her eyes squeezed shut. She had a better chance of hitting herself in the foot than shooting an intruder, which she'd tried telling him. He'd made her practice several times a day. She was a terrible shot every time. Thank God she was surrounded by a veritable army of men who looked as though *they'd* have no problem at all remaining steely-eyed as they pulled the trigger.

Standing outside the cabin door were two men in black. A few yards away, on the small balcony, stood the shadowy figure of the man stationed there to protect her. He and his big gun stood motionless in the shadows between her and the vastness of the night sky and the blackness of the ocean.

"I could go and talk to Wes. What do you think?" He was in her old cabin next door. But it was two in the morning, and he was probably sleeping. She could get up and go and peep in the open door . . .

Preternaturally awake, Daniela pulled the light blanket up around her shoulders, and willed herself to relax. Eyes gritty, she was too wired. Her heart pounded for absolutely no reason, and she had a jittery sensation in the pit of her stomach. The kind she'd had as a child when she had to get up to go to the bathroom in the middle of the night. That sliding-her-feet-to-the-floor-even-though-she-knew-a-monster-hid-under-the-bed bad feeling.

Victor was somewhere out there in the dark. Not literally—God, she prayed not—but symbolically. She could almost hear him breathing. "That's just the air conditioner," she told Dog, who was oblivious to her flights of fancy.

She felt foolish, lying there, frozen in place, held there by named and unnamed fears. She was the cause of her own anxieties. She had to stop it. She'd get up and turn on more lights. She'd take a cool shower. She'd jog in place. Write a novel. Compose a sonnet. God.

How girly and ridiculously, annoyingly codependent. She wanted Logan to come back. She wanted the feel of his hard, strong body hugging her close. This time, she swore, she wouldn't be embarrassed that there was a man just a few feet away who might turn and glance through the closed slider and see them. This time, she'd savor the closeness and sleep.

The cabin was surprisingly quiet but for the faint throb of the generator deep in the bowels of the ship and the faint noise of the air conditioner.

Suddenly all the lights blazed on, and a siren split the quiet, the sharp sound reverberating in her ears and resonating through her bones. Daniela shot upright, her hand over her manic heart. Dog stood over her extended legs, lip curled back, ruff up, growling low in his throat, head down.

Dear God . . .

There was a loud *thwack* over her left shoulder, and when she swiveled her head to see what it was, she saw a small black hole in the upholstered headboard. Frantically, Daniela scrambled to get untangled from the blanket and Dog, and at the same time fumbled under the pillow for the gun.

"We—" she stared to scream for Wes, when the sliding door from the balcony was shoved aside with a bang, and the black-garbed man raced into the room. With the door open she could hear gunshots and running footsteps as he let in an assault of loud noises, and the smell of—she had no idea, but her nose wrinkled as she stared uncomprehendingly at him.

To make the noise worse, Dog went ballistic, barking and lunging. "It's okay, it's okay." She was saying it more for herself then the animal. "What's happening?"

"Ma'am, we've been breached," the man yelled, leaning over the mattress to grab her wrist and violently yank her over the other edge of the bed. He cuffed Dog aside as the animal tried to grab his black jacket in his sharp teeth. "Gotta get you outa here! Come on! Hurry."

There was something—in the chaos she couldn't pinpoint what was off. But she resisted his inexorable pull on her wrist. "Logan said to stay here, no matter what!"

The siren was so loud they had to yell to be heard. Poor Dog, confused by the noise and yelling, was barking and trying to bite the guy. "You're *both* taking care of me, boy. It's okay. It's okay." But it wasn't.

The security guy jerked her roughly, pulling her to her feet. His hold was painfully tight, and the angle at which he held her arm hurt; he was almost wrenching it from the socket.

Dog, who'd been knocked several feet away, came out of nowhere, flying at him across the rumpled bed.

His teeth sank into the man's shoulder. That was good enough for Daniela. She screamed blue bloody murder at the top of her lungs, struggling to get the man's hand off her arm. She clawed at his fingers with her nails, and when that didn't work, brought a knee up sharply to his groin. He turned quickly, and her strike deflected off his thigh. He cursed and slapped her so hard her head jerked back from the flat-handed blow.

She went for his eyes, but he was taller and much, much stronger. He planted his elbow in the middle of her chest to hold her back, and at the same time wrenched her arm behind her. She screamed out her rage as Dog came charging, yellow eyes feral, teeth bared.

The man's leg shot out and he kicked Dog in the head with his heavy boot. "Noooo!" The dog dropped like a rock and lay still, out of sight at the foot of the bed.

Daniela's body sagged, so he had to support her just by the cruel grip he had on her wrist. Red-hot pain shot up her arm, but she used the weight of her body and writhed and twisted until she broke his hold and fell on all fours to the carpet.

She was already on the floor, but the bed had drawers. No crawl space. She crawled until she managed to stumble to her feet. He had her blocked in. He was between her and—everything. She was between the bed and the open slider. The gun was still under the pillow.

"What the fuck—!" Wes came charging into Logan's cabin, a gun in his hand, and took in everything at a glance, rage on his face. "Get down! Get down!" He fired several shots. One slammed into the sliding door several feet away. Glass shattered, showered the carpet with glittering shards.

He dropped to one knee, and his gun fell from his hand as blood poured from his shoulder. "Run!" he yelled, then toppled over on his side and lay still. Daniela jumped up on the bed and bolted across the mattress, only to be pulled back by a hard grip to the back of her shorts. She fell, and the man grabbed her by her hair, dragging her to his side of the bed. "On your feet."

She dug her nails into the backs of his hands and screamed at the top of her lungs.

"You're lucky I was told not to mess up your face." His features distorted with fury, and he fumbled inside his jacket. For a gun? She went even colder. "Bitch, if you don't shut the fuck up, there are other ways of making you cooperate." He took a small bag out of an inner pocket, flipping it open on the bed.

"Then you better use *all* of them, you son of a bitch," she yelled, fighting him. "I'm no . . . t go . . . in . . . anywh—mff!"

He slapped a soft cloth, *hard,* over her mouth and nose, held it there, cutting off her erratic breathing. Daniela held her breath until the room spun and her lungs burned. He twisted her arm behind her back between them, yanking her against him.

The desperate need for air compelled her aching lungs to suck in a breath. Just a small breath. She fought him like a wild woman, but her intent and fury wilted as the edges of the room, and the sounds of the siren and shouts rapidly imploded.

Logan . . .

Weightless. Darkness edged out light. Knees lique-fying.

Help.

Body dissolving into shadows.

Dimly she heard boots crunch over broken glass. Felt the cool night air on her face. Had a sensation of flying. And then experienced nothing at all.

Sixteen

The clanging of the ship's emergency alarm bells cut through the din like a blunt surgical blade. No one gave a second's pause. Oblivious, the men kept going. Punches. The crack of gunshots. Screams and grunts. It was a fucking cage fight without the damn cage.

Sharp, rapid-fire barking carried across the din, catching Logan's attention. Fear gripped him by the throat as he absorbed the facts. Dog's bark was frantic.

Dog was supposed to be with Daniela.

Logan spun around just as Dog leapt from the dive platform, landing on the deck on all fours, soaking wet. How the hell had he gotten from the locked cabin into the water? His ruff was up, his lip curled to reveal white teeth as he continued to bark ferociously.

Fuck. Fuck. Fuck.

Daniela!

Logan called for Dog, who ate up the deck between them in long bounding strides. The animal leapt from six feet away, body slamming Logan so he had to stagger to maintain his balance. Clamping his hands around Dog's neck, he eased him back on all fours. "Let's go get her," he yelled, because if Dog was out here, something had—

Fuck.

This bloodbath was nothing more than a goddamned diversion. A costly one.

He turned and ran like a wide receiver going for the end zone, Dog hard on his heels, barking as if warning everyone to get the fuck out of their way.

"Little help here?!" Jed yelled, arm twisted behind his back by some dude in a water-beaded wet suit as they scrabbled on the landing at the foot of the stairs. A second man pulled back his arm to punch Jed in the belly. Blood poured from Jed's swollen nose, and he was trying to make eye contact from his one open eye.

Logan closed the gap, grabbed the puncher by the shoulder, spun him around and slammed his elbow up into *his* nose. Dog danced around them, barking and biting. Logan heard the satisfying crunch, then warm blood splattered onto his bare chest as the man shrieked like a girl. As he doubled over, Logan jerked up his knee, and had the satisfaction of hearing bone and cartilage crunch. The man went down without a peep.

"You good?" he yelled at Jed, who now had the other guy in a headlock.

"Yeah. Go get her." *Daniela. Jesus. Daniela.* He started running again, Dog glued to his side. Flat out, legs and lungs pumping. Heartbeat manic. Fear tasted metallic in his dry mouth. He jumped the sprawled, upside-down guy on the stairs whose throat was cut, then passed three men locked in hand-to-hand combat. Logan vaulted over the legs of a guy barely conscious and attempting to claw the smooth teak wall for purchase.

Three stairs at a time. One flight. Two. Heart pounding. Vision focused, legs pistoning. He saw more men up on the upper decks, some dead, some fighting. He passed those he could, and paused barely long enough to interact when he couldn't. When he fought, Dog circled, barking and snapping, urging him to hurry.

As he ran, he prayed like never before.

At last they reached the long corridor to his cabin. Key card in hand, he saw that one of Wright's men was sprawled across the doorway, facedown. A giant fucking hole in the back of his neck. Blood pooled obscenely on the floor around him. The other man was gone. Logan bent to grab the guy's gun out of his cold dead hand. Dog was going ballistic, barking and body slamming the door.

Logan yelled her name even as he unlocked and wrenched open the door. Barking, Dog dashed inside, racing across the cabin.

Logan took in the room at a glance. The shattered door, the glass on the carpet, and the shredded sheer curtains blowing in the wind. "Daniela!"

His heartbeat stumbled, a hard, painful knock inside his chest. It took seconds to start again. "Daniela?! Oh, Christ. Wes!" His friend lay sprawled near the door connecting the two cabins. He'd been shot in the shoulder. Logan's gaze darted about the room searching for any sign of Daniela even as he crouched beside his unconscious friend. He pressed two fingers on the pulse under Wes's jaw. Alive. Thank God.

He activated the comm in his ear. "In my cabin. Wes has been shot," he told Piet, his voice eerily calm to his own ears. Inside, he was filled with fear and an awful sense of foreboding "Daniela's gone." He disconnected, not waiting for a response. Piet would send help ASAP.

The bed was a rumpled mess. The sheets tossed on the floor. A small, obscene black hole had been drilled in the white leather headboard, causing his already erratic heartbeat to stop and then roar back at full speed. A marksman with uncanny skill had made the shot.

It felt as though a fist grabbed him by the balls and squeezed. "No sign of blood," he told himself. "That's good. That's really good." He laid his hand on Wes's massive shoulder. "Hang on buddy. Help's on its way. I need a minute."

Running to the door, he yanked it open, fastening it in the open position, then he raced into the bathroom. Empty. Ran into the cabin next door, then went back to his own cabin to stand beside Wes, head lowered.

Logan felt gutted, his vital organs scooped out and left trailing. He hadn't expected to find her, but God, he'd—

Dog barked from the open doorway to the balcony. He ran.

Another of Wright's men, dead, slumped in the corner. An obscene dark hole between his eyes. Someone had scaled the side of the ship, shot him, and entered through the slider to grab Daniela.

"Quiet!" he instructed the frantically barking dog as he curled his fingers over the wood topping the Plexi, and scanned the water with burning eyes.

Pleasepleaseplease.

He saw nothing but moonlight dancing on agitated black water.

What the invading bad guys couldn't know was that Derek Wright had more than one group of T-FLAC operatives on standby. A group that was patrolling the coastal waters, so that when the attackers fled *Sea Wolf*, they were scooped up before their boats hit land.

Daniela hadn't been with them.

Dawn broke in a display of coral streaks against a purple and yellow sky, similar to the bruising to be seen on the men on board. One of the counterterrorists was a doctor, and he was still busy in *Sea Wolf*'s small infirmary, tending Wes and the other men injured in the fracas.

Piet made some order out the chaos left behind by giving the men clear instructions. The authorities were already on the way to retrieve the bodies and take statements. The crew had the ship cleaned in record time, and Hipolito and the stewards kept fresh hot coffee and hearty foods replenished as the men limped into the common room, which was being used as a war room and command center.

The atmosphere on board was grim. Logan couldn't sit, so he paced until Jed took him by the shoulder and shoved him into a chair. "Listen, and we'll go from there," he instructed his friend, not without sympathy.

"As nonexistent as my imagination is, I can't help but—"

Jed squeezed his shoulder. "Focus on what we can do, not what could be."

Sound advice. "I'll give it my best shot."

Dog sat beside him, ears pricked, eyes intent on the slider to the deck. Dog was looking for Daniela too. There was a strong possibility that she was dead. Logan pressed his fist to the pain in his chest. Surely he'd feel it if she was dead.

No. Stamps had taken her. Stamps had her. And if that was the case, then the senator wanted her alive. Logan had to cling to that scenario. Nothing else was acceptable.

Derek Wright walked in and one could hear a pin drop. Logan got to his feet, walked over, and punched him in the solar plexus, hard. He almost broke his hand on the man's rock-hard belly. All Wright did was grunt before muttering. "Promise broken. Got it. We'll find her."

"You'd fucking better." Logan stalked away before he tossed the son of a bitch overboard or worse. Acid churned with fear and regret in his belly. Daniela wasn't Wright's to protect. *He* was the one who'd let her down. *He* was the man responsible.

Logan's mind raced like a fucking rat in a maze. Cool it, he cautioned. Running around like a chicken with its head cut off was counterproductive. Clear, cool thinking was what was called for now. And clearly, it made fuck-all difference if Wright and his men were present or not. Despite every precaution, she'd been snatched from beneath their very noses.

The only broken promise in the entire clusterfuck was his to Daniela.

Since it was impossible to sit, still or otherwise, Logan stood, his mind going a mile a minute. Who she was with wasn't the issue. The question was, how to get her back.

He stared blindly across the room as Wright raised a hand to get everyone's attention. Rubbing his belly, the T-FLAC operative propped a shoulder against the doorjamb. "Here's what we know. Daniela was taken to a private airfield in Punta de Bombon. No flight plan was filed. That plane just landed in Lima. Plans are being made for her retrieval, and you *will* be on hand when that goes down. Let me fill you in on our visitors while the details are being ironed out.

"One hundred men were dispatched from those two pleasure crafts off your starboard side."

"We got that," Logan said tightly. He knew, because

Wright had told him when he'd come back, that there hadn't been that many men on board. So they'd snuck on after Wright and his people had paid the ships a call. "Didn't see them because they used SCUBA gear and approached underwater. *Again*. Should have fucking thought of that." Logan sounded as feral and savage as he felt.

"We did."

"Not fast enough to protect Daniela. They threw her from the third-deck balcony, for God's sake!" Dog must've gone in after her.

Wright acknowledged the statement with a small nod, and sympathetic glance. "Senator Stamps has arranged a press conference at the Grand Hotel in Lima this afternoon."

Logan's mouth was dry as he fisted his hands in his pockets. *Alive. Thank you, God.* "Is he going to show her off or kill her?" he asked evenly, hearing the surge and race of his blood through his veins and the annoying pounding of his heart in his ears. He'd never been so afraid in his life. Not the day his mother had grabbed him and his brothers and snuck them all off Cutter Cay away from their abusive father. Not the day their father had snatched them back. Not the day their mother had died in that car wreck.

This was a whole different fear, because now he knew enough to know what evil lay in wait for Daniela, and he was too far away to do anything about it.

"We believe he's going to use her appearance to announce that he's running for president," Wright informed him.

"She won't be part of it." Logan clamped his teeth together.

Wright met his eyes. "She might not have a choice."

Every minute, fuck, every *second* that Victor Stamps had his hands on Daniela, there was a chance he'd do worse than brand her, or suffocate her for a few thrills. "Let's go."

"Chopper'll be here in thirty minutes."

Not nearly soon enough. "I have my own. It's leaving *now*."

Wright pushed off the doorjamb, with a shake of his head. "Not enough fuel to get a group of us to Lima. Thirty minutes isn't going to make any difference. We have his location, and we know that he won't do anything to harm her until after the press conference at four." He held up a finger, then touched his earpiece and listened for several minutes.

"That thirty minutes may not matter to you, but to her that's hell on earth. Do you know what that fucker did to her?"

Wright's eyes narrowed. "We know what he's done, or we wouldn't be here. But we need that thirty minutes for the tactical advantage. You go in there right now, you're one guy, maybe four at the most. You wait thirty minutes and my team will be ready to back you up completely."

"Confirmed and in place? Because I've heard this fucking song and dance before. And look how well that panned out!" Logan knew these guys were good, but they weren't off the hook for fucking up. Now he was in charge.

Wright gritted his teeth. "Here's what we have. No investigation was ever started on the senator. Special Agent Price and his family were discovered by their neighbors. Suspected home invasion. All dead. We're looking into Price's financials now. I suspect a payoff from Stamps."

"If Stamps was paying off Price, and I don't doubt that for a moment, why the hell kill him?"

"Perhaps Price had a crisis of conscience, and was about to blow the whistle. Perhaps he refused to give up Daniela. Doesn't much matter, does it? Guy's dead."

"What about the drugs at Daniela's gallery? Price had to have told someone else what was happening." This shit only happened on *CSI*.

"The Blue Opal was drug free as of yesterday at o-eight hundred. Swept. Not a trace that anything illegal was ever there."

Logan clenched his fists in his pockets. "If Daniela said there were kilos of heroin, I believe her."

"So do we," Wright assured him. "The senator's been a clever, sneaky boy. But my people are smarter and a lot sneakier. We're building a case, and it'll be solid and airtight."

"And how's that going to impact Daniela?"

"In her favor, I hope."

Logan got right up in Wright's face, nose to nose so his meaning couldn't be mistaken. "Not *hope*. Allow one hair on her head to be hurt again, and I don't give a fuck *how* much training you have. It might not be quick, it might not be finessed, but I assure you, I *will* kill your ass."

Sour nausea crawled up the back of her throat in a burn of fear. Disoriented, Daniela struggled to open sticky eyes, but dizziness pinned her down like a rock on her chest. No—a *hand* on her chest. Panic was cloaked, almost, by drug-induced layers of calm. She fought against the lethargy, but knew moving would give her away. Fear made her heart race, and sweat made her skin itch. She lay limp and still.

"I *told* you—you gave her too much!"

More powerful than the nausea, more frightening than being held down, Victor Stamps's voice, so close, made Daniela's heart stop. To hell with it. Fear dictated that she move, and fast. She struggled to break free from her stupor, but no matter how desperately she wanted to, she realized she couldn't move, and opening her eyes was a Herculean task no matter how hard she tried.

"She's awake," an unfamiliar male voice said defensively.

"I know she's awake." Victor slapped her cheek hard. "Open your fucking eyes, bitch." Face hot and stinging from the blow, Daniela managed to slit them at half-mast, seeing him through the screen of her lashes. Not because he demanded it, but because to be blind to his next action was as frightening as knowing something worse was coming.

Victor sat on the bed beside her, his hand splayed between her breasts. Even though she wasn't capable of movement, Daniela's felt as if all her organs were shrinking out of reach. Her skin crawled, and her heart beat so fast she was afraid she'd pass out. As her eyes focused fully, she was able to see his face more clearly.

Handsome in a preppy way, Victor was a cunning, charming reptile. The horn-rimmed glasses were nothing more than a prop, and did a good job of hiding his real expression from those around him. When he looked at someone, it was opportunity he was looking at. Opportunity, advantage, or a soft spot to deal a blow. Either physical or psychological.

His "sun-streaked" hair was perfectly styled, his tan looked natural. He was as handsome as a Greek god, and as scary as a child's worst nightmare. No. *Daniela's* worst nightmare.

"A ship in the middle of the Pacific?" His upper-class Boston accent dripped contempt he no longer had to hide. "Clever, Daniela. I never would have looked for you anywhere near the ocean because of your phobia."

A Victor-induced phobia.

Her damp hair stuck to her throat and neck. Her shorts and tank top clung to her goose-bumped skin like a shroud. She'd clearly been immersed in water recently. A full body shudder preceded teeth-clicking shivers. A mixture of cold and dread. Her eyes shot to his. Had he . . .

"*How*?" It came out a hoarse whisper. Her throat was raw, her mouth so dry it hurt to push even that one word out.

"How did I get you from there to here? My people created a little diversion—Oh, you mean how did you get so *wet*? Bob, apparently, threw you off a balcony. Then it was a simple matter of hauling your inconvenient ass into a fast boat and heading here by private plane. Oh, *here*, is the Grand Hotel in Lima."

Hundreds of miles from Logan. He'd never find her. If he was even alive. "Happen to t—ship?" To Logan? And Jed, and Wes, and Hipolito? Her eyes smarted. *Dog.*

"Jesus, Daniela, who cares! I hope you're happy at how much trouble you've caused me at the most crucial time in my career. It's cost me a fucking fortune to find you." He pressed his hand down on her chest, making it painfully harder for her to breathe, his eyes cruel slits behind his glasses. "I had to use resources earmarked for other things." She flinched as he lifted his hand, but it was only to comb through her hair, and hold her head steady so she had to look up at him whether she wanted to or not.

"You owe me, and you owe me fucking *big* time. It took an army and dozens of payoffs to pull this off." He yanked so hard at her hair, tears sprang to her eyes. "And their discretion didn't come cheap. They were sent to retrieve you. You're retrieved. End of story."

She met his cold gaze. "How did you find me?" It was frightening how weak her voice sounded to her own ears. How long until the drug wore off? How long until she could attempt an escape? If they were in a hotel, there'd be people around. All she had to do was elude Victor and his minions and get out of the room. *All.* She wanted to laugh at how much weight that one small word had.

If she was with other people, he wouldn't . . .

"Your sailor boy and his brother went looking for info on you online. Guess you lied to him, too, huh, bitch? One of my more gifted hackers was watching for Internet searches on you, me, and your gallery, and it didn't take a genius to connect Nick Cutter to Cutter Salvage, with its boat off the coast of Peru. I should have figured you'd head home to Mommy's family." He leaned closer and sneered at her. "If you'd just told the man what he wanted to know, it would have taken us a lot longer to find you. As it happened, Mack happened to be paying a visit to Special Agent Price's home when Cutter called him." Daniela got even paler and Victor paused, his eyes glittering in a perverse way that let her know worse news was coming. "The first group of guys who hit that damn boat weren't able to say for sure if you were on it, but that call made it a lock. Unfortunately, Price had a home invasion later that evening," he murmured with exaggerated sympathy. "He, his wife, and those three sweet little towheads were brutally murdered. Terrible."

Focus. Don't internalize. Focus. Stay in the now. "Must've told other people . . ." The DEA didn't work in a bubble. There were strict protocols. People would investigate the murder of a federal agent. They would search for the killer . . . And how long would that take? More than the next hour, she bet. And how would they connect Daniela Rosado to the case?

"About the drugs? No," Victor scoffed. "No need to worry about that. Price came to me the day you ran. We made a solid business arrangement. But he did have a soft spot for you, my love. Tried to help us both. It got him killed in the end. You know how I feel about disloyalty. I gave his wife and little kiddies to Mack as a bonus, right, Mack?"

Mack had been the one jacking off in the room as the stench of her own burning flesh had filled the air when Victor had branded his initials on her ass. Like his boss, Mack was a psychopath.

"Good bonus, boss."

Victor yanked on her hair again, so she had no choice but to look up. "You've caused my Gallup poll numbers to drop dramatically. Voters like having a golden couple. And sympathy votes only lasted so long." He withdrew his fingers from her hair, pulling the strands hard enough to make her eyes water again. Her head fell limply back to the pillow. Daniela bit the inside of her cheek to contain her fear as he traced a smooth finger down the side of her neck to the swell of her breast.

"They need their king and queen back, baby. Everyone wants another Camelot."

His nail grazed her nipple through the damp cloth of
her thin top, and the best she could manage in defense
was shooting him a heated glare and uttering a hoarse,
"No!"

Victor grabbed a fistful of her shirt, pulling her off
the mattress, his warm spittle flecking her cheek.
"You've caused enough trouble, Daniela. We're going
to give the people what they want. The press is already
gathering in the ballroom downstairs. They want the
scoop on where you've been for the last few weeks, and
they want the kidnapper handed to them."

"Wasn't . . . kid . . . napped."

"Cutter and his band of cutthroat pirates kidnapped
you, transported you halfway across the world, and
tried to extort five million dollars from me.'"

"*Delusional,*" was all she could manage. Even though
the kidnapping was cut from whole cloth, Victor's team
would spin any grain of truth in it into whatever he
wanted.

His political idol was JFK, and he emulated him in
every way he could. Up to and including the president's
sexual fetishes and aberrant behaviors. Victor's PR machine had started weaving and fabricating Kennedy
comparisons the day after they'd started dating. God,
his sense of entitlement, and his misconception that
they were the perfect, golden couple, would be laugh-
able if it wasn't so totally terrifying.

Someone cleared his throat, startling her. Daniela
didn't dare take her eyes off Victor. Her throat was dry,
and her voice sounded raspy and frighteningly weak as

she pushed out the words, "Lo—They'll find me." Logan will find me. Please God, Logan *will* find me.

In time?

Probably not.

Behind his glasses, the color of Victor's brown eyes confirmed he was still as full of bullshit as he'd always been. He kept his gaze on her, but asked someone behind him. "*Will* they find her, Mack?"

Mack with no neck and rough, cruel hands, who used to hold her down. Daniela couldn't even stomach the sound of him, much less the sight. "No, sir."

"I'll take that off my list of concerns then," Victor answered smoothly, his eyes scanning her face. "How long will it take to get her ready?"

"She's a mess!" Daniela recognized the voice of Mena Bobrov, Victor's stylist. The woman sounded fearful of what would happen if Daniela didn't look her best.

This hair color is similar to Victor's, Daniela, she'd said a year ago. *This buttery color will look good with her skin, and she won't look quite so . . . Mexican.*

I'm American/Peruvian—Daniela had inserted, annoyed that they'd talked over her.

Blondes have more fun. Victor had stood by and adjusted the cuff links at his wrists, then bent to kiss her cheek. They'd conferred without her input, and Daniela remembered exactly how uncomfortable she'd become. But she'd loved him, and if being a blonde got him more votes, what did she care what color her hair was? She hadn't understood then how far he'd go to achieve his goal of becoming the youngest American president. He just needed the right accessories.

In the mirror, Daniela had caught the two of them

making eye contact behind her. That should have been her first tip-off.

You know what he means, Mena had said smoothly.

It meant he wanted a blond Hispanic woman on his arm.

Nothing too ethnic, nothing too specific.

"I'll need at *least* four hours," Mena said now, sounding panicky. "Five hours would be better. I have to color her hair, do something about her skin—"

"She was kidnapped and kept in deplorable conditions," Victor snapped, as if repeating himself. "She shouldn't look perfect, just suitable. The press conference starts at four. That gives you three hours to work your magic, and do the job you're paid for." He reached over. Daniela froze, but instead of striking her, he disdainfully flipped her hair between his fingers. "Do something with this."

"I just sai—" Victor cut off Mena with a glacial glare. "Of course."

"Not too much makeup. She's in a delicate mental state, make sure she looks the part. A few strategically placed, suitably brutal bruises, I think. Visible, but not on the face. I want that clear for pictures. Ligature marks on her wrists would be interesting and photograph well."

"Real, or makeup?" Mack asked hopefully, rubbing his hand over his beefy fist.

"Now don't be greedy, Mack. I'll let you have her when I'm in the White House. Let Mena do her thing. You can do whatever you like with her. Later."

"How alert *do* you want her?" an unfamiliar voice asked diffidently.

Daniela tried to sit up, to get off the bed. To—she could barely move. God . . . "No. Can't . . . do . . . this—"

Victor turned, sneering as he wrapped his fingers around her windpipe, holding her by the throat so she couldn't breathe. Daniela mentally counted to fifteen before he let go, scared that he might not. Black snow danced in her vision.

"I can do whatever I want—you should've figured that out by now." He looked to the voice. "I want her incapacitated, so she's not difficult. At three thirty? Mobile." Victor got to his feet. "Capable of walking on stage on my arm, smiling. Out of it is fine. She won't be required to say too much. And thanks to your statement last week, they already think she's mentally unstable."

"One more shot now, then."

"Do it."

Someone took her arm.

No!

A sharp prick in the bend of her elbow made her flinch. Not because it hurt, but because of the intent. She struggled against the insidious darkness . . .

Then nothing.

Seventeen

Daniela surfaced slowly, disoriented, but already frightened. It wasn't that difficult to remain limp and unresponsive as they moved her around the hotel room like a rag doll. Brain sluggish, she had no control over her body thanks to the drug they'd administered. Her brain felt dopey and slow, but she was capable of listening and comprehending what was going on around her, even if it took several seconds for her to understand some of what she heard.

Mena colored her hair, allowing the dye to sting Daniela's scalp, not bothering to add Sweet'N Low to cut the chemical burn as she used to. While the color processed, Daniela allowed her heavy lids to remain closed, conserving what little strength she had. Time must've passed, because Mena was painting her nails the next time she swam to the surface. French manicure, she knew without looking. Victor had an image of her he liked to have presented to his voters. She should have known there was something the matter when he'd referred to her bright cherry nail polish as Hooker Red. He would know.

The timer dinged, startling her as the sound broke through her stupor. Oh, God. She'd been out at least thirty minutes that time. She lost all concept of time as she drifted in and out. From nothing black to drifting formlessly in a soft brown fog.

The stylist used too-hot water, which would have really hurt if Daniela was fully aware. Still, it was unpleasant enough to help clear the fog. Unfortunately, the sound of running water made her desperate to pee. It took everything in her to control the urge without moving and giving herself away. The last thing she wanted was another damn shot.

Mena wrapped a towel around Daniela's wet hair, then roughly dried the newly blond strands. The yanking at her scalp was enough to take her mind off her bladder, but accentuated a dull headache throbbing behind her eyes. She drifted, everything around her insubstantial, and just out of reach. She kept her eyes closed, her mouth slack. Victor had never drugged her before. He'd scared her, branded her, and attempted to control her before she'd escaped. But feeling disassociated from her own body, unable to stay awake or focus, was by far more terrorizing.

He had all the control, she had none.

If he'd done all those things while she'd been able to think, what new torture would he devise now that she was vulnerable? Helpless? Daniela realized, even in her doped-up state, that there were several levels higher than mere fear.

She'd never liked Mena, and had only allowed her to color and style her hair because she was Victor's stylist, and he "trusted" her. Victor had always been paranoid about his privacy and he had no real friends, none that Daniela had ever met. The people he kept around him had been with him for years and were incredibly loyal.

She'd assumed it was because he paid them extremely well, and suspected, after her discovery in the storeroom of the Blue Opal, that he probably supplied them with just enough drugs to keep them needing him. Or maybe he flat out threatened to kill them or their loved ones if they made a single mistake.

Mena had always been cold with her, but Daniela had chalked it up to jealousy. It was pretty obvious that the older woman was very much in love with Victor. Good luck with that.

She flinched as she suddenly felt rough hands slide under her back and knees. Smelled Mack's sour breath, as he carried her to what felt like an easy chair, propping her up while Mena started to dry her hair. Minutes drifted by in a listless fog, because the next time Daniela was aware of what was going on she could feel the hot rollers in her hair. And then what felt like a second later, Mena was finger-combing the curls and spraying. Not sneezing or gagging on the cloud of hairspray was a feat. Daniela was so thirsty she was almost tempted to open her eyes and demand a glass of water. But if they knew she was conscious, they'd drug her again. She toughed it out, even when she heard Mena pouring herself a soda inches from her ear. Her throat constricted with thirst and her tongue stuck to the roof of her mouth.

Mena grabbed her chin, shoving her head against the upholstered chair back. Her breath smelled of onions and breath mints. She used a clip with teeth to hold Daniela's hair off her face. Daniela welcomed the bite. Everything, anything that would bring her mind and body back in sync was welcome. Even Mena's intentional small cruelties.

"How long's that gonna take?" Mack asked. "I need a smoke."

"The senator told you not to leave the room."

"Gimme a break. Look at her. She ain't goin' nowhere."

Oh yes she was. The second she knew Mack was well away from the door, she was going to bolt out of there so fast they wouldn't see her dust.

"Ten minutes. And don't be late. I need help dressing her."

"I'll hurry back for that." Daniela heard the leer. Her stomach turned over.

"Go."

Daniela heard his footsteps cross the carpet. The door opened. Shut.

Get up.

The pop-fizz of the effervescence in the soda so close to her ear made her thirstier and thirstier.

She still couldn't move.

The other woman turned on the radio to some local station playing hip-hop, which blocked the sibilance of the bubbles popping. "He thinks he's gonna get to play with you awhile." Mena muttered, amused, as she returned to airbrush foundation on Daniela's skin. Cool. Don't breathe. She struggled to corral her thoughts, but floated instead.

"The senator found himself a new guy. Sniper." Mena's amusement switched to excitement as she applied eye shadow to Daniela's lid. "Name's Harry Smith. Probably not his real name, do you think? Nah. He's the one they sent to help get you off that boat. And *he's* the dude who's gonna pop you in the back of the head and ruin my most excellent color job tonight. He is *hot*, mama! Not 'cause of his looks. He's kinda nondescript, has to be you know? 'Bout my height, sandy blond hair.

Not hard on the eyes, but nothing to write home about. But his *equipment* is the stuff of this girl's dream. And the man is a *machine* in the sack."

Daniela tried to sift through the monologue but it was like mentally wading hip-deep through quicksand. Someone was going to ruin her hair? What? No, wait—pop her in the back of the head? Her skin grew clammy. *Pop . . . pop? Shoot?* Oh, God. They were going to shoot her?

So the offer he'd made to his bodyguard that he could have her after Victor was in the White House had been a lie. She was a loose end and she'd served her purpose. Victor would parade her triumphantly to the eager media. And just when everyone was rooting for them, just when everyone had their happy ending, she'd be shot in front of them. Leaving Victor to mourn her death all the way to the White House.

It was masterful strategy.

And one she couldn't allow to succeed. Daniela had enough awareness to realize that she had to get out of the hotel room before either Mack or Victor came back.

"Gotta pee, don't go 'way." Mena laughed as her footsteps crossed the room. The second the bathroom door clicked shut, Daniela's eyes fluttered open. The toilet lid clattered. She had minutes, possibly seconds to get out of the room. After that she had no idea. But now—

She tried to push up from the chair and found that the drug had left her muscles flaccid and uncooperative. It was impossible to lift her arms, let alone walk. She fought to flex her fingers and toes. Okay. Those worked. Not well, but at least she could control the movement and crawl her way across the room if she had to. How

long did she have to wait for the drug to wear off so she
was really mobile?

She couldn't move her legs, or lift her arms.

The toilet flushed. Water ran.

Hurryhurryhurry!

The bathroom door slammed open, hitting the wall.
"Where were we?" Mena asked rhetorically, coming
back to stand beside her.

She started applying shadow to Daniela's other eye.
"Man, you're really out of it, aren't you? I told him he
should a killed you that first night, but he liked you as
a couple. He thinks you're classy. For a foreign chick.
Well, la-di-da, he doesn't want no *classy* in the bedroom. He forgot about that little piece of his Camelot
pie, didn't he, you classy bitch? You didn't like his
games, and he didn't like you snooping in his bees-
wax."

The door opened. "She awake yet?" Mack asked. He
stank of cigarette smoke.

Daniela's heart sank. She'd left it too late.

"Why?" Mena asked sarcastically. "You wanna did-
dle her before the senator gets back?"

"Hell, yeah," he said eagerly, his voice coming closer.
"Think I've got time?"

A flesh-on-flesh slap. "Moron. I was *kidding*. Especially the way you manhandle a woman. You'd mess up
my work and then he'd kill both of us. Go stand over
there and let me do my job. You'll have your wish in a
couple of days. Play with yourself till then."

"Bitch."

"Idiot."

After a few seconds, Daniela heard the sounds of

Angry Birds as Mack played the game on his phone. Mena turned up the radio and came back to finish applying her makeup.

The helicopter landed at a small private airstrip thirty miles outside Lima. "Can we haul ass now?" Logan demanded of Wright, trying to be civil. He felt feral and wild with panic.

They'd been delayed two *hours*. The first chopper had a busted rotor. They'd taken Logan's into the small town while a second Huey had been flown in from Lima. Then it had to be refueled for the return trip. He, of legendary Cutter calm, was just about jumping out of his skin by the time it was ready and they'd lifted off. He could practically hear the metronome in his head ticking away the seconds.

Fortunately, there were several vehicles waiting for them on the edge of the tarmac, and finally—finally— they were en route to the hotel, where Victor had Daniela.

"There's a large turnout at the hotel already," Wright told him. The T-FLAC operative was tuned in to his men on the ground, and had been giving Logan play-by-plays since they'd left the *Sea Wolf*.

"How's he going to explain her disappearance?"

"The Peruvians have a vested interested in one of their own being kidnapped on Peruvian soil, and her kidnapping and disappearance were sprung on the press only this morning. They'll have a million questions. The news went out on the wire, so the U.S. press is already here in Peru. As well as news media from all over South America. Stamps is a popular senator, and they were a popular couple."

"That makes me feel so much fucking better," Logan said dryly. "The more people, the harder it'll be to get close enough to protect her." But the more people, the less likelihood that Stamps would harm her. Logan held on to that. That she'd been "found" locally had everyone clamoring for the story. "And I suppose *I* make the perfect scapegoat."

"That's a given."

Fucking great. Add that she was supposedly engaged to one of the bright stars of American politics, the man many people believed would become president, and people had come to the hotel in droves to see the show.

"We'll make it with thirty minutes to spare," Wright assured him. "I know it's nerve-wracking, but I swear, we'll get your lady."

"Unharmed? Will you swear to *that?* Because I'll settle for nothing less."

"I hear you. Been in your shoes, and know how you feel, believe me. I get it. If the tables were reversed, I'd be just as pissed. I'd go to any lengths to protect my wife."

That snagged Logan's attention. He swiveled to look at the man seated beside him. "You're *married*?"

Wright shrugged. "Almost ten years. Lily's the love of my life. Four boys. Nine, seven, and four-year-old twins."

"And she doesn't mind your line of work?"

"She's a busy veterinarian and busier mother; she hardly notices when I'm gone."

"I doubt th—We're here," Logan said with surprise as they pulled up under the portico, then realized Wright had kept him talking for the short trip to distract him.

"Stay cool. My men are already in position. She's in

room seven thirty-four. We go up, you take her, you leave. The senator is on the sidelines in the ballroom, getting ready to make his big announcement. They have a woman with her, and one of his security guys. We'll clean up the mess. No fuss, no muss. Ready?"

"Hell, yeah. Let's do it."

"Shit," Mena said, sounding impatient, and annoyed. The brush she'd been holding clattered into the box. "I left her engagement ring in the safe in my room."

The Angry Birds game was silent as Mack responded shortly. "Not my problem. Go get it."

"I'm not leaving you alone with her."

Mack's laugh was as unpleasant as he was. "I'm good, but even I can't do her in the five seconds it'll take you to go next door and come back. Get it, then we need to get her changed. Hurry up."

"Come with me."

"You're kidding, right?

"No."

"Jesus, woman, you're paranoid."

"Look who we work for," Mena said dryly. "Get the lead out."

Mack turned the game off and there was another clatter as he tossed his phone on the table near Daniela.

Daniela waited until the door closed behind them before opening her eyes. *Gogogogogo!*

She managed to lift her head, ignoring the pinwheel- ing of the room. She tried swinging her legs to the floor. They didn't move. She screamed *NO!* in her head. Was she able to move her arms? Cold sweat misted her skin as she heard the door open in the next room.

Thank God. She could move her arms. Not wildly,

but enough to weakly grip the arms of the chair and try to push herself to her feet. She fell back panting, her pulse racing. *Think, Daniela, think.* She glanced at the toolbox Mena used for her makeup supplies, looking for a weapon within easy reach.

As she visually searched the heavy box, she picked up Mena's Coke, greedily gulping down half of the cola. It quenched her immediate thirst, and maybe the caffeine would kick in. The can scraped as she slid it back on the table.

Mack's phone! It lay six inches from her hand. It felt like a mile. It took everything she had to reach that far and retrieve it. It slipped out of her nerveless fingers several times, sounding terrifyingly loud as it clattered onto the tabletop. It took several impossibly long tries to fumble it into her palm, and bring her arm back to her side. She panted from the effort, and her heart threatened to choke her, it was beating so fast.

The metal box was too heavy and too bulky to lift. Inside were brushes and pots of cosmetics. The only thing useful was the airbrush battery pack. But it was too far away.

The door slammed open. Daniela pushed the phone deep between the cushion and upholstered arm of the chair as she forced her breathing to even out.

". . . a fact! All I said was *maybe* that was going to happen."

"He promised *I* could have her." Mack said petulantly, his footsteps heavy as he crossed the room. The bedsprings creaked as he sat down.

"Jesus, you dickhead! Don't sit on her clothes, I spent an hour ironing everything just the way the senator likes them."

They were so busy arguing they didn't hear the door opening. Or notice the soda and phone were gone.

So far.

Daniela smelled Victor's distinct cologne from across the room, and figured they wouldn't notice anything amiss with him present. She hoped.

"We'll take it up with the senator. I just repeated what I thought I heard—Hello, Senator. We're just about to get her all dressed and pretty for you."

"She looks like a whore! Lose the red lipstick."

Mena instantly started wiping her mouth with a damp makeup remover cloth. "Better. The light lipstick. Nude palettes are what's in this season."

"I thought you were sending up someone to get h—"

"I want to be seen walking through the hotel with her," he said, clearly annoyed by the question. "Has she said anything?"

"No. She hasn't woken up yet. She's still out of it."

Victor grabbed Daniela by the wrist, lifted her arm, and let it fall. She hadn't been startled by his touch because she always expected to be roughed up when Victor was anywhere near her. "Get the doctor back in here." His rage climbed several notches. He stormed across the room, came back to the chair. "Now!"

She waited for him to hit her. He didn't. But he would. It was just a matter of time.

She heard Mack on the hotel phone. "The senator wants you in her room. *Now.*"

"Tell him to bring an antidote. Something to wake her the fuck up."

Mack repeated the order. The phone clattered. "He's on his way, boss."

Daniela reminded herself that Victor didn't want her drugged again. He wanting her mobile. Thank God.

She had a phone. Not a weapon, but at least contact with the outside world. If she ever had the opportunity to use it.

Mena pulled her still damp T-shirt over her head, and bent Daniela over like a rag doll to unfasten her bra. "If you hand me the bra over there, I'll get that—"

Mena was going to strip her in front of Mack and Victor and there wasn't a damn thing Daniela could do about it, so she blocked out the activities and Mena's grunts. It was apparently completely impossible to dress a deadweight. Aw, wasn't that a shame?

Mena was doing up the zipper down her back when the door opened. The sheath dress was rucked up her bare thighs until she stood up. Mack was probably leering at her legs and the view of her exposed underwear.

"Wake her up." Victor told whoever had just walked in, his voice cold and clipped. "You have five minutes to get her moving. Do it."

"She shouldn't have been out this long. Did you feed her befor—"

"Just goddamn give her whatever, so I can get the show on the road! I've got thirty minutes to airtime, and fifteen to get her downstairs."

Cold hands straightened her arm.

Eighteen

Damn it to hell. "They're taking her down early," Logan observed tightly, speaking quietly into the lip mic supplied by Wright.

He fingered the hotel room door open another quarter of an inch, observing Daniela and Stamps's entourage as they came toward him. Stamps had one arm around her waist, his hand splayed possessively on her hip. He was practically supporting her entire weight down the carpeted hallway, headed to the elevators and the room where Logan was situated.

What the hell had they done to her? Her gorgeous dark hair had been dyed a pale blond. She looked like a different woman. She tripped on her high heels, her ankle twisting until her foot nearly rolled beneath her. Logan winced but bit his tongue. Jesus, that had to hurt, but she didn't make a peep.

Something was wrong. Daniela was either too terrified to make a sound or had been drugged to the gills. Either one fucking pissed him off. Stamps tightened his hold, saying something close to her face that made her stiffen. Logan's finger tightened on the butt of the gun in the small of his back.

"Easy, Cutter. Easy." Wright said in his ear.

Logan's hand gripped the doorjamb. She was surrounded by a phalanx of armed men just like those he'd encountered on the *Sea Wolf.* They were heavyweight security. In such a confined space, it would be impossible to grab Daniela without the possibility of her getting hurt . . . or, if Stamps was in the mood, killed.

He knew he had to be patient a few minutes more, but seeing her in such terror, being so close and yet unable to swoop in and grab her away from Stamps, made his blood run cold.

Two middle-aged couples exited the elevator, chatting as they approached the large group. Stamps bent to whisper something else against Daniela's glossy hair. She nodded. Don't talk to them, he guessed, because she didn't even make eye contact as the couples squeezed past the men all dressed in dark business suits. No one who didn't have cataracts would ever think these were businessmen. It was obvious they were all carrying, and their muscles made them look like caricatures of bodyguards. The couples hurried by, all tittering whispers and stolen looks. Victor gave them a slight smile and nod of his head. The two women's eyes widened.

She was only five feet away now, her expression distant, eyes slightly unfocused. Drugs. Rage surged through him anew.

He'd never seen her in a dress and heels. She looked stunning, elegant, and as lifeless as a doll. The cream-colored dress fit her curves like a glove, and the butter-soft black leather jacket looked both timeless and hip. Gold glinted at her ears and a diamond flashed on her finger. Her right hand was firmly tucked in her pocket, her body language clear. Anything to have a barrier between herself and the senator.

I'm right here, sweetheart. Logan willed her to feel his presence just feet away.

Wright's men were in various rooms on either side of the hallway on the way to the elevator. Every exit was being monitored, every floor, every stairwell, the elevator. The rest of his men were covering the ballroom on the mezzanine floor, where the press had been gathering for the last hour.

Two of Wright's men had been riding the elevator for the last twenty minutes. There was nowhere now that Daniela could go that Wright's men wouldn't be with her. After what had transpired on the *Sea Wolf,* Logan was supposed to be satisfied with that? He wasn't. Not by a long shot. He wanted her back on *Sea Wolf.* In his cabin. In his bed. In his arms.

He just had to be patient.

Something he'd always excelled at and never considered a trial. Until now.

He'd failed her. *Again.* The knowledge was bitter on his tongue and agony in his heart.

The group waited for the elevator. The door opened, giving Logan a glimpse of two men inside. Wright's men. Daniela stepped into the car, the doors slid closed. Wrenching open the hotel room door, Logan raced toward the *salida* sign and the stairs, Wright and his men close on his heels.

They hauled ass, seven flights at a dead run.

Whatever the second shot was, it had done the opposite of making her flat and floppy. Now Daniela was wired for sound, and ready to rumba. Neither boded well for her continued good health.

She, Victor, Mena, Mack, and four of Victor's bodyguards were in a room behind the ballroom, waiting for Patti Reed, Victor's longtime publicist.

"I have to use the bathroom," Daniela told Victor listlessly as he made a circuit around the small space. Energy radiated from him as he held her by his side as if she might bolt. He was a psychopathic asshole, not stupid. By the way his lips were twitching and the focused look in his eyes, she knew he was rehearsing his speech silently to himself. He hated being interrupted when he was concentrating. *Too bad.*

He turned his head and gave her a look vicious enough to make her take a step back. "You can wait fifteen minutes."

If he had his way, she'd be dead in less than that. "I honestly can't." Acting lethargic and still partially drugged wasn't easy when her blood was racing, and she now wanted to do freaking jumping jacks. "I'm going to pee my pants any minute. *Seriously.* How long was I out, four maybe five hours?"

Victor gripped her upper arm, his fingers painfully tight as he propelled her a short distance from the others. "If you do anything to ruin this day for me, I'll kill you slowly, painfully. You got that? Anything that makes anyone take a second look at you will get you killed. Mena! Mack! Get over here." He shoved Daniela at Mack, who grabbed her breast in passing. She stepped on his instep with her stiletto.

"Take her to the john. Both of you go in with her. Three minutes. Don't fuck up. Go!" He turned to his bodyguards. "Wait outside for her."

Daniela was frog-marched to the bathroom across the hall. It was empty. Victor's men stood outside while she, Mena, and Mack went in.

"Be quick," Mena told her.

"I'll speed pee," Daniela assured her sweetly, closing

the door in the other woman's face. She did have to go—and badly. But more importantly, she took Mack's phone out of her pocket. She deserved an Oscar for her performance in the room, because getting the phone from between the cushions and into her jacket pocket unseen had been a major production. She set everything up to record, then put the phone back in her pocket. All she needed to do was press the right button.

She finished and flushed, and went out to wash her hands.

Mena scowled at her. "Here, fix your lipstick yourself."

"That's so nice of you," she said, not too sarcastically, taking the tube from the stylist and opening it as she leaned over the sink to apply it in the mirror.

The diamond ring on her left hand sparkled in the lights over the sinks. She'd never seen it before. It was a suitable size for a wealthy man to give his beloved. But not so big and ostentatious that people would frown.

"It's not for you. It's for the senator."

Daniela met her own eyes in the mirror. God. She looked as she'd done before she'd run for her life. Honey-blond hair sweeping her shoulders, eyes smoky, lips creamy beige. Nails pink. As ordered by Victor. The dress and jacket were her own. Items he'd taken from her condo. The knowledge that he'd felt free to invade her personal space when she was gone infuriated her, until she remembered who she was dealing with. Taking a few of her clothes was the *least* of his infractions. She kept her expression bland. "Of course. It always is."

"Let's go!" Mack snarled, hand on the partially open door.

They walked quickly across the empty hallway and back into the anteroom of the ballroom. Whatever the doctor had shot her up with made her feel a little giddy and almost euphoric. Daniela reminded herself that she had to get a grip, and focus. She'd only have one chance to get this right.

Victor was pacing, Patti by his side. The publicist was a stunningly beautiful black woman with mahogany skin and a centerfold body that was squeezed into a fire-engine-red power suit with a short skirt. She'd apparently forgotten to put a blouse on under the jacket. Patti had always looked like an expensive call girl. But she'd once been an entertainment attorney, and had worked for Victor for ten years.

The two were lovers, and Daniela had seen Miss Reed bare-assed naked and being held under the water in Victor's bathtub several times. She was adept at holding her breath with those large . . . lungs.

"Daniela," the other woman said coldly. "You've caused the senator a great deal of trouble and expense."

Daniela casually stuck her hand in her pocket and gave the woman a withering look that clearly had no impact. "So I heard."

"I'll go over what we want the press to know. You're a clever girl, I'm sure you'll deliver the short statement, and let Victor do the talking."

"What if I don't?"

"Don't what, for fuck sake?" Victor spat, eyes narrowed like the snake he was. He shoved his glasses impatiently up the bridge of his aristocratic nose.

"Don't want to lie? What if I stand up there and tell them that you were bringing drugs in from South America, and using Blue Opal as a distribution center?"

Fury erupted behind his eyes and his fist jerked up, up ready to strike. She drew in a sharp breath, raising her hands defensively and stepping back before he hit her.

"Don't hit her now!" Patti snapped, grabbing Victor's wrist.

"How about I let them know that you ordered thugs to kill DEA Special Agent Price, and his wife, *and* their three lovely children? Bet they'd love to run with *that* ball."

"I've already had it leaked to the press that you're mentally unstable. Who do you think they'll believe? A woman taking antipsychotics and antidepressants? Or a well-respected senator?"

"You've got a point there. Wow. Antipsychotics *and* antidepressants. You *are* thorough. Clearly I'm a mess." Daniela shoved both hands in her pockets.

"How about I tell them how much you like to play in the water?" she taunted. "You and Miss Reed here with her personal flotation devices. Hard to drown *her,* I imagine. Have so much fun taking near-death experience to a whole other level. Holding someone's head underwater is called—what was it again? Oh, yeah. Autoerotic asphyxiation. A dangerous, nasty little game you so enjoy. Wouldn't your voters love to know that you hire prostitutes to play with the two of you?" She took her hands out of her pockets and hooked her thumbs in them instead.

"Nobody gives a rat's ass what I do when I'm not doing my job. And I do my job well."

"Drug reform. Importing heroin?" Daniela weighed each choice on her hands. "I bet they'll be interested in the drugs. Oh, and that you put the money from that last fund-raiser straight into your pocket earmarked swimming lessons?"

"I'll drug you again," Victor said coldly.

"Well, you *could*," Daniela mused. "But won't it be hard for that sniper you hired—What's his name again, Mena? Harry Smith? Nah. I don't think that's his real name. So awkward to shoot me when I'm lying down somewhere unconscious. I suppose it could be done. But not with nearly as much flair as if I was standing meekly by your side acting the doting fiancée. Thanks for the ring by the way. Is it real?"

Light glinted on his glasses, but she didn't need to see his eyes to know his expression. "How the *fuck* do you know about Smith?"

Patti slid her red-tipped fingers up his arm. "Shut up, Victor. You're just incriminating yourself, and confirming—"

He turned on Patti and practically grabbed her by the lapels of her jacket. Not that there was very much of it. He dropped his hands, but his face was flushed, his mouth twisted with fury. "Don't tell me to shut the fuck up. Remember who signs your paycheck."

"You have to go out there now. What are you going to do?" Patti's attractive face looked quite homely when she was pissed and scared. Poor Patti.

Daniela flinched as he spun around to grab her arm in the vise of his fingers. "Let me tell you *exactly* how this is going to play out. We'll walk in there together, hand in hand. I'll tell everyone how my people searched the globe for you, and discovered you'd been kidnapped and held hostage on a boat called the *Sea Wolf*, where you were terribly abused. I'll discreetly not go into detail.

You'll have ninety seconds to tell everyone how grateful you are that I found you. That we're planning a June wedding because we can't stand to be apart. You'll tell them how much you love me, an—"

"No."

Victor backhanded her, sending Daniela stumbling into Patti, who jumped out of the way. "No?"

"It's a complete sentence." Daniela righted herself, straightening her jacket. "I'm not going to lie to the press to save your criminal, unpleasant ass. What are you going to do about it, kill me? You already plan to anyway. You see, I don't have anything to lose, Victor. So I'll be damned if I'm going to stand there calmly while a sniper is lining up his shot as I bullshit everyone, so that I die in your arms and you look like a hero. I won't do it."

Patti's hands fluttered as she leaned in, brushing her breast against Victor. "Victor, we have to go out there, we're already late—"

He glared at the publicist. "I didn't tell you to speak. Shut the fuck up." He turned back to Daniela. "Nothing left to lose?" The sneering smile he gave her had never been seen by the media, she was damn sure. But she'd seen it often, and knew what it foreshadowed.

Her blood ran cold.

"I have your parents at my Back Bay house. If I don't call to assure their keepers that everything is going according to plan here, they have instructions to torture and kill them. They'll waterboard your father first—he's almost seventy, isn't he? Your mother might enjoy a little autoerotic asphyxiation."

Daniela hadn't known her capacity for hating someone until she'd met Victor, and never more than at this moment. "Nice try. Right now they're visiting Mykonos."

Patti gave him a pleading look. "Victor—this is all going to fall apart if we don't go out there *right now*!"

He stuck his hand into his breast pocket and withdrew his phone. "Call the house and speak to your mother."

Daniela's fingers were cold as she took the phone and hit the speed dial for Victor's Boston home. The phone was picked up on the second ring.

Patti shifted restlessly, her eyes going to the double doors and the noisy crowd waiting in the ballroom.

Victor folded his arms, looking smug and self-satisfied.

"Let me speak with my mother," Daniela told the man who answered the phone, holding Victor's gaze with murder in her heart.

Her mother must've been standing right there. "Dani, honey! We're having such a wonderful time at Victor's house." It was her mother's fake voice. The voice she used when Daniela's father had had a heart attack last year and they didn't know if he'd make it. *That* voice. The voice that said what the hell is going on, and how do we stop it? Scared. Worried.

"Mom. I thought you were on the cruise?" Her belly tightened. The people she loved most in the world were thousands of miles away. Unprotected and terrified. She'd brought this on them, and the realization that Victor not only could, but would, kill them on a whim was beyond terrifying.

"He persuaded us to cut our trip short and come home for the wedding. You naughty girl—why didn't—"

"Everything's going to be okay, Mom. I have to go.

I'll call you later, okay? Give my love to Daddy." She handed Victor back his phone, and said dully. "Promise you'll let them go—after."

"Someone has to mourn at your funeral to make it look convincing for the press. I promise." Which was as worthless as his fake glasses, and his cheap charm.

"Okay. I'll do it."

Nineteen

They walked in hand in hand. Logan hated to admit that Daniela and the senator made an attractive, hell—*whole-some*-looking couple. The press surged forward. Sixty or seventy people, equipped with cameras and mics, pushing for a better view as Stamps and Daniela made their way to the podium set up on a small raised platform at one end of the ballroom.

Stamps smiled benignly at the crowd, then lifted his and Daniela's joined hands in a show of triumph and solidarity. The cynical press cheered, and started yelling questions.

The fucking American dream. JFK and Jackie. Impeccably dressed, modest jewelry—except for the flash of a diamond engagement ring. The senator raised his other hand as he whispered to Daniela. Her smile was strained, but she, too, waved at the cameras.

Logan gritted his teeth, feeling trapped and hating it. What hold did Victor have over Daniela, to keep her so docile?

The senator tapped the mic. He was a president straight out of central casting. Neat suit, discreetly expensive. His shoes were shiny, and so were the lenses of his glasses. A neat trick so that no one could see his eyes, Logan would bet money on it.

Stamps waited until everyone had quieted down and

introduced himself with self-deprecating humor, making everyone laugh with him. By the movement in her jaw, Logan could tell Daniela was holding back the bile surging in her throat. He imagined that vomiting from the podium onto the crowd would not go over well with Stamps's squeaky-clean public image.

He explained how the love of his life had been kidnapped by, unfortunately, radical Peruvians, and brought to this country. He placed the blame squarely on the *Sea Wolf* and her crew. Why in the hell a multimillion-dollar corporation like Cutter Salvage would give a rat's ass about kidnapping a senator's girlfriend was something the press would have to think through for themselves.

They'd eat the bullshit he served up on a plate and smile. Until they dug deeper.

Stamps talked about the ransom demands, and when he mentioned her distraught parents, Logan saw the stiffening of her shoulders, and the pulse throbbing at the base of her slender throat.

Stamps had Daniela's parents. Fuck.

Logan made eye contact with Wright, who was positioned about a hundred feet away. The other man indicated he was already on it, and Logan turned back to Daniela and the dog and pony show. He wanted her to know he was there. But since he had no idea what her reaction would be in a drugged state, he stayed out of sight as much as he could in the seething, churning mass of reporters.

The senator held up a finger for the media to wait, then slipped off his glasses to wipe away a tear.

The press should be wearing waders, for God's sake. Surely they weren't buying any of this? Clearly Daniela was there under duress—unless they bought everything

Stamps was telling them, in which case she looked exactly like a rescued kidnap victim leaning against her fiancé for strength.

Instead of a woman being held forcibly restrained by his unbreakable hold on her hand.

Logan was going to roast the son of a bitch's balls over a spit and make him eat them.

"Thank you all for coming. Many of you came great distances to share this extraordinary day with us. Due to the ongoing investigation of the kidnappers, I can't divulge too much information, but . . ."

Logan tuned him out.

Daniela was glued to Stamps's side. She looked a little pale, but otherwise composed, and calm. Had they drugged her to keep her so calm? The Daniela he knew would be fighting tooth and nail to break free. Logan had to trust that she knew what she was doing by standing there so still and achingly beautiful beside a psychopath.

She appeared to be listening to Stamps intently as he spoke eloquently to the crowd. As if she really cared what the son of a bitch was saying. Logan's gut burned.

"Daniela would like to say a few words. She's being very brave, standing here with me after her ordeal, but she insisted." Victor gave Daniela a loving glance before returning to the people in the room.

"No questions please. She's very tired." He raised his free hand and gave her an encouraging smile.

She ignored both as she stepped a little in front of him. "I'd like to thank all of you for coming." She stopped suddenly, her attention caught by a familiar face a few feet away. Wright! He looked at her intently and clearly mouthed, "They're safe." Her parents were safe!

She didn't stop to question how he'd found her, how he'd known about her folks, how he'd saved them. All that mattered was that she was free to tell the truth. She looked up, leaned into the mic to make sure that every word she said would be heard.

"Somewhere out among you is a man named Harry Smith, a sniper, hired by Senator Stamps with orders to shoot me while I'm talking to you. I hope that doesn't happen because I have a lot to say—" There was a pregnant pause as her words resonated with the press, then all hell broke out.

Stamps grabbed her arm, lifting a hand for silence. "My apologies. I was concerned that my fiancée wasn't up to a press conference after the traumatic ordeal she's been through, and unfortunately, the doctor was right. She's on medication, and under the doctor's care. I'll—"

Daniela wrenched her arm out of his grip, and withdrew a cell phone from the pocket of her jacket. "I recorded a conversation we had just minutes ago. I'd like you all to listen."

Logan pushed his way closer, but she still hadn't seen him. She fumbled with the phone, and a second later the familiar tones of Stamps's voice were heard. Loud and clear. He was clearly dictating something to be transcribed, and it was about a bill he was trying to push through, not an incriminating taped conversation.

The color drained from Daniela's face. Stamps tried to wrestle the phone from her. "Give me the phone, honey, you're just embarrassing yourself." He turned to a woman in a red suit behind them. "Please get Doctor Calvert down here right away." He motioned for his bodyguards to come and restrain Daniela as the press surged forward en masse.

Camera flashes went off as though they were on the red carpet. Boom mics were extended over heads, handheld-camera operators pushed and shoved to get closer. A CNN reporter almost got trampled by the BBC news crew. Logan stepped up onto the podium beside them, taking the phone Daniela was struggling to hold away from Stamps. She turned and her look of fear melted away as she saw him. With a glad cry, she flung herself into Logan's arms. He wrapped one arm around her, glanced at the phone for a moment, pressed buttons a couple times, and held it up to the mic.

"Don't what, for fuck sake?" The senator's voice.

"Don't want to lie?" said Daniela. "What if I stand up there and tell them that you were bringing drugs in from South America, and using Blue Opal as a distribution center?"

"Don't hit her now!" a woman shouted.

"How about I let them know that you ordered thugs to kill DEA Special Agent Price, and his wife, *and* their three lovely children? Bet they'd love to run with *that* ball."

"I've already had it leaked to the press that you're mentally unstable. Who do you think they'll believe? A woman taking antipsychotics and antidepressants? Or a well-respected sena—"

Wright and his men, accompanied by a dozen officials, circled the podium. Logan handed him the phone, with Stamps still talking.

"Well done," Logan said into Daniela's ear. She nodded, her entire body shaking with adrenaline. The senator tried walking off the stage as cameras flashed, but T-FLAC ensured he was going nowhere until the police had him in custody.

"I knew you'd come." She spoke calmly, but fear glittered in her dark eyes as she said rawly, "He threatened my *parents*, Logan."

Senator Stamps refused to be taken off the stage, jerking his arm back from the two T-FLAC men accompanied by local police officers. One police officer asked if he would like to be tazed, and the ballroom quieted as they waited, eager to hear Stamps's response. This was a press conference that was probably already being Tweeted around the world.

"Fuck off."

"Cuff him," the police chief ordered. He eyed the senator with disdain. "You want to be treated with respect, *Señador* Stamps? You must earn it." The officials hustled Stamps away, and Wright and his men followed to make sure he remained in custody.

Flashes sparked as cameras picked up every frame as Stamps was shoved toward the exit. Logan wrapped his arms tightly around Daniela as she buried her face against his chest, her hands fisted in his shirt in the small of his back. She wasn't crying, but her entire body shook. He tightened his hold around her, pressing his lips to the crown of her head as he observed Wright and his men accompanying the locals.

Stamps would be returned to the States to stand trial. He'd be in jail a very long time.

Not long enough as far as Logan was concerned.

Suddenly the crowds pressing around the men erupted into screams and chaos, as some people in the crowd of reporters raced forward, while others pushed and shoved their way out of the seething masses.

What the hell?

Stamps's head had *disappeared*, seconds before he dropped to the floor out of sight.

Daniela lifted her head. "What's happening?"

"I believe the senator's hired hit man just tidied up a loose end," Logan told her grimly as the room erupted into a madhouse, as every cameraman and film crew tried to get the money shot of the senator's lifeless body.

Twenty

Daniela's lashes lifted to reveal whiskey brown eyes glazed with passion as Logan skimmed his hand over her hip. "We're going to be—hmm—late for your brother's wedding."

Midmorning sunlight flooded Logan's bedroom in his house on Cutter Cay, spilling over them as they lay, limbs tangled, on his big bed. The warm tropical breeze drifting through the ceiling-to-floor French doors cooled the sweat on their skin. "Island time, remember?"

"I'm sure they're eager to get married."

He kissed her throat. "I know what I'm eager for again . . ."

The room was filled with the scent of their lovemaking, and the heady fragrance of the ginger flower he'd plucked last night and tucked in her hair.

Accompanied by Dog, they'd arrived on Cutter Cay late the night before. And since the lights were dark at his brothers' places, they'd come straight to Logan's house high on the bluff.

He'd invited Daniela's parents to join them later in the week, but for now it was just the two of them. Dog had trotted off in the dark to find Teal's father, Sam, and hadn't returned.

Logan kissed her soft mouth gently. Lazily exploring her damp curls, he found her slick and hot, and ready again. They'd made love enough times that they were both sweaty, breathless, and utterly replete, and yet . . .

Her fingers tangled in his hair as her muscles pulsed around his fingers, drenching his hand. She moaned low as his fingers found the exact right place, and exerted the exact right amount of pressure. Then, because it felt so damn good, he did it again. And again, until her eyes lost focus. One of his favorite looks for her. After several minutes of soft sighs, she murmured against his throat. "I have to do my face and hair. And you're making me all hot and sweaty again. We'll have to shower again too."

Yeah. A shower. Again. They might miss Zane's wedding altogether. A slow grin curved his mouth. "My brother won't care." They'd had it hard and fast before breakfast. Showered, and started to dress, and then one thing led to another . . .

"It's his wedding, he won't be looking at us," she admitted breathlessly, as she shifted her hips, and parted her legs a little more to accommodate his hand. "But there'll be other people there too. You don't want to meet your new brother smelling of sex, do you?"

He picked up her hand, which was now languidly sifting through the hair on his chest, and stroked his tongue over the delicate blue vein in her slender wrist. Her fingers curled in reaction and he unfurled her hand to taste her palm, then each finger. She tasted like pine-apple vanilla. "I'll smell of you."

"Now. Fine. At the wedding, definitely not." She put her hand firmly on his chest. "Move, Logan, I—no fair," she murmured, as he raked his teeth across her shoulder.

He rolled her on her back, saw the glint in her eyes,

and reversed position, with her straddling him. She slid her leg over his hip, then seated herself and she slid down, fitting him like a glove. Her body pulsed and throbbed around him. He settled his hands on her slender hips, and flexed, pushing deep. Her nails scored his chest and her back arched. They took their time, rising and falling like the tide.

He glided his palms up the curve of her hips, over her ribs, then captured the gentle swell of her breasts. Her nipples were a deep coral, and pebbled beneath the brush of his thumbs. "Good?" He barely managed to push the word out, because the sensation was so sweet, so exquisite it bordered on pain.

"Perfect."

She was soft and strong, a sea goddess as she rode him without mercy. "Yeah." She *was* perfect. In every way.

Holding her gaze, he pulled out in a slow, measured stroke, then just as slowly pushed back deep inside her. Her breath caught, and she rose, then slid down his length in retaliation.

A slow, long, rolling climax surged through him like high tide. Head thrown back, Daniela arched as the climax swept through her. Her skin glowed like a creamy pearl in the sunlight filtering through the shutters, and her hair, once again dark, was a wild tangle around her shoulders.

Still buried deeply, Logan whispered, "Hi," and reached up to brush her warm flushed cheek. Her mouth was a plump and deep pink, damp from his kisses, and her eyes sparkled.

She lifted her hand to stroke her fingers over his jaw. "I love you, Logan Cutter."

He tugged her down so that their lips touched, feeling the heavy flutter of her heartbeat against his chest as he kissed her gently. His heart soared, and he tangled his fingers in her sweat-dampened hair. "I had no idea how big love could be until I met you," he told her softly. "I saw what my life would be like without you in it when you disappeared from the cabin that night. Bleak, and empty." His heart was so full, he could barely put together the depth and breadth of his love for this courageous woman. "I love you, Daniela. Marry me."

Her arms tightened around him. "Without hesitation. But not today. Today is for Zane and Teal."

"Soon."

"And then it will be Bria and Nick's turn . . ."

And they'd have to go to Washington to help unravel the mess Stamps had left behind. Logan wasn't sorry the man was dead. Even a life sentence wouldn't have been long enough. And he didn't want Daniela to spend the rest of her life looking over her shoulder waiting for Stamps or one of his minions to retaliate. Stamps having his head blown away by his own hit man was poetic justice, and richly deserved.

Logan stroked her cheek. "You're killing me."

He'd introduce her to his family tonight. To Zane and Teal. Nick and Bria. Jonah. They'd love her as much as he did.

"We have the rest of our lives," she murmured against his lips. She tasted of the pineapple they'd shared for breakfast, and rich coffee. She tasted, Logan thought, brushing her hair from her eyes, like the love of his life.

They actually did make it to the wedding. With minutes to spare. Daniela was glad. There was no way

Logan would miss the wedding of his youngest brother.

It was close to sunset, and the sky was a glorious blue fading into a cinnamon red over the pale turquoise water. A couple of gulls wheeled lazily high above and there wasn't a cloud in the sky. Daniela had never seen such fine, white sand. It felt powdery soft under her bare feet, and still retained the heat of the day.

Dog bounding around them, running in circles with doggie joy as they walked hand in hand down the sand to the foot of the bluff, where a stand of trees shaded a small group.

The cloudless sky was the couple's wedding canopy, the susurrus of the waves lapping at the shore their music. The ocean was a crystal-clear aquamarine as far as the rust-streaked horizon. The warm breeze off the water made Daniela's pink-and-lime-green tropical print *pareo* flutter around her ankles.

She was naked under it, and they both knew it. The fact that the wrapped fabric could drop from her body at any second made going out in public an adventure. She shook her head at herself for accepting Logan's dare. She felt wild and free, and so happy it was as if she were filled with helium. With her fingers twined with Logan's, she felt both insanely light and securely, blissfully tethered. "I'm surprised you haven't called Jed or Piet to see how things are coming along."

Logan's eyes crinkled as he grinned. "Swimmingly."

"Funny man." It would be business as usual while Logan was away. The *Sea Wolf* was a well-oiled machine, and all the parts worked like clockwork, Daniela knew, even if Logan was absent. "How long can we stay?"

"I want to show you the island. At least a couple of weeks."

So he wasn't ready to send her back to DC alone. Her heart lifted even more. "It's beautiful here." The sugary sand stretched before them for what looked like miles. The water was the most exquisite color with just a lacy froth spilling onto the shore. In the center of the small island, the volcano rose like a jewel surrounded by lush emerald-green vegetation. Cutter Cay was Paradise.

Being with Logan was—bliss.

They were close enough to the small crowd up ahead that Daniela could separate the faces. Several people had turned to watch their approach.

"Chief?" she called. Dog bounded after a seagull. "Aries? Hercules? How about Zeus?"

Logan laughed. "I don't think he's interested. Don't confuse him. He knows his name." He brushed his fingers against her sun-warmed shoulder as they walked. "What happens if I move this little piece of material aside . . ."

"The whole thing will fall off and everyone over there will see the woman you love bare-ass naked." She gave him a sassy look under her lashes. "Go ahead. I dare you."

He shook his head, holding up his free hand. "I know how you enjoy calling bluffs. I withdraw my dare."

"Thought you might. How about—Skipper," she called out. "Okay. How about Ahab?" The dog frolicked through the water, splashing and barking happily. Oblivious to her best efforts.

Logan shook his head.

"Buoy, come here Buoy." The dog stopped, then spun

around, bounding toward them, tongue hanging out. "He likes it!"

"Because *Boy* isn't that different from *Dog*," Logan pointed out, still grinning.

"You boys spell it your way, and I'll spell it mine. Ah," she lifted her face for his kiss. "Compromise is a wonderful thing."

Buoy trotted back to them as they closed in on the wedding party. A couple, both dressed in jeans and white T-shirts, stood before a man in a bright pink Hawaiian shirt. Everyone turned at Buoy's wild barking.

Zane yelled, "Wolf's here!" Logan's brother raced across the sand to give him a bear hug. "God, I'm happy to see you."

Logan hugged him back, then took him by the shoulders and held him at arm's length. The two men grinned at each other like fools. No one seeing them would ever doubt that they were brothers. Same dark hair, identical searing blue eyes. "Wouldn't miss your coming of age for the world, Ace." He pulled Daniela closer to his side. "Daniela, my miscreant brother, Zane. And this gorgeous woman is my soon-to-be sister, Teal. Hi, beautiful." Still with his arm around Daniela, he leaned in to give the other woman a kiss right on the mouth, sending a laughing glance at his brother.

Logan extended his hand to a frail older man who'd come up beside Teal on the arm of a heavyset woman who was all smiles. "Sam. You look good."

The man smiled as he shook Logan's hand. Daniela saw how gentle Logan was with him, and her eyelids stung. Sam said gruffly, "And here I thought you despised liars."

"You look good to be here." Logan smiled. "Zane and Teal and the rest of us are grateful for every moment. So yeah, you look great."

"Hey, big brother."

Logan grinned as another blue-eyed man and dark-haired woman approached. "This must be your princess."

The woman extended an elegant hand. "Bria. So you're the big bad wolf."

There was much hugging, and laughter.

"And this," Logan looked up, unsmiling at a man standing a little bit out of the tight circle. "Must be our long-lost brother, Jonah."

Like Zane, Nick, and Logan, Jonah Cutter was tall, dark, handsome, and blue-eyed. Daniela would've picked him out of a crowd as a Cutter without a moment's hesitation. He stepped into the group, hand extended. He looked a little wary, but Logan shook his hand without hesitation, then yanked the guy into a bear hug.

"I'll probably beat the shit out of you for lying. Later." Logan told him, half seriously, Daniela thought, amused. "But for now, welcome to the family. Okay, people. Let's get these two married."

They moved as a laughing, loving, *noisy* group to the man waiting to join the happy couple in marriage.

Daniela suspected she'd be seeing the minister several more times in the coming weeks.

Filled with a joy that she could barely contain, she tugged at Logan's hand, holding him back for a moment. She turned, lifting her face. "I love you, Logan Cutter. There's no one else like you in the whole world."

He grinned. "Not true," he glanced over his shoulder at his three brothers waiting for him. "Apparently there are more just like me being added every day."

"*Nothing* like you. Their eyes might mimic yours, but you're *my* one and only."

"That's the only one I want to be," he told her thickly. His Cutter blue eyes darkened as he dipped his head to kiss her. After several moments he lifted his head. Cupping her face in his palms he stared down at her with eyes filled with love. "I'm going to spend the rest of my life loving you, Daniela Rosado. The rest of my life and beyond."

"Hey, you two!! People trying to get married here!" Zane yelled.

Hand in hand, Daniela and Logan ran across the sand, Buoy at their heels.

Life didn't get any better than this.

Don't miss the next book in
The Cutter Cay series by
Cherry Adair

Stormchaser